WHAT REMAINS

WHAT REMAINS

TRACEY LEE

MYS
Lee

Library of Congress Control Number: 2015920656
ISBN: Hardcover   978-1-5144-4395-8
                Softcover   978-1-5144-4394-1
                eBook   978-1-5144-4396-5

Print information available on the last page.

Rev. date: 12/19/2015

To order additional copies of this book, contact:
Xlibris
1-800-455-039
www.Xlibris.com.au
Orders@Xlibris.com.au
718141

To Greg, Ellen, and Patrick
for teaching me about patience,
optimism, belief, and hope.

CHAPTER ONE

I don't believe in the portents of the weather, but I find I'm susceptible to deep and unproductive thinking when the elements pique my nerves. This day was one of those. It was 2:00 p.m., and a large lunch—a carbohydrate-rich one, at that—was dulling my mind and encouraging me to remain still in my new deck chair. I deliberately faced north to capitalize on every discernible degree of heat. The sun warmed me with its milky winter rays, and I was almost persuaded that it wasn't June. In my mind I denied that the worst of winter was ahead of us. Despite the sun's promise of a perfect day, I knew that frost and temperatures in the negatives were only hours away. But it wasn't the vague and yellowish sunlight that stirred me. The occasional, almost imperceptible breeze that tingled my skin with an unexpected icy touch aroused my senses. I could have been lulled into a nap but for the occasional *tap tap* on my skin by that chilled hand. It was as if the tiny gusts were waking something in me. It wafted not only against my bare skin but also into my mind to keep me awake and search for some kind of memory. It was a don't-go-to-sleep kind of cold lick. It was a time for being alert, as if something was coming.

Now, June is always a time for hibernating. We are eight hundred metres above sea level out here on Lake Road, and neither winter nor summer can be taken for granted. In the height of summer, we can swelter in the upper thirties to low forties, and there's no breeze to move a blade of grass. But in winter, we are at the mercy of relentless fogs and frosts that refuse to leave and frigid rainstorms that take visibility down to a few metres. If you are leaving the lake in winter, then do it in autumn, because moving anytime from July to September requires an expedition. The road becomes impassable to anything but a fairly robust four-wheel drive. So a sunny day that comes to us with an endless blue sky is a celebration and brings the few of us who remain out on the lake to our front porches, armed with sunglasses and fewer than three layers of insulation. The view is inspiring, and over the decades that my family has lived here, it has been varied.

The lake comes and goes with the drought. The years it rains, we have a lake; the years it doesn't, we don't. It seems to be a pretty simple equation. Rain makes a lake. The weather brings the fortunes of a substantial, if somewhat shallow, body of water to my front door. As kids growing up in the 1970s, the lake was our adventure playground. We were allowed to row out a few hundred metres, fish, and make believe that the centre of the world was right there in Lake George. The boys from the local township of Bungendore would row out from their end of the lake and engage in some social discourse that included ramming our dinghy, mocking our fishing skills, and flirting tragically with the girls from Lake Road. We didn't go to the local schools in the town, so only during this summer boating did we get a good look at our neighbours across the lake. By and large, they were a handsome if somewhat rowdy lot of country boys—all blue-eyed and tow-headed. They weren't brothers, but they could have been. We liked the look of them, but there was no way we were ever likely to meet on terra firma, as they had the same distance embargo that we had. At that age, we were still obeying our guardians, and none of us had the courage to deny the rules. It was only as the lake dried up that the distance between us became terra firma and the risk of drowning was all but gone. Access to each other was easier to disguise as a stroll through the weeds and tea trees.

Our childhoods were composed of risk and bliss. People drowned. People went into the lake during the summer and winter and were upended into the murky pool. It wasn't the depth or treacherous movement of the lake that took lives; it was the mud. Deep, clay-like, reed-infested mud took them—and in my lifetime, it took four. Father Hagan and Liam Reilly were involved in the second incident I remembered hearing about. An altar boys' outing on the lake went horribly wrong when Liam leaned over the side of his rowboat to hurl his salty egg sandwich out of his stomach. The heat, the egg, and the movement of the boat combined to ensure someone would vomit. And it was wee Liam, a non-swimmer from a poor family in which he was the baby brother of six sisters. His fall was poetic, according to witnesses who were in his boat and the other one, which was expertly rowed by Father Darragh O'Day. Liam simply leaned out too far in order to ensure his regurgitated and soured lunch did not land anywhere on his best shirt, and his body upended virtually in slow motion into the brown water. Father Hagan, urged on by Father O'Day, simply brought the boat around and prepared to scoop up the waif, but in the seconds that it took to execute the manoeuvre, Liam was gone. Darcy Hagan, new from County Kildare in the Republic of Ireland, was not a strong swimmer, but he was a strong believer in family and couldn't bear to think of how the Reillys would cope with the church losing their only son, so he clumsily launched himself into the spot he thought Liam had disappeared. The remaining seven boys and Father O'Day had a laugh at the inglorious stylings of the young father's dive, but the laughter died quickly, as neither man nor boy reappeared. A flurry of oars was poked into the water where it was believed the two had gone over. It took twenty minutes before Father O'Day could comprehend that the two had gone and that he would have to get the stronger boys in the first boat to row themselves towards the Bungedore end of the lake. It was a long and terrifying row by boys and man. By the time they reached the shore, the children were howling and were good for nothing when it came to raising the alarm that would send the local men out to search the lake. The police eventually sent divers from Canberra, and the bodies were found twenty yards apart, both entwined in weeds and mud, both looking skywards hopefully as if to beckon the searching boys who started looking too late and too far away from where the pair died—a sad story, a dire warning, and a tragedy.

The most recent tragedy was a little closer to home. I was a new baby, only six weeks old, and therefore precluded from a family summertime sail around the lake. I lay at home in my newly painted bassinet under the protective gaze of my aunt Billie and uncle Darcy, who were in fact not husband and wife but brother and sister. Neither had married or had children, so my older brother, who was five when I was born, and I were much doted on by our unmarried relatives. As a pre-Christmas treat for my brother, Brannen, my father had taken him and my mother, Moya, out onto the lake for a bit of fishing. It was, no doubt, also a blessed relief from my incessant wailing. Only my father came back. Cillian Fitzgerald O'Hara rowed back from the outing alone, having had to leave his son and wife behind. Either they were below in the water or they had disappeared. There was an accident of some sort that he couldn't bear to talk about, not even to the police when they bore down on the little Lake Road community with all their accusations and feigned concern for the bereft man and his new daughter, Lily. But the kerfuffle died down, disorder became order, and the hubbub became gossip. Apparently, my father could see no sense in raising his only child, and shielding me from the grief and ignominy of loneliness, he hanged himself when I was nine months old. The bodies of Moya and Brannen were never found.

How was it possible that a shallow lake that came and went under the auspices of the weather could take two lives and never return them? For a long time, I asked myself, *How could it be?* And then I stopped asking, stopped thinking about it, and allowed myself to pretend that it was not important to the life I was leading. It was the past and, as such, had no place in my present or future.

Luckily, in a tale that contains little optimism, my aunt and uncle raised me in their homes, which stood thirty metres apart on Lake Road. I didn't know how they did it, since it appeared that they had so little, but I was educated at a private girls' school and chauffeured to Canberra by either Billie or Darcy every Monday of the school year and then back every Friday for what seemed an eternity. Boarding school, it seemed, was a way of normalizing my life, according to the family I had left. It would be a way of immersing myself in real life away from the memories of the lake, and it would perhaps give me the opportunity to find friends who didn't know about the tragedies of the past. But those sorts of things can't remain hidden in an all-girl environment. The farm girls and the daughters of the international elite who were installed at the boarders' dorms were easily entranced by grisly secrets. The small glow I had because I was the only orphan, made spectacular by the mysterious disappearance and suicide, kept me interesting to my peers for eight years. Real friends were not easy to make, as I wasn't quite like those other young girls, who were silenced by the expectation of easy pathways into the future. They were travelling straight lines to universities and marriages, etched into concrete, as they had been for the generations of women before them. I was not of that ilk. There was no roadmap, and the future for the Lake Road orphan remained uncharted. But I was never bullied, hurt, or lonely. It helped that I was clever and good at sport and that I could sing and play several instruments. It was a relief to be accomplished. It probably saved me. I was on several sporting teams and made the school and state swimming teams each year. While I wasn't close to any girls in particular, I was included in all school activities. I was, however, left out of all private events. The local girls had parties and sleepovers that I was excluded from, but I was impervious to the slights implied by the exclusions. I had a couple of friends from the boys' grammar school down the road. They too had accomplishments but were always outsiders. Our connection through the schools' combined band led us to have our own kind of clique—the outsiders' club. It wasn't the worst place to be.

My unusual relatives were happy to keep my friendship group limited to this meagre collection of other unique individuals who lived on the lake. The other kids' Irish Catholic parents allowed the relationships because they believed that God must have something special in mind for such a wee child who had suffered so much.

Perhaps all the evil and bad luck of my life had made me a safe bet for their girls to befriend. What else could happen, they might have been imagining. So on most weekends and school holidays, I settled back into my life, residing mainly in Billie's house but allowed to wander between her rambling weatherboard, my parents' unchanged home, and Darcy's ramshackle, quaint cottage. All three houses were filled with the collections of the O'Hara generations. Furniture, papers, photos, and treasures remained as sentinels, waiting for a day when they would be needed.

I was not afraid of the lake, and obviously Billie and Darcy thought nothing of letting their orphaned niece play on the water in summer. Strangely, I never thought of the events that took my mother, my brother, and ultimately my father during those strange summer days, rowing out to smile coyly at those Bungendore boys.

After all, this place had a long history with my family. The first O'Haras arrived on the lake in 1825 after brief stints in both Sydney and Port Dalrymple. There was no clear information about the nature of our arrival in the fairly new colony. One story had the first family arriving as part of the constabulary assigned to make the new free settlers safe; this probably the sanitized version of our exit from beloved Ireland. The more likely story is that one or both ancestors arrived on the convict ships filled with Irish Catholics who had committed crimes, real and imagined. They eventually built this new life in houses constructed from sturdy local timber by using all the skills they had learned in Ireland. These houses would stand forever. Their legacies perhaps would too. The property was called Stone Orchard Farm.

It was those lives that I thought about on that June afternoon—how my ancestral path had led to this spot, this quiet and perfect place. The winter breeze bought memories of Billie and Darcy and vague stories of my parents and brother, whom I'd never known. I thought about the life I'd chosen to live—a life of strange privileges, an excellent education, loving guardians, eventually good friends. Despite the tragic past, it was a very happy life. Life was not perfect, but it was one that I felt essentially comfortable with. I understood loneliness and was content enough to be alone.

When my school life finished, I left the lake for a university education in Sydney. I rarely went back to Billie and Darcy, but we spoke weekly. I made visits for their birthdays and for mine. The life there was a memory for the five years I studied. I was just a student, like everyone else on campus. I rented with acquaintances, became a vegetarian, went back to eating meat, fell in and then out of love, learned to drink, and then realized I couldn't drink, when hangovers lasted weeks. I became arty, geeky, studious, and frivolous and put on a multitude of other guises. I tried on every known personality type and social milieu and finally, at twenty-two, settled on quirky know-it-all. It worked for me and won me a few exceptional friends, who I kept out of my past. I didn't tell them about my parents, and for several years, they assumed Billie and Darcy were my mother and father. I hadn't corrected them, for it seemed unreasonable to do so.

After graduation, my skills led me to move back to Canberra to work in the National Museum curating key exhibits. I was happy with this, and the little O'Hara gang was pleased that I'd be nearby. I would see my family most weeks for brief catch-ups and the occasional meal. Billie and Darcy didn't ever come into town to visit me. The times I was back out at the lake, I was so busy describing my new life that it took me a while to notice how things were changing. I slowly came to realize that Darcy was not well. He was only sixty, but he looked older. I had always imagined that he started life as an old man. Of course, he hadn't. He was only thirty-eight when he took on raising me. Billie was a year younger. My father was thirty-five when he died, Moya only twenty-nine. They had not been much older than I was now, which was a strange realization. At any rate, stomach cancer cares very little about age, and after Darcy's diagnosis, he lived only a short month. His funeral and burial in Bungendore seemed to diminish Billie. She was not above middle age, but a year after Darcy died, a bout of pneumonia sent her to lay with her brothers and sundry other relatives in the weeds and headstones that so aptly reminded me that I was the end of the line. The O'Haras were buried together on the Catholic side of the cemetery. Two plaques on temporary but long-standing white crosses simply stated, "In loving memory of Moya" and "Brannen: loved son of Moya." My father's name was absent from both little engravings. No bodies were found, so no burial could occur. But their disappearance and assumed deaths were etched and commemorated to ensure the O'Haras would not forget them.

After Billie's death, I spent some time visiting the family graves in the somewhat dilapidated cemetery. The weeds were sometimes higher than the gravestones, and the years had tipped many of the older stones over so they leaned at haphazard angles. There was my family, lined up in rows of granite and marble that marked simple losses, simple epitaphs of dates and belongings. Two of the most important simply identified the "Beloved auntie" and "Beloved uncle" of Lily O'Hara. The third simply said "Cillian Fitzgerald O'Hara. There were dates and facts but no emotion. Many had assumed and the police had concluded that my father was a murderer who, so burdened by the fear of discovery, killed himself. There in granite was etched the truth of a loneliness that could, if allowed, consume me. But there were things to do, and mawkish hovering about a cemetery would not get them done. I had a job, three houses, and a life to get underway. I was twenty-six and was aware that growing up was not something to do later; it was today's job.

CHAPTER TWO

o in my grown up life, I moved back to Lake Road. I took up residence in my parents' house and lived in the sunny front room and spare bedroom that ran across the side that faced the water. I renovated the bathroom and kitchen, but other than painting, everything else remained locked in its era. I was the curator of the O'Hara museum. But unlike at my job in the National museum, I did not handle the exhibits; I did not research them. I simply kept them free of dust, water, and contaminants that might damage them. I didn't look at the items in any of the three houses; I just minded them.

My friends and colleagues thought I was crazy, living out on the lake and driving everyday into the city for work. I parked my gas-guzzling four-wheel drive in any parking space big enough for it and paid exorbitant fees just to ensure that I could get in out of my road during the four months of awful weather. In the summer, I drove the ancient 1958 Mercedes that Billie and Darcy had left me as part of the O'Hara estate. I had it rebuilt by an ancient German mechanic who lived on a property in Captains Flat. I used to imagine that he had escaped the evils of World War II and had found peace in the isolation of the limestone plains of NSW. It was more likely that he had been serving the German army with his brilliant mechanical skills and was, in fact, hiding more than I'd ever know. Nonetheless, the O'Hara estate, as I frequently called it, was well serviced by men

9

like Arhen Beltz and others tradesmen who dutifully came to fix a range of problems around the place whenever I needed them. Many of them had known Billie and Darcy, or their parents had known them. That connection was always honoured in places like this.

As for the estate, Stone Orchard Farm, it stood firmly on the lake shore at the very end of the road. I had inherited all three houses and the land and orchard that surrounded them. The upkeep was enormous, but I couldn't bear to part with them. Nor did I think it reasonable to lease the properties and then have to tolerate strangers wandering around my life. To be fair, I didn't really want to have to clean out the two houses that had been owned by my aunt and uncle. Their places had been filled with furniture and treasures from the lives of generations past. Other than housekeeping, I didn't really do much in either place. Occasionally when I was cleaning, I would open drawers and dispatch bits and pieces to the garbage bins. I would notice what needed repairing and call one of my legions of tradesmen to come over and fix it. I ripped up worn and dusty carpet and polished the boards. I painted the walls in fresh neutrals, and I kept the dust at bay. Other than that, I didn't really infiltrate the past lives of the dead. I was aware that Billie had packed some boxes. After Darcy died, she had tried to put things into boxes and label them. She did the same in her home, and she had long ago packed up my parents' things and had carefully written on each what was, more or less, in the box. I opened none of them. I simply kept things ticking over, even though I knew that the time would come when common sense would have to prevail. Ultimately, I would have to pack up the two "spare" houses and throw away the lifetimes of both Billie and Darcy. I thought, too, that I would also one day sell my family home and move to something more modern and easier to manage. I suspected that my friends were right that burying myself out on the Lake Road was not a proper life and that I should simply leave. Most winters I agreed, and yet something always held me back. It was as if I was waiting for something—something that I couldn't identify, but definitely something.

CHAPTER THREE

O f course something did come. It had been hinted at by that biting wind and my ruminations about the future. It was also there in full view from my front veranda; the lake was in a dying stage, and the water that had been so apparent in my childhood was now all but gone. Mud flats and deep-cracked earth with the beginnings of weeds and grasses made up the prevalent vista. The lake was going, or more correctly, had gone, its evaporation part of its life cycle, part of the comings and goings of drought and flood that characterized much of the Australian landscape. It was no surprise to those of us who lived out here, but it was mesmerizing to those who knew so little about the area. The "disappearing lake" was a magnet to the environmentally disposed and to artistic folk who wanted to catch the evolution of climate change.

So scientists, journalists, painters, protesters, and photographers made constant pilgrimages down Lake Road and inevitably parked in front of one of my houses. Some of the bold, usually the journalists and others who thought their enthusiasm for knowledge somehow circumvented the rules about trespassing, simply traipsed up my driveway and espoused their unique theories about the water's coming and going. Some wanted to know about my understanding of the mystery. Occasionally I'd be kind and explain what an endorheic lake was. It had no outflow, and evaporation played a role in the water level. The less polite came to accuse me of being complicit in the crisis, because the flood of new families moving to the lake seeking the rural lifestyle had committed residential vandalism by tapping into the water table and sucking the life out of the lake. I wanted to defend my name by saying the O'Haras had been here for 170 years—hardly newcomers. All I could do was stare in utter bewilderment at the boldest and the craziest ones and concur with the most lucid. My silence seemed to send most of them off to do whatever it was that floated their boats. I was fully aware that that was not the best analogy, given the lack of water. However, if my unwelcome visitors had done a tiny bit of research, they might have known that the lake had been here for a million or more years and that the indigenous people of the area knew of its fickle ways. They might even have found the pictures that showed that the newly settled capital city of Canberra had a yacht club on the lake in the early part of the Commonwealth. But few had any research to back up their ideas, and most of the time I was just a witness to the visitations or a hindrance to their intrusion.

There was, however, one visitor who seemed more earnest and more interesting than the rest. He was a young photographer who had known about the lake and simply wanted to capture the changing face through photos. His questions were generally about the stories, true and exaggerated, that coloured the lake's history. I trusted him enough to share some of the photos and newspaper articles hidden away in the O'Hara archives, these being Billie and Darcy's respective houses and cupboards. They revealed the early twentieth-century incarnation of the lake. I didn't give him the Canberra Times that followed the disappearance of my mother and brother or the one documenting the death of my father. I hadn't read them myself, and although I knew Billie had them, I didn't know where. It was still something I thought should stay buried. But other parts of the dusty collection inspired and enthused the young photographer. He seemed to appreciate my interest in his work, and when he discovered that I was a curator and archivist, he seemed to think my opinion carried not only the weight of experience but also of expertise.

His name was Eddie. He was trying to make a living as a landscape photographer. He was one of the few who had courageously, or stupidly, thought he would make a career out of his passion. Each time he arrived on the lake, I secretly wished him well. If anyone deserved to make a living this way, I thought Eddie did. On his last visit, he bought some of his work to show me. It was beautiful, and one in particular was of the lake from the dried shore outside my driveway. The sun was setting, and the night sky was hinted at in the lengthening shadows. The colours were stunning, and I told him that the photo captured my favourite aspect of the lake. His most recent visit was during the work week, and in my absence, Eddie had left me an exquisitely framed one-hundred-by-forty-centimetre version of that photo. It was sublime, and I spent a long time examining its detail. I was also unsure if I should accept such a gift, as it seemed too generous and simply too beautiful to be given in exchange for a little information. But there was not much time to get too concerned about the rights and wrongs of the gift or its implications, if any existed. He seemed a little keen on me, and despite his good looks and creative soul, I was not looking for a boyfriend. I didn't want to hurt anyone, but I was not interested in romance; the complication of relationships was not currently on my radar.

After Eddie left the picture resting against my front door, he went down to the driest entry point and made his way carefully across the lake's nearly dry surface to photograph a day's worth of changes and varying angles. There was greater access to the middle point, now that the water was decreasing daily. Mud was cool and deep in places, arid and fractured in others. Eddie had decided the contrast between soggy and parched would make art. His previous work captured the changing colours of the days and months. Seasons brought changes in tone. He would search for the most intense contrasts for his work, but what he found on that day was more than art—it was both the end and the beginning of a mystery, both an answer and a question, both calamitous and glorious. In the world between mud and desiccated earth, Eddie found bones. Human bones. Bodies that had seemingly become indistinguishable from one other. As the flesh disintegrated, the two sets of bones had collapsed into each other, but even to the novice's eyes, it was clear that one was a small adult and the other obviously a child.

And there was something else. He was initially shocked, but then realizing the importance of his find, he let his camera capture what he could hardly believe to be true. When he returned to his car, he had two hundred images of the tangled skeletons, images he would share with the police that afternoon and with me the following day. That change I thought was coming had arrived.

CHAPTER FOUR

O f course, the bodies were undeniably old. Forensic scientists
and police officers worked to release the skeletons from their
once-muddy tomb. Removing the rusted chain that entwined
the bones was more difficult. The photos taken by both Eddie and the
police would be a significant part of the evidence. Evidence of what?
Evidence that would, in the minds of those who remembered what
happened to the O'Hara family, confirm that my father had murdered
my mother and brother and that, in a guilt-fuelled admission, Cillian
had taken his own life. There would be questions for which there
would be no answers. There was no one who could truly know what
happened. Billie and Darcy were gone, and if they knew any more
than what the papers had reported in 1975, they had never told me.
But the story would make the front page one more time. Journalists
and writers who thought they could make a story from my family's
past made a beeline to my doorstep. Voyeurs and ghost hunters, locals
and ghouls flooded down the potholed Lake Road, dropped by the
houses like long-lost friends, and burrowed into my life. I thought I
would go mad. I felt exposed and hunted. The guilty secrets of the
past threatened to drown me, to suck me down into the mud as it
had Moya and Brannen.

Moya and Brannen were identified after extensive testing. The
case of disappearance, presumed drowned, was now pronounced
a murder case, and the empty graves were filled with the pathetic

bones of my mother and brother. They lay beside my father, Billie, and Darcy. Some of the older residents of the town were appalled that I had allowed the body of my father to remain in the family plot, now that murder had been confirmed. How could a murderer, even though long dead, be allowed to lie beside his victims? What was I supposed to do? Dig him up? Fling his bones into the mud or perhaps hold a ritualistic burning to purge myself of the evil? I was bereft of ideas and methods to cope. I had long buried any notion of the means by which I had been orphaned. But the past, it is said, cannot stay buried. Nor can it stay submerged in mud and reeds. The truth was surging like a tidal wave, and denying what seemed to be a forensic reality was idiotic. Only a fool would deny the proof. It was more than a reasonable assumption that the two were murdered. In the absence of absolute truth, one had to believe that what appeared to be true was true.

The young detective who drove himself back to Lake Road to inform me of this version of events was obviously uncomfortable about delivering the findings. He took up a considerable amount of space in my sunny front room. His mouth was set in a firm line, and his tone of voice was frighteningly matter-of-fact. I almost felt he was going to tell me that I had killed them. I couldn't look at him while he was reading from documents he had in a folder. These were the initial coronial enquiry, the investigative reports from 1975, forensic results, and the final conclusions. I kept my eyes firmly locked on the centre of the lake, where only a lick of water was left. When he was quiet, I turned to look at him. Detective Sergeant Phillip Swan was all business and fairly formidable, but his eyes gave him away. He was not much older than me, and despite his imposing form, he had a boy's face and eyes that were the strange blue of deep water. His eyes reflected pity and, I thought, genuine sorrow for the awfulness he had to share with me. It was if he was delivering information about a recent tragedy. I felt sorry for him.

"I didn't know any of them, you know." This was my attempt to make this easier for him. "I don't remember anything about them, and what I do know comes from some grainy photos my auntie kept. They raised me, my auntie and uncle."

He didn't respond. I suspect it's a copper's training—don't interrupt the suspect as they might inadvertently confess.

"I'm not sad," I said, though even as I said it, I knew I was lying. "I have always suspected that they were out there."

Actually that was the second lie I had told DS Swan within a minute. I think I had somehow believed that my mother had run away. That when the little sail boat made its way to the deepest point and was rocked by wind, she swam with Brannen to the furthest shore of Lake George and simply walked away from her life. Perhaps in my childhood and adolescent fantasies I had imagined that she was a spy who had to leave her newborn and husband to save them from some foreign power that was hunting her down. When I was quite young, I thought she and my brother were angels that could only be on earth for a very short time. In other bleaker versions, emerging during a period of adolescent negativity, I imagined that she had a terrible disease and my father had her locked away somewhere— some appalling institution that would eradicate her from our lives. Of course few, if any, of these versions adequately explained Brannen's or my father's death. I looked at Phillip and tried to smile, to give him some reassurance that he was doing a good job of delivering bad news.

"Perhaps a cup of tea?" I said. It was a tentative question that I had already answered myself by walking into the kitchen and putting the kettle on.

"Lily," he began, "this can't be easy, but I thought you were aware that your father had always been suspected of murdering your mother and brother."

Suspected. Now apparently confirmed. "I really didn't believe that he had. I cannot believe that there was anything so terrible in their lives that would make him do such a thing."

Phillip simply looked at me and raised his eyebrows. I imagine it was my naivety and delusions that made him look so bewildered. I know it seems impossible to believe anything else. My mother and brother fell into the lake, drowned, and could not be recovered, and in response, my father took his life. I was unable to look at any other scenario other than this one. Everything else was supposition until the bones weighted by chain were found.

"What did you know, Lily?" A fairly gentle question from Phillip. "What did your family tell you?"

The answers should have been equally simple, but for much of my life, I had stoically denied any knowledge or understanding of the saga. What had Billie told me, and what had Darcy ever said about his brother? I would need time to recall, and perhaps the place to start would be with the newspapers that initially reported the deaths. My memory would need some prompting, and in the absence of family, I would have to find other witnesses to these events. Perhaps this is what I could do. I could use my head instead of my heart to find the answers to all the questions.

"Lily." Phillip's voice reminded me that he was in the room and that I was supposed to be making him tea.

"I'm trying to remember what I might have been told and what I have simply assumed all these years. I might need your help, Phillip. I might need to know a few things about the earlier investigation." He simply nodded but looked doubtful.

He drank the tea and had a second cup. We ate cake and chatted about his job and the increase in petty crime. I asked him about his ambitions and his family. It was a pleasant distraction from the awfulness that brought him into my home. He was an interesting man who had entered the police after university. He had a degree in sociology and a master's in criminology, and he joined the NSW police at twenty-five. Now at thirty-three, he was a detective sergeant and was happy working in his field. He wasn't married, but he had a failed engagement to a fellow officer, who had left him for fireman. It was obviously still a bit of an ugly subject for him, but he brightened up as he talked about his family.

"I grew up on the south coast, went to school in Moruya, and spent most of the year surfing. Stayed out of trouble, unlike most of the guys I grew up with." He went on to talk about his parents, who stilled lived in Broulee, and his older sisters—three of them—who all continued to live on the coast. They had married local boys and had babies. Their husbands all owned local companies, and between them, they had a number of trade businesses covered on the coast. All the girls worked in the companies, and their kids were happy growing up on the beach. Phillip would go home, when time permitted, to get his board out and teach his nieces and nephews about fishing and surfing. He had a boat at his parents' and would take his dad out for quiet days and happy conversations. I could see he was relaxed when he talked about them. But he suddenly stopped when he seemed to realize that he was talking about something I didn't have and that he had recently confirmed I didn't ever have.

It was strange that I felt no sense of envy or bitterness. In fact, I had always enjoyed hearing about my friends' families and listening to them recount the eccentricities of parents and siblings. My favourite stories include the Christmas and birthday chaos that most of them said they had to endure but ultimately loved. My celebrations were nearly silent affairs with Billie and Darcy. They were generous with their gifts, which were always practical, and provided festive food, but they were stingy on conversation and frivolousness. We didn't put up decorations or have elaborately wrapped presents. Instead we had long silences and periods of being together while I played something for them on violin or piano. I always wanted to play guitar and sing something modern, but the two of them would look rather bewildered at my choices. In fact, they looked tortured, so I rarely inflicted it upon them. I was more likely to go out to the veranda and strum happily for hours, humming to myself. Christmas and birthdays were quiet, but Easter was downright gloomy. It included two visits to St Joseph's across the lake, fish on Friday, and a small chocolate egg on Sunday. My guardians weren't mean or even penny-pinching; they just didn't buy into something that was incomprehensible to them, and I was satisfied with that.

"Well, I'd better go, Lily." Phillip's voice brought me back into the room and face-to-face with his hovering frame. "I hope you're okay. I'm sorry if I was rambling on about my family. I'm sorry for not being able to give you better news."

"I'm fine. I guess I always knew that there was not likely to be a happy ending to the story. I just think I was happier with the lack of facts. *Disappearance* is a much better word than *murder.* You can be as delusional as you like when you don't say murder." I tried to smile to reassure Phillip that I was coping, that I was strong, and that the revelations of the last weeks were not weighing me down. "I am serious about the initial investigation. I would like to know more about it. Can you tell me where to start?"

Phillip looked pretty unsure that this would render anything new, but he said he'd email me the contact details and anything else he thought might help.

"Bye, Lily. I'll be in touch." He reached out his hand and put it on my shoulder. Then he gave it a little squeeze.

With that, he opened the front door and strode down to his car. He paused before getting in and looked out at the lake. He then looked back at the house and seemed momentarily to be lost in thought. I followed his line of sight and looked out into the middle of the now-dry lake bed. I realized what he was seeing, and the shock of it surprised me. My mother and brother had been in sight all these years. The front door of my parents' house and of Darcy and Billie's homes all looked north east, directly towards the spot where their bodies lay, entwined and weighted with iron, faces turned hopefully towards the shimmering light of sun and moon. Twenty-six years of seasons coming and going, water rising and falling, they waited for the day that the lake would go dry and they could be discovered. I was saddened more by the fact that they had waited so long and was oddly comforted by their constant vigil. Perhaps they had known me all along. It was this that made me think that I had to know more about their lives and deaths.

I was ashamed to have been so ignorant about them—about all of them, my father included. I am both a curator and historian; my life is all about knowing and investigating and placing each fact and artefact in its rightful place in time. I rebuild the lives of those individuals whose lives come to museums. I make the past come back to life. This is what I do, and yet I have never thought that it should be done with my own past. Billie, Darcy, Cillian, Moya, and Brannen had their lives ensconced along with the lives of my ancestors in the trove with which I lived. In these three houses, and perhaps in the recollections of investigators and the remaining locals, I could reconstruct the lives of my family. I could try to answer the question that no forensic report mentioned. Why did he kill them? What possible reason could there be to murder your young wife and son and leave your new born daughter a motherless waif? Why, when it seemed you had gotten away with it, would you kill yourself? As Phillip drove away, kicking up dust and avoiding potholes on Lake Road, I was committed to my new course. I would find answers.

CHAPTER FIVE

efore investigating anything, I would have to deal with work and friends. I knew walking back into the museum would cause a small ripple of interest; and by ripple, I mean deluge. I hadn't been obstructive, only secretive about my life and childhood tragedy. I had revealed nothing about my family because nothing had been asked and assumptions had been made. Everyone assumed that I had lived some bohemian existence and called my parents by their first names. They imagined Billie and Darcy were artsy folks who loved the isolation and quiet of life on the lake and had raised me with a reasonable degree of efficacy, as I was fairly normal, moderately intelligent, and generally civilized. But my silence about life before uni and work was just part of my mystique, and no one really thought to question it further—until now, of course. Now the truth of the past had drawn itself out of its muddy hole and been splashed onto the front pages of local and national newspapers. Why it was a story and why anyone was interested in such things was beyond me. I suspect the dark nature of such an event had whetted the appetite of many, and the current obsession with voyeurism and self-revelation made my story worth examination.

Returning to work was simply an opportunity to escape the unexpected visitors and the incessant phone calls requesting interviews. Here in my office, I would have relative quiet, and most of my colleagues were sensitive enough not to swamp me with questions the minute I appeared. And work was something I could do with a certain confidence that any mystery could be solved. I could bring order to this world. Our current focus was Australian bushrangers, and the excitement over the discovery of Ned Kelly's body and its reburial in Victoria had brought hundreds of related items out of storage. Taking time to reacquaint myself with the life of our most infamous and beloved bushranger was the task I needed to take my mind off the investigation into my own life that I was about to begin. I was just beginning to review the conservator's notes about handling the homemade armour worn by Kelly and his so-called gang when I became aware of a little gang of my own that had shuffled into the work space I'd set up in.

"Lily?" The rather tentative question was offered by my senior researcher and very dear friend Helena Howard. "Can we interrupt you?"

I really wanted to say no, but her earnest and reddened little face made that an impossible choice. And as she was backed by two other colleagues and pals, I simply had no heart to shut them out.

"Of course you can. Hi, Jimmy. Morning, Brendan. Come on in. Interrupt away." I made a weak attempt to sound light-hearted and like my usual self, but I could tell from their faces and their awkwardness that I looked anything like my normal self. A lack of sleep, coupled with heartache, forensic examinations, revelations, and burials, had worn its way into my face. No amount of hair tidying and make-up could eradicate the strain.

I felt worn and brittle. It was if I could finally identify with the most fragile artefacts I dealt with at the museum—things that, if held with too much pressure, would simply disintegrate and fall into floating meaningless pieces. These things, held together with acid free paper and protective covers to ensure the integrity of the objects, were luckier that any human artefact. Nothing was available to us to protect the human object from the onslaught of rough handling. Seeing my little band of extraordinarily clever and eccentric friends, who looked at me as if I were a broken thing, nearly brought me to my knees. All I could do was stare at the notes in front of me.

"I'm okay, guys. I'm rattled but okay." It didn't sound like the truth, and the rush forward to hug me, console me, and offer assistance impacted what I thought was steely resistance. I cried, and they cried—even Jimmy, who was not known for his sensitive responses to weeping. They were making the right sounds of consolation and empathy, and their closeness made me feel protected. Their sorrow at my hurt made me realize that I was right to feel so much pain and misery. I had begun to think that I had little right to feel so bereft. They confirmed that this was a big deal and a shockingly wounding one. The outpouring actually made me feel normal for the first time in several weeks.

"Okay, enough of this." The crying was good; it broke the seal on the tomb that held the long-buried mystery. And strangely I felt closer to the three of them. It was as if failing to reveal the truth about my life had kept an invisible buffer around me. "I'm going to be okay. I just need time, and I feel so overwhelmed."

"Why are you at work?" Jimmy asked.

"Because I need my friends, and I need to be busy. Otherwise all I do is dwell on how exposed and frightened I feel."

Helena just patted my hand. "You do need to be with us. We can keep all the inquisitive bastards away, if you want." She was the only person I knew who could swear and still sound like the queen. She had been a teacher for years before starting work at the museum. She was fifty, looked forty, and behaved as if she was twenty. Jimmy and Brendan were equally as riotous. They partied with Helena and then brought their hangovers, along with tales of their exploits, to me at work to patch up with painkillers, lighter workloads, and reproving lectures. I had met the boys while I was at school—the band of outsiders—and we had kept in touch and, ironically, fallen into the same line of work. When I came back from Sydney to take up this job, they more or less sought out jobs here so we could work together.

The four of us were an excellent team and were really good friends. I felt momentarily guilty when I realized how much of their lives I knew about and how little I had given them. Helena had been so forthcoming about the awfulness of her first marriage and the son she had lost contact with. Her husband had been violent with her but had flourished in the business world. He had money, so when she garnered the courage to leave him, he totally discredited her. She lost custody of her boy. He was only six at the time, and now he would be twenty-six. She left him in London with her husband. Penniless, she returned to Australia, rebuilt her life, and put her past to rest. Of course, she thought about Louis, her child, every day, but misery was a poor motivator. A second and third husband ensued, but there was no other child. I often wondered why.

As for the two boys, Jimmy and Brendan, well, I knew their parents and siblings and even more of their extended families. James Hall and Brendan Holmes were, God forbid, scholarship boys. They were excellent rugby players from the same western NSW town, and city schools would often scout for sporting talent. Luckily, they were both musical and clever. They were respected, but they never really belonged. We were made for each other when we were at school. They were in the brass section of the band; I was in the strings. In our private time together, we sang and played guitars. There was an unspoken but shared hope that we would become rock stars—a shared delusion.

So I knew the three of them very well. They shared everything with me, and I hadn't given them anything. I felt like I had cheated them badly. The recent revelation proved the real test of friendship. After the consoling came the questions—the usual things: What did I know? Was this a complete surprise? Did I know that Billie and Darcy weren't my parents? What was I going to do? To reward them for their faithfulness, I told them everything I knew about my past and everything I was going to do find out truth.

"We're in," Helena said, speaking for the three of them.

"Pardon?" I wasn't sure what she meant.

"You can't do this by yourself, Lil. We're in. We'll help you." I was organising my response to reject the offer, but Jimmy and Brendan confirmed Helena's statement.

"You don't have to do everything by yourself, Lily. This is how friendship works, you know. You let people into your life, and you don't keep secrets," Jimmy said. He was fairly emotional.

"We forgive you for not telling us," Brendan said calmly. Then not so calmly, he added, "So we are going to help you, and all the head shaking in the world won't stop us."

I had spent so much time alone, both physically and emotionally, and I wasn't sure I could cope with the new direction these friendships were taking. But there was a strange relief in letting people into my life. I felt that the decision to be a grown-up was momentarily superseded by the need to be a child—a child finally embraced by protective arms and a fierce kind of angry love. It was a bit new and quite nice. Work would have to be on hold while we talked about the past.

The winter went, and spring came. I had a birthday and turned twenty-seven. A bunch of beautiful white roses, interlaced with pink and purple freesias, arrived on my desk. The note said simply, "Happy Birthday, Lily." The card was signed, "Phillip."

CHAPTER SIX

nd so the days of discovery began. Past lives would unfold in varying degrees of clarity and obscurity. Some secrets would float out of my investigation without resistance, and others would need to be tweezed out of their hiding places. The starting place came from one of a number of pleasant visits from Phillip Swan. We had been emailing each other for a while after I had graciously accepted the flowers. We were generally exchanging courteous inquiries about each other's work and meeting for coffees and brief lunches. I felt Phillip was keeping an eye on me, making sure I wasn't falling into some malaise or maelstrom from which there was little hope of rescue. I was quite surprised by how happy I felt each time I opened my emails and found something from him. He talked about the cases he was working on in the briefest terms, but he was obviously really enjoying dealing with crimes that had obvious perpetrators and some hope of prosecution. The latest bikie shootings and bashings predominantly caught on CCTV cameras were nothing short of a bonus for the police and the DPP. I wondered how much danger he might be in when making these arrests and again found myself bewildered as to why it mattered so much. I eventually had to acknowledge that I had formed a little crush on the gentle giant who had been so kind to me. So much for avoiding the complexities of relationships.

Before I could respond to his latest email, he left a message on my work phone asking if I was going to be home on Saturday afternoon, as he had some news. I didn't want to say that I was home every minute of the weekends, in case it sounded needy, but I happily let him know that I'd be there and that maybe he could come for lunch. I was ridiculously pleased when he confirmed he would arrive at noon and would bring something his mother had made.

In order to gather my thoughts, I spent a little time talking to my friends, Helena, Jimmy, and Brendan, who had generously offered to help me with the forensic-like examination of the O'Hara homes. We had set a date after the exhaustion of Christmas and New Year to start. It would be hot out at the Lake, but the houses were dark and cool. Moreover, we all had time off work to undertake the labour required to dig through the years of history hoarded and compacted into the three O'Hara homes. I tried to dissuade the group from giving up their meagre few weeks of holiday to bury themselves in the dusty remnants of the dead. They insisted, however, that now that they had named themselves Hall, Holmes, and Howard Investigators, they had to help. It was impossible not to, once you had taken on the serious business of a title. It had evolved after a week of discussions and some ardent fighting about the actual order of the names. They wanted to add O'Hara, but I refused to be named last, despite the alphabetical rightness of it. We argued and laughed for days until it was settled. It was a silly distraction that fought away the enormity of the task and the fear of what it might render. I wondered what Phillip might make of such a frivolous approach to such a serious thing. I thought I might ask him.

Saturday came. I had tidied the front room and kitchen more than I had intended. It was a beautiful early summer day, and the drought wore on, making everything just a little dustier and a little crisper. The sky was a startling blue and cloudless. It felt like a day of promise. I was up early, as I wanted to prepare something excellent for lunch. It couldn't look like I was trying to impress, but I wanted to. Somewhere in my head was something about men's hearts and their stomachs being inexplicably linked. Perhaps the paella I had planned might forge this connection. Following it with leatherwood honey panna cotta and gourmet chocolates might help too. It seemed silly, but I wanted some light in my life. I wanted to escape the burden of the past and the fear of what was to come. I just wanted to be a young woman who was making lunch for a young man. Was it too much to ask?

When midday came and Phillip was pulling up in the driveway, I felt a bit self-conscious, because my efforts looked so very obvious. I think desperate might have been a less kind way of putting it. But in the few moments it took him to stride from the car to the house bearing a huge smile and a large cardboard box of things, I let go of the tension of appearances and decided to enjoy the act of welcoming a new friend into my home. The air of officialdom that usually accompanied him out here was nowhere to be seen. Without his suit and carefully concealed gun, he looked like the teenager who had grown up at the beach. He moved like he was a man who expected the world to go his way. There was no sense of the complexities of his job about him.

"My mother insisted that I bring you some things she's made. She insists that the known world should know how great a cook she is." This certainly explained the clinking jars and the large Tupperware cake container that took up the central part of the box. Mrs. Swan had sent me jam, pickles, and a rather substantial pound cake. Phillip must have told her about the young woman he had been helping, and she, perhaps like many mothers, thought food would make everything better. I thought perhaps she could be right; after all, look at the son she had made.

Phillip carried everything into the kitchen and simply set to unpacking it. He was obviously very proud of his mother and maybe used to delivering this type of gift. He had a bottle of white wine, and he casually made his way to the fridge with it before speaking again.

"Give it a couple of minutes to get its chill back," he said. He barely took a breath. "And how are you?"

I was able to tell him that I was better. I felt confident and ready to start some real investigation into the deaths of my family. He didn't respond immediately but looked carefully at my face. I think this silent staring thing is definitely a detective's way of sizing up the enemy. It wasn't the first time he had done this to me, but I stared back and simply raised my eyebrows in defiance.

He laughed and said, "That's good, Lily. I'm glad you are well. You look great." He paused fleetingly and then qualified his adjective by adding, "The first time I saw you, you looked terrible. Like a half-starved stray." That certainly took the possibility of a romantic moment right off the table. But I did laugh.

He was probably right. I was quite a wreck. Months of sleeping poorly and failing to eat had led to considerable wear and tear on my twenty-six-year-old body. All my clothes were too big, the black rings under my eyes made me look like I'd been in a brawl, and I hadn't bothered to try to tame the mane of red curls that simply tangled its way around my head. Today, however, I had been to the hairdresser, had put on make-up, and had selected a dress that did not swamp my dwindling frame. I looked like I might just survive. I think Phillip thought I might too. He put his hand out and touched my face.

"What's for lunch, Lily? I want to eat before we talk about what I've found out." I liked how he said my name as if it amused him. I liked everything about him, particularly the way he made me feel as if I was a normal woman, living a normal life.

I was actually happy to wait for information in case it spoiled the flirtatious mood. I cooked while he talked about his work, his family, and the renovations he was doing on his house. We enjoyed a couple of glasses of chilled wine, ate, and then waited until later in the afternoon to eat dessert. I found it difficult to believe that for a few sunny hours I could put everything out of my mind and simply enjoy the company of a kind and clever man who seemed to be able to do most things. He even thought he could teach me to surf. It would give me another chance to spend some time with him, no matter how unlikely he was to be successful in such an endeavour.

"I suppose you have been waiting all afternoon for me to give you some information," Phillip said, breaking the peaceful afternoon. I had to confess that I hadn't given his reason for coming out much thought at all, but I expect I had to get my head of the clouds and talk about what he had discovered about my family.

As it turned out, it wasn't much of a discovery. The archived reports had little to offer, in the scheme of things. The lack of bodies meant that the investigation was rife with speculation. One couldn't even conclude that there was circumstantial evidence that my father had killed his wife and son, but the terminology and tone certainly cast the pall of suspicion on Cillian O'Hara. There was nothing obvious in the lives of the family that would point to this. Several people had been interviewed. These included the most likely to have information, Billie and Darcy, as well as people around the region who had known my parents, people who had come and gone, and those who even I recognized as individuals who had something to say about the disappearance and suicide that orphaned a baby girl. These names provided a starting place to learn something more than I knew. It seemed unbelievable that in all the time I had sought the help of locals, I had never once asked what they knew about my history. With Billie and Darcy gone, I would have to rely on the memory of those people who had floated about the periphery of my life. They were the neighbours and workers who were there in 1975 and were generally still in the area.

Phillip could obviously see my mind ticking over at a million miles per hour. "Human memory is a flawed thing, Lily," he said. "Don't get too hopeful."

It was a little late for that warning. I felt that somewhere buried in the old paperwork was an answer. If it didn't contain all the puzzle pieces, perhaps there would be one fact, one thing that I could know for sure. There was one name: that of the lead detective on the case in 1975. He had recently retired from the NSW police force and continued to live locally. Detective Michael Flynn, retired, was alive and well enough to be a source of first-hand recollections. He interviewed my father and family in the hours, days, and weeks after the disappearance. If anyone knew what my father had done, Detective Flynn would know.

"Do you think he'll see me, Phillip?" I asked. I sounded like a child asking if Santa was real. I was both apprehensive and excited at the prospect of first-hand knowledge, a primary source who might just tell me something that had never been reported or recorded in any of the surviving documents.

"I've already asked him," Phillip replied. "He said to ring him this week."

I don't know if it was the two glasses of wine or the thrill of having a place to start, but I launched myself at Phillip and hugged him as hard as I could. I experienced a different kind of excitement when he returned my spontaneous squeezing by wrapping his arms around me and kissing me firmly on the lips. I think it surprised us both, but it was obvious that neither of us would protest the action. I was feeling something very much like happiness and perhaps a little like hope. Phillip merely looked pleased with himself. He had one more thing to add.

"I've told my family that you will be joining us for Christmas. I was hoping you wouldn't refuse. There's plenty of space at my parents', and the beach will do you good."

I initially felt the refusal making its way to my mouth. I had spent every Christmas since Billie died by myself. I preferred the lack of human contact on that day. Being with other families rendered my lack of relatives way too obvious to all. But in an unguarded and incautious moment, I simply said yes. Christmas was ten days away, and I had time to think of an excuse not to go if I felt I couldn't manage it. And these days would be filled with meeting Detective Flynn and sorting out some Christmas treats for Jimmy, Brendan, and Helena. This year I would do more than purchase expensive wine and organize a boozy lunch. This year I could be brave enough to bring them out to the lake, feed them here, and exchange real gifts that actually showed them how much I loved their friendship and how much that friendship had saved me. I also thought I'd buy Phillip something.

My mind was racing; my logical manner of processing everything had splintered in a rush of cyclonic happiness. I don't think I've ever felt like this. Not ever.

CHAPTER SEVEN

hen my happy Saturday ended with Phillip waving from his car, I was not only happy but motivated. I liked a man who might just like me, and the promise of a proper Christmas seemed possible. Moreover, in the coming week I would meet a former detective who had been involved in the 1975 investigation into my family's troubles. I felt that Sunday might be a good day for finding some of the old newspapers that reported the incident and captured some photos. I knew Billie had kept piles of old papers all over her house. Some I'd already thrown away since her death. They were ones that had dealt with things she was interested in and that had been important at the time. The attempted assassinations of the Pope and Ronald Reagan in 1981 constituted the first heap I'd turfed into the recycling. The royal wedding followed soon after. Billie had only kept the cuttings from a number of popular magazines and papers about Diana's dress and the hoopla that went on about the young couple. I couldn't really believe she had been a royalist, given her pragmatic and rather brusque way of dealing with romantic notions. Other than the Diana and Charles file, there were many other piles, and if I was going to find the right pile, I'd have to brave the two unused bedrooms that were a hoarder's paradise. I'd have to do it all before Monday and my phone call.

Sunday was, it seemed, designed for staying indoors and keeping out of the weather. A hot, dry wind arrived early in the morning and swirled about the properties and the dry lake like something engaged in a desperate search. Willy-willies were spinning dust and fragments of plants and seeds in all directions. These whirlwinds that sprung up and seemed to have lives of their own. They have been called dust devils and are known in several cultures, including indigenous tribes, as representations of spirits. Sometimes bad spirits spring from the vortexes and lay claim to those who have misbehaved. I didn't subscribe to such notions of evil omens, but I was vexed by the eddying wind that swept into me as I made my way across the yard to Billie's house. Dirt and dust caught me by surprise and left me watery eyed and wild haired. I felt roughed up by the time I leapt up the four steps to Billie's front door. It was enough of barrage to make me feel as if I shouldn't be trespassing. I felt momentarily like I had been rebuked for what I intended to do. But common sense prevailed, and I continued my entry into Billie's world. The pop of the key in the front door and the slight resistance to my push made me realize that I hadn't been inside for a while. The dust that lay in an obvious layer on most surfaces was a clear reminder that I hadn't been over here to clean for some time. I resolved to do some work in the coming weeks before Hall, Holmes, and Howard started helping me with the collection. It would be unfair to make them wade through dust and grime as well as sort out collectible from crap. Darcy's home would be even worse, as I hadn't done anything there since months before the bodies had been found. Resolutions made, I made my way to the rooms where I knew Billie had left her paper collections.

The first room had been mine as girl growing up. It still had my single bed and a hint of pink in the curtains and the paint. There were pictures of fairies and puppies in white frames still on the walls. It had been forever since I'd been here. A couple of Michael Jackson posters clashed horribly with the little-girl decorative touches that had obviously been Billie's choices. She had created a pretty room for a little girl who wasn't her own but who she had determined to raise when there was no one else to do the job. There were no obvious signs of teenage rebellion in this room. It was not really possible to consider Michael Jackson a threat to conformity. I was not a teenager filled with angst or thoughts of anarchy. I think I might have been terrifyingly calm and focused. I'm sure the people who knew what had happened might have expected me to eventually displace my anger and act out, but I didn't. You can't use something you rarely thought about as a catalyst for craziness. I didn't ever consider myself to be a person with a reason to be angry or sad. This room seemed to reflect that very clearly.

Billie hadn't left many papers in here. In fact, she had stacked plastic boxes of clothes and books in my old bedroom. One pile of papers was stacked neatly on the shelves where once I left my instruments and music folders. My violin and two guitars, along with hundreds of sheets of music, were now part of the house I lived in. This group of papers was tied with twine and had curled and yellowed edges. Billie had written "1984" in her tight and tiny handwriting. The papers dealt with the killing of Indira Gandhi in India and the death of Rock Hudson from AIDS. It was strange that these two events had piqued Billie's interest enough for her to keep these papers. I speculated that perhaps she had been a committed feminist and had admired the Indian prime minister for leading the way for women in political life. Perhaps she had been a big fan of Rock Hudson and was unable to believe he was gay. I knew I was distracting myself from the task at hand, which was to find the papers from 1975, but I loved the way a life could be rebuilt from the examination of the artefacts left behind. It was my work but also my passion. In the future, there will be no need for people like me. With the advent of the internet, the explosion of users across the globe, and the new social media concepts being touted, there will be no secrets left to unearth. We will be revealed, and no one will need to guess why a pile of newspapers held such meaning for the collector. Speculation will be lost art. However, this is not the case for Billie's life, which was somehow wrapped up in the things she had gathered, treasured, concealed, and celebrated.

The second room was more challenging in volume. It was room devoid of light and furniture. It had always been an empty room when I was girl. It was the music room, for all intents and purposes.

35

The family piano remained in the front room, but I spent hours of my life in here practising instruments and writing songs that I hoped would propel me into a pop career. By fourteen, I had come to realize the truth about that aspiration. I had talent and I really had the voice to be professional, but I had no pizzazz. The eighties had given birth to Van Halen, INXS, Prince, and Cyndi Lauper. I was no contender in the beauty and eccentricity of this new world of music. Best stick to writing about unrequited love, singing all the parts, and playing all the instruments. As I stood among the carefully stacked papers and magazines, I wondered what had happened to my songs. I really hoped that they had gone away and were not stored here in Billie's history collection. I wondered what she had seen as important enough to stockpile.

Luckily she had some sense of order in her cataloguing. Dates were penned neatly to each pile. Here in the old music room were the 1986 reports on Chernobyl—not just the breaking news stories but the stories about the hideous fallout for the Russian workers and the children of the region. Flicking through the fifty or more papers, it was easy to see that the West was panicking about the implications for our own nuclear power safety and the economic impact of such large-scale disasters. Perhaps it was events like these that started people thinking about global responsibility. I would have been eleven, and as I read through some of the front pages, I recalled Billie and Darcy talking about radiation sickness and the fear that that the whole world might be poisoned by this one terrible accident. I don't recall feeling worried about this calamity at all. The later groups of papers brought about more genuine memories: the Lockerbie plane crash in 1988, the bicentenary for Australia, the fall of the Berlin Wall in 1989. Each subsequent pile neatly dealt with key events of each year. And strange little memories came back. The 1990 pile documented the launch of the Hubble Telescope, which had lead me to decide I wanted to be a scientist. The next piles documented Desert Storm, the Bosnian genocide, and World Trade Centre Bombing in 1993, which together had been the catalyst for me deciding that I wanted to contribute to world peace. It was the year I finished school and was applying for university courses. Everyone thought it would be the music conservatory or medicine, but I did a strange U-turn and decided history and curatorship was my thing. I must have driven Billie and Darcy crazy that year with my indecision and final choices. Perhaps they were just glad I was moving away and that the responsibility would finally be over. I wondered if they really were pleased that I was finally an adult at eighteen and that they could leave the decision making to me.

I knew I was heading in the wrong direction, at least chronologically speaking, when I got to the 1996 pile on the royal divorces and the 1997 stack that was all about the death of Princess Diana. It was a big year for Billie. I was graduating from university, and Darcy was suffering an illness that would see him die early the next year. I wondered if Billie could ever have imagined what was coming as she read through the terrible reports of the young mother's death in a Paris crash. While she was mourning the Princess's demise, did she ever contemplate the further sadness that was coming the O'Haras' way? Did she ever think about what would happen when I was all alone in the world? Could she ever have imagined what would happen when Moya and Brannen returned to me? How could anyone contemplate these things? And soon enough after Diana's death, Billie herself would be gone.

This slip into what might be labelled self-pity was not helping me find 1975. In fact, it was getting the way. I had let my research take me in the wrong direction, which had led me to 1997, and I had to go back. Billie, thus far, had arranged her treasures chronologically with 1984 as the starting point. Logically, the previous years must be back with 1984 in my bedroom. Thirteen years of papers were wedged into the music room, so it was possible that ten years of papers were either in my room or hers.

Another quick sweep of my room revealed no dusty mounds of paper. Perhaps it was reasonable that the more important ones were somewhere else in the house. I hadn't been into Billie's room for more than a year. I didn't go in there as a child very much, only occasionally when I was very little if I had a bad dream. But then she sent me back to my own bed with a strong sense that I could cope and didn't need coddling. I never went there as a teenager and never had the desire to. I went into the room to find clothes for her to be buried in, and I vacuumed there every couple of months in the year after she died.

As I stood outside the door, I couldn't even recall what the furnishings looked like. All I could remember was a story that Darcy had told me one Christmas that had left the two of us doubled up with laughter and Billie unmoved by our amusement. Apparently when I was three, I had vandalized Billie's bedroom. She had one brand-new lipstick. It was red and extremely fancy, as it came in a gold metal case. I could not recall Billie ever wearing lipstick, let alone bright red. I must have had something in my head when I woke very early one morning as a three year old. Allegedly, I went into Billie's room, and as she slept, I discovered the red lipstick, unsheathed its glorious greasiness, and used it to draw a line around the walls of her bedroom. One wiggly three-year-old's poorly controlled lipstick line around the walls from one side of her bed to the other. Then in a flash of symmetry, I decided to draw a line across the floor. This required me to drag my now-blunt lipstick across polished boards and a tufted, woollen mat and then up and inside each of Billie's best shoes, which unfortunately sat right in the middle of my artistic trajectory. Darcy laughed till he had tears running down his face. It took the two of them weeks to clean and repaint the whole room. The mat and shoes were ruined. Billie apparently never had lipstick again—that is, until she was prepared by the mortician's assistant for burial. I provided a brand-new, gold-cased red lipstick to complete her final make-up. I hoped she and Darcy would laugh in heaven at my final apology for lipstick sins. I asked that the lipstick and few other small treasures be arranged in her hands before the casket lid was secured. It was the only thing that made me smile.

Now on re-entering Billie's room, I smiled again. It was terrible that I had let dust gather. It was terrible that I hadn't cleaned out her clothes or let light or air in here for so long. There was so much to remember, and much of it was good. But where had Billie put ten years' worth of papers? It was not obvious, like it was in the other two rooms. I would have to open cupboards and pry into her life if I wanted to really find 1975 and 1976. It was actually easier than I thought it would be. Her wardrobe had three mirrored doors. It was a monstrous oak thing with bevelled mirrors and ornate carving. Perhaps if I'd ever played in here, I would have thought that Narnia was just on the other side of one of these doors. But there was no snowy fantasy world beyond the neatly stowed clothes. On one side, Billie had hung a small range of good-quality going-out clothes. This included a beautiful tailored coat in grey wool with a ruffled silk collar. It was stunning. I remembered her wearing this to church and to parent evenings at school. I had probably been embarrassed by my country guardian, but I recalled seeing her arrive in the visitor's car park and exit the old Mercedes with a grace that I'd never hope to achieve. Billie was a proud woman and was not ashamed of who she was or how she had raised her niece. How strange that one item of clothing could help me remember so much, so fondly.

I was struck by the neatness of her wardrobe. Everything had a specific place to be, and each item was folded with precision and laid on shelves lined with rose-covered paper. There was a scent as well that wasn't quite masked by dust—not the usual lavender or rose scent one might assume ladies of Billie's ilk might use, but rather a fresh herb smell. It was rosemary.

Among the clothes were the newspapers, stacked neatly under the hanging garments. There weren't many. Of course, there wouldn't be. There was more important news in 1975 that would have pushed the mysterious disappearance of a woman and her child out of the headlines. After all, that was the year Microsoft was founded, Pol Pot rose to power in Cambodia, and Jimmy Hoffa went missing in America. And in 1976, when the supposed murderer Cillian O'Hara topped himself, Nadia Comaneci was getting the first perfect scores in gymnastics, the first cases of the Ebola virus were striking the Sudan, and 240,00 people died in the Tangshan earthquake. Even the local papers couldn't keep a local story going under those circumstances.

How could such a little tragedy on Lake Road compete with global events like that?

But there they were, carefully preserved and seemingly more well read than the others I'd put aside to move to the recycling. I couldn't really believe that I'd never seen these front pages before. The first one on the top of the 1975 pile was dated Monday, December 8. It was not going to be a happy Christmas that year.

LAKE GEORGE CLAIMS MORE VICTIMS—not an inspired headline but certainly poignant enough. The journalist, Thomas West, was not trying anything clever, he was simply stating the obvious. The photo that accompanied the front page story was a rather bleak black-and-white image of the scene with our house in the background and police and others milling around the lake's shore in the foreground. The watercraft and men in what looked like diving gear seemed to be the focus of the camera, but there were other things that perhaps had not meant to be captured. Only by squinting at the grainy, unfocused image could I see Billie standing on the front porch of my house holding what appeared to be a baby. A man sat beside her with his head in his hands. It was not my father, so I imagined it had to be Darcy.

A smaller photo of Cillian was incorporated into the story as it moved to page 2 of the paper. He was leaning on the front of a police vehicle. His arms were folded across his chest, and it was obvious that he was listening to man who was waving his arms in the general direction of the eastern side of the lake. My father's face looked ashen, and his expression was one of confusion. He looked like a man who was being told something incredible. But other than that, I couldn't see anything that told the story one way or the other. I'm not sure what I was expecting—that one look at his face and I would be able to see the truth? In fact, all I could see was a young man who could have been doing anything except trying to explain why his wife and child had disappeared while sailing.

The story was factual in its reporting, and I was momentarily impressed by Mr. West's lack of embellishment and innuendo. He was not building a story; he was merely telling what was known.

He interviewed the lead detective, Sergeant Flynn, and two locals, Jimmy and Sarah Murphy, who had been long-term residents of Lake Road. Words such as *tragedy* and *wonderful family* were key in the reports from the Murphys. They said little about Cillian other than that he was a hard-working man who was known for his carpentry skills. Moya, they said, was a model mother. She doted on her little boy and was very proud of the new baby. Detective Flynn simply outlined the facts as he knew them and concluded that the investigation would continue once the bodies were recovered. West had allowed himself some literary flair in the description of the treacherous nature of the lake and some glimmer of emotion when he commented that the joy of Christmas would not be so joyful for the families of the district.

So there was little to be gleaned from the first report. The second report followed the day after the disappearance, and there was a clear but unstated shift in sympathy. Divers were confused that they were unable to see any sign of the bodies in the area Mr. O'Hara had directed them to. The unlikelihood that the bodies would not float up to the surface was woven into the story as an accusation of some interference at work in the drownings.

Someone had provided an older photo of my parents and Brannen taken at a school fete. It showed a dear little boy with a fat face being held close to his mother's side. She had gripped his shoulders to hold him still for the photo. Her face was flushed with the effort of wrangling a four-year-old, and she was trying to smile. Her hair was loose over her shoulders, and she was managing a slight, crooked smile. She looked tiny in her jeans and shirt—more like a child herself. My father, on the other hand, was tall and lean. His hair was long too but curly and quite unruly. But his face was the thing. He was smiling like a man who had everything he wanted. His eyes were bright with the simple joy of being. He looked like a father a little girl would have adored. He was good looking and truly handsome. There was nothing in his face that would have spoken to anything being wrong. But something in the photo caught my eye: it was the fact that in this family portrait, my father's left hand was wrapped tightly around Moya's right forearm. He was holding her in place as much as she was holding Brannen. It seemed that they were grasping each other like lifelines. I wondered if he was holding her up or holding her in place. I could only speculate on what would happen once the photographer walked away. Were they having a little fight? Had she just told him that he would be a father again? The time frame was right. Would that have made him happy? Had she done something that made him angry?

There were only four more reports that had the story in the first few pages of the paper. There were similar images of the lake and the searchers. No personal photos were included in any of the other stories. Detective Flynn had assured the family that although the search was being called off, he would continue to investigate.

"Young mothers and their sons do not just disappear. We will find out what happened to Mrs. O'Hara and her son. The family is continuing to assist us with our enquiries," he was quoted as saying.

I don't know whether he meant to sound accusing with the clipped nature of his words, but he did. The family, Cillian, Darcy, and Billie, were providing information, but whatever this was, it was not being reported by Thomas West. The story was not a story until the bodies were found. But the dark speculation was rife. A photo of my father walking away from the water was the last image captured by the newspaper, or at least the last one published, on Christmas Eve 1975, seventeen days after Moya and Brannen disappeared. The same photo reappeared on September 26, 1976, the day after my father killed himself. The same reporter broke the news to an unforgiving public, who assumed that his hanging himself was an admission of guilt, despite the headline that attempted to elicit sympathy: TRAGEDY CONTINUES ON LAKE ROAD. I assume he wasn't talking about Cillian. Cillian was described as a suspect in the disappearance of his wife and son. The tragedy according to Mr. West, one assumes, was that a nine-month-old girl was now seemingly adrift in the world without parents. He seemed to conclude that the tragedy was deepened by the fact that she would be adopted by the suspect's sister and brother. The public, I imagined, must have had Dickensian visions of my servitude and loveless existence at the hands of two strangers who knew something and were protecting the killer, despite his suicide. While they were not effusive in their love, I did not doubt that Billie and Darcy loved me. I was theirs and was the only tangible link to both the awful past and the hopeful future. I wondered if Mr. West was still alive and if I could ask Phillip to track down another lead for me.

CHAPTER EIGHT

he Sunday ended with several trips to the recycling bins set up on my three properties. Most months I barely had half a bin to be taken to the main road for the garbage collection trucks to pick up. But this week would be a bonanza for the recyclers. The only papers I was keeping were those in the meagre pile from 1975 and two from 1976. While I thought they offered little in the way of the sort of evidence I was looking for, I still couldn't bring myself to throw them away. And I was sure that my friends would want to see them when they came in to help turn the places over after Christmas.

The last thing I did before settling in for another quiet evening was ring Detective Flynn. I was adamant that I would prefer meeting him rather than discussing things over the phone. There was always more to be gleaned from being face-to-face with someone when they were trying to recall the past or conceal it. It was much easier to brush over the truth when you didn't have to look at the person who was seeking information. Lies were easier to tell when someone wasn't searching your eyes while listening to your words. So after some deft persuasion, he gave in and made time for me on Tuesday afternoon.

Despite it being a week before Christmas, Detective Flynn seemed to accept the inevitability of having to come face-to-face with the child he hadn't seen for over twenty years. I wondered if he had thought about the incident—the crime, as he might see it—during that time frame. I made a mental note to add that to my questions.

He gave detailed directions to his rural property, which, ironically, wasn't that far from where I lived. I would leave work early on the Tuesday and get to his place by four o'clock.

The two days at work before the meeting were slow, and this gave me the opportunity to think about what I would ask the detective. Perhaps the most burning question was whether he thought my father was a murderer. Did he think it then, and did the discovery of my mother and brother at the bottom of the lake confirm his initial beliefs? I also wanted to ask him if there were people he interviewed who I could also talk to. But all of this would have to wait until I met the man himself. Phillip had been sensible to warn me about the nature of memory. It was shaped, of course, by the events themselves, the reasons we were creating the memory, and then reshaped by the ensuing years. It is infrequent that what we believe to be a true account of something is the actual truth. Anything approximating the truth had to be viewed from several angles and perspectives. I expect this was never more true than in the minds of the police who build cases against criminals by knowing everything and everyone involved. Surely one wouldn't simply believe the account given by the perpetrator, nor that given by the victim—that is, if a victim was capable of giving his or her side of the story.

I left work at three o'clock on Tuesday, despite knowing that weaving my way through the new suburbs in Canberra's north-west to get to Gundaroo, where Detective Flynn lived, would only take me thirty minutes. I didn't want to be late or to feel rushed when I arrived. I had it in my head that he would not take me seriously if I arrived in an anxious state. I didn't want to be seen as someone hopelessly floundering around, trying to make sense of the long dead. I wanted him to see this as more forensic in nature, more objective, not some strange quest for absolution or closure. I just wanted to know the people who were my family.

As I approached the area now subdivided into reasonable farmlets, I consulted the directions I had been given. Plain Farm, the Flynn property, was on my right as I exited the village. At this time of the afternoon, a small posse of kids had just left the primary school, and they were kicking up dust as they dragged themselves home through paddocks and long, winding driveways. They still had two more days of school before the Christmas holidays finally began. I had a small pang of envy as I thought about the anticipation of that kind of freedom. When you are young, the thought of six weeks of hot weather, cloudless skies, and endless opportunities for adventure is the motivation to slog out the last few weeks of the school year. I could see that very thing in these young ones, in their navy blue shorts and sky blue t-shirts. The white socks and polished black shoes that would have started the day clean were now grime covered and heavy with a day's play. Their backpacks, full of a term's work, were being taken home to weary parents who wondered what to do with the dog-eared exercise books and poorly preserved projects. No doubt they wondered how they'd be entertaining the troops for the entire holiday.

I waited until the last little group filtered away or got onto buses or into waiting cars. The dust settled, and the town fell to silence. I thought about the power of rural solitude. I wondered why people still sought this type of urban escape. I lived out on the lake, but it wasn't by choice; it was by birth. Maybe I'd ask him why he moved out here.

Detective Flynn's house was at the end of a fifty-metre driveway. It was rutted and dusty, a further testament to the number of rainless seasons that had recently passed. The property was neat and unfenced. Obviously he was not running livestock on his little farm. He had built himself a new home that resembled the homesteads built in this area in the past. It was placed square on the site with the front door facing the drive. The house was bordered by geometric garden beds built of treated pine and corrugated iron. The plants were thriving and varied in colour and size. The man was obviously a keen gardener and had an eye for landscape aesthetics. The house was appealing too, in its symmetry. A wide veranda wrapped around three sides of the house and was covered by a bull-nosed roof—very traditional and very practical. It kept the heat out of the house in summer and made the timber porch useable if ever there was rain. The veranda was unadorned except for two timber benches on either side of the front door. As I got closer, I could see they were old church pews that had been preserved and polished. I couldn't say exactly why I thought this looked like a man's home. There didn't seem to be anything feminine in the matter-of-fact way the house presented itself. Of course, I had no idea about the detective's personal life; he might have had a harem inside, for all I knew.

As my car engine stopped and I got out of the car, he appeared from the side of the house. He was dressed for outside work. For a man in his sixties, as I guessed he must be, he looked fit and had an air of youthful agility about him. Perhaps it was working outdoors that had made him look so good. He didn't smile when he saw me but waved his hand in the direction of the front door to indicate that I should go up onto the porch to wait for him to remove his hat and gloves. As he climbed the steps at the far end of the veranda, he removed his sunglasses too, and I was surprised to see such a good-looking man. His hair was greying but still thick and well groomed. His eyes were dark and stern. There were deep lines etched into his face, and it was hard to tell whether it was from laughter or worry. He said nothing as he approached me, but I could tell he was sizing me up in the same way I was taking him in. I wondered what he thought. *She looks like her mother?* Or *She looks like the daughter of a killer?*

"Lily O'Hara," he said. A statement, not a question. He went on, "Detective Swan has filled in the gaps, so there is no need for you to explain the background. Although I'm interested in why you think I can tell you more than you already know."

I wanted to interrupt him, but he had obviously thought about how he was going to circumvent a long discussion. I wanted to tell him that I knew very little and that I harboured hope that he might be able to remember something that would offer a light, even a slight candle flicker of light, on the past.

"Detective Flynn," I began.

"Mick. I'm not a detective anymore, Lily," he said, interrupting my opening gambit.

"Once a copper, always …" I inadvertently verbalized. He smiled and nodded in agreement. The ice broken, I was invited inside, out of the warmth of the afternoon sun. Late afternoon was always the time when the temperature peaked, even in early summer, so it was nice to enter the cool dimness of the house. The home was as uncluttered as the garden. The entry opened into a wide, open room with all the key elements in it. The kitchen was on the left, the dining table in the middle, and a lounge chair and enormous open fireplace at the right. A hallway on the far wall seem to lead to other places, such as bathrooms and bedrooms. The few artworks, fewer photos, and absence of ornaments seemed to confirm my thoughts that this was not a place that had a woman's touch. It was beautiful but bland. On reflection, it revealed as much about the detective's life and mind as everyone's homes do. The chaos of my own houses was a clear indication that I couldn't see the truth of the clutter I'd allowed to grown around me. Mick had certainly picked his life clean, and the bare bones of his past and present were evident in the well-ordered sparseness of his home.

Mick asked me to sit down at the kitchen bench. He went around the other side and put on the kettle. He had assumed that I would be staying long enough to require the pleasantries of a hot drink. While the kettle began to boil, he ascertained whether it was tea or coffee, white or black, sugar or not.

Then he led with, "What do you want, Lily?"

It seemed like such a simple question, and the answer was equally simple. I wanted to know if thought—if he knew—what happened in 1975. What had people said to him? How had he responded to my father and my aunt and uncle when he met them? I wanted him to remember and explain to me what he felt on those days when he drove out the lake in search of my mother. My silence must have conveyed everything that was happening in my head, because he simply said that he would tell me what he could remember.

He started with the most obvious. He remembered driving out from the Queanbeyan police station to meet the local coppers who had been called to the house when Cillian returned alone. The officers were Paul Matthews and Terence Bailey. They had called for a detective, and it happened to be Mick who got the call. Mick knew the area well, but he had never driven down Lake Road before. Despite growing up in Canberra and knowing the history of the area, he was unaware of this access to the water. Most people had no idea about the little community, and few had an interest until there was a story.

Mick continued by describing the scene as he had written it in his notes. Matthews and Bailey were interviewing Cillian by the police car. Two other people were standing close by, rocking a pram. The only noise was that of a crying baby.

"Your father went and picked you up and continued the interview with you in his arms. You stopped crying immediately. He seemed to relax more when you were quiet." So my father held me. Obviously he felt better with me in his arms. This was an assumption with little or no basis in evidence, but I liked the thought that he gained some level of comfort from holding me.

The local officers had already sketched the details of the events when Mick arrived. He had been in contact with the AFP, who were likely to share resources with their colleagues over the border and provide divers if it seemed a search was warranted. This, of course, happened later that day.

"Did you ask him questions?" I said, interrupting Mick's description of the facts. I wanted to know something about my father's voice, his demeanour. Mick described him, choosing his words fairly carefully. He said that Cillian was passive. *An odd word*, I thought. He elaborated by saying that he was incredibly still, even with the baby in his arms. He didn't rock and move his weight from foot to foot, he merely stood stock-still and looked out to where he thought he had lost them. There was little expression on his face; it was blank and emotionless. Perhaps it was shock, I offered as an explanation. Mick nodded, but not in a way that reflected agreement. He said people in shock act differently, not with this unusual calmness. It was as if Cillian was describing something that had happened to someone else. He was very disconnected, but his explanation was very precise, with detail down to the sounds and recalled conversations.

My father had described the afternoon to the three listening officers in minute detail: The day was warm, and the breeze off the lake was very gentle. Billie had offered to watch the baby, and she had suggested Cillian take Moya out for a sail. She was tired and irritated by the lack of sleep that comes with a new baby. Some quiet time for the parents would be good for everyone. They weren't going to take Brannen. He could stay and play with Darcy on the front veranda and watch his parents on the lake. But he wanted to go with them. He was sick of hearing the wailing of the nuisance baby that had come to disrupt his life. Moya didn't want the little boy to go. She tried to make him stay at home, but he had a crying fit and wouldn't let go of his mother's dress. He kept saying "Mummy, I want to go with you. I don't want to be alone."

"See what I mean about the detail," Mick interjected. "He remembered things like what your brother said and your mother's reactions. But he couldn't recall anything about what happened on the lake."

I was still sure my father's reactions must have been shock, but Mick continued with his storytelling. Cillian was able to describe how he loaded Moya and Brannen into the little dinghy. It was anchored just five metres from the shore and was easily pulled close enough for him to carry both his wife and son to the boat and load them safely inside. He waded about in the reeds and drew the light anchor and chain up from the mud. These were new additions to the boat. It had been painted and reappointed with new oar locks as well as a new anchor and chain. He fitted the oars into the locks and started to row to the eastern shore. It was deepest there, and the little boy could put a line in and catch a fish perhaps. Perhaps he might also be lulled to sleep by the gentle rocking that was established as Cillian created a reasonable pace, the blades slipping into and slapping out of the water. He was certain Moya had fallen asleep about ten minutes into the row. Brannen was sitting on the anchor chain making patterns with the shiny new links. He was humming to himself.

Mick remembered feeling odd about how precise Cillian was on the timing of things. They went into the boat at 2:00 p.m. They had eaten lunch, and he had had a beer with his food and another after that. He had been drinking but was apparently sober enough to row a dinghy. He slowed his rowing as they made it to the east basin. They were just in view of the houses on Lake Road but far enough away for the activities there to be unseen and unheard. Brannen was asleep on the floor beside his mother. His little head was resting on her knee. Cillian described the moment as one of relief. Everyone was relaxing, tension was gone, and there was no need for anyone to worry about anything. He was so relaxed that he thought he would close his eyes for ten minutes and just let the boat drift a bit. It was 2:35 p.m. exactly when he "allegedly" closed his eyes. The word *allegedly* brought tension back into the room.

"Why would you say *allegedly*? Didn't you believe him?"

Mick's patience continued as he explained, "Allegedly because I had no proof either way. You have to realize that I didn't know your father, and two people had gone missing. I had to make some assumptions based on limited facts and gut reaction."

"Did he say anything else?" Of course I knew the answer to this question. My father had given the detective further description of the events after he had woken. The boat was simply empty. Cillian had surprisingly slept for fifty-two minutes as the dinghy floated further into the south-eastern side of the lake. He was woken when the little boat scraped against reeds that grew well out into the lake on that furthest side. The time was 3:27, according to Cillian. The boat was empty. He seemed to think that Moya and Brannen had simply vanished. He even questioned if they were even in the boat with him. He made mention twice that, because they were so close to the shore, Moya perhaps got Brannen out of the boat and walked, soaking wet, through the mud flats and rushy lagoon to the properties south of Bungendore. He was convinced that she was playing some kind of trick on him. He called her name for nearly fifteen minutes, and at 3:45 he put the oars back in the locks, rowed out of the reeds, and headed home. When the police asked him to consider that Moya and Brannen had fallen from the boat and drowned, Cillian O'Hara seemed to be unable to comprehend that anything like that could happen. The place they had floated to was so shallow that even Brannen could have touched the bottom of the lake. Moya could swim; she was small but strong. He seemed certain that he would have heard something if they had gone over the edge. He would have woken up.

The next question seemed to baffle him even more. Officer Bailey asked him outright if he had anything to do with his wife and child's disappearance. Cillian remained impassive, and his response was both curious and suspect. Cillian simply said that killing someone would be better done in a place that the killer could not be proven to have been. Mick stopped his narrative for a moment.

"What did you think then?" I asked, but I didn't want to know the answer.

"I knew your father had killed them." It was so blunt a response that it felt like a blow to the solar plexus. I felt air forced out of me like I'd truly been punched deep in the gut.

When I could breathe again and speak without a tremor in my voice, I suggested that my father's comment surely pointed to his innocence. Why would he talk about the ease of killing someone or the purpose of an alibi if he was truly guilty? I sensed that I was becoming a little shrill and defensive of a man I didn't know. Mick poured more tea into my cup and put the teapot down. He put his hand on mine and looked at me as if I was a stupid child.

"Lily, your mother and brother were found in the lake weighted by a chain—a chain that your father didn't mention was missing in those first interviews. He knew the time down to the minute when people fell asleep, woke, and called out, but he didn't observe the missing anchor chain. You have to accept that he killed them. He was clever, and he was calm. But when the coroner finally concluded that Moya and Brannen were dead, Cillian O'Hara killed himself."

It was a *fait accompli* for Detective Flynn. He couldn't prove that her father was a killer in 1975, but by 1976 he was ready to lay charges, despite the lack of bodies. And now in 2001, he had bodies, he had the proof, and he had his gut feeling. Without a shadow of a doubt, he believed my father murdered Moya and Brannen.

"But why?" I knew I sounded dejected, pitiful—like a child again. But if this terrible thing was true, there had to be a reason. Surely people didn't go around killing people they love without a reason. How could a father kill his son? Mick didn't have an answer. I felt more pain than I'd expected to, but more had to be said.

"What did the other people you interviewed say? Did any of them confirm that he would be capable of this." I couldn't use the term *my father* at this point. I thought I was going to throw up all the tepid tea I'd consumed. I had to use Mick's bathroom to calm myself; if I was going to vomit, I didn't want to do it all over his kitchen bench. He pointed me down the hallway, and when I closed the door, I gave myself five minutes to find some composure. I really wanted to ring Phillip. I wanted to tell him that I was afraid of what I was hearing and that I wanted him to be with me. Instead, I splashed water on my face, used the toilet, and spent another minute looking at my face in the mirror over the sink. I didn't know who was looking back. It was a new face—one I hadn't seen before. It was a woman who was a killer's daughter. I could live with *orphan*, and I could live with *lonely*; but I wasn't sure I could bear this. From photos, I knew I looked a lot like Moya and not a lot like my father, but something of him had to be a part of me. I could only hope the rest of my discussion with Mick would render something better. There weren't really any further depths we could explore after his last disclosure.

When I came out to the bathroom, Mick had moved our cups and a hot pot of tea to the lounge area. He had settled himself into a huge leather chair, which was obviously the spot he always sat in. He was leaning forward with his arms on his knees looking at the table as if it might be about to tell him something. When he looked up, I could see a little worry in his eyes, and before he could ask the question, I informed him that I was fine.

"It's a bit like being hit, I think. I knew I might get punched if I started a fight; I just didn't think the force of it would be so unexpected." That was my weak explanation for a long stint in the bathroom.

"How could you be surprised, Lily?" I guess it was a reasonable question. But there's a huge difference between an academic understanding of something and a real-life, emotional connection to it. Why was disbelief in something so terrible a crime? Why couldn't I be surprised and shaken by such a thing?

"Do you want to know more?" he asked. Of course I did. Fortified with more tea and now sandwiches that Mick had somehow rustled up in my absence, I thought I was able to hear more. What I didn't know was that in my absence he had called Phillip to tell him that he was worried about my reaction, that he thought this was too much for me, and that perhaps Phillip should discourage me from investigating further. Mick thought that the sleeping dogs should lie and that the bodies now buried and long dead should be left alone. No good could come from this. Phillip, wisely, had said that he didn't think I could be stopped. He would, however, try to talk me into letting the rest go.

Despite his rushed conversation with my new friend, he continued to answer my questions. I wanted to know who else he had interviewed and what he could remember about their responses to Moya's disappearance. Mick was patient, and I suspect that, despite looking at a file of papers he had produced, he knew pretty much what he was going to say. I think his words were rehearsed but also truly familiar. This case seemed to have stayed with him, and I wondered if that was because a woman and child were involved or because he remembered all his cases this well.

As if he was reading my mind, he said, "The finding of the bodies last winter brought much of this back to me. I was already connected to this case; it never really left me. It's hard to let go of something that is so inconclusive. And I mean that. The coroner was emphatic in his decision, but I wanted to know why all this had happened to your family." So Mick was not so different from me. He knew something about the deep longing that comes when answers are not provided.

He started going through his interview notes methodically. He recalled Darcy's reaction easily. He was a man who was bereft about the disappearance of his sister-in-law and of the wee boy. He was barely able to answer questions coherently, and Mick recalled that Darcy's responses to questions didn't match. When he asked Darcy if he was close to his brother, Cillian, all he could say was "they're alone out there." The police were sure that Darcy knew something, but when asked "out where?" he became defensive of his younger brother, claiming that Cillian was a wonderful, kind, and decent man. Mick had put his mixed answers and unpredictable responses down to shock. Darcy seemed to be a very private man who did little living outside the lake community. He didn't work, other than to produce highly sought-after fruits and vegetables from his huge market garden, chicken and duck eggs, poultry meat, and apparently an assortment of self-made alcoholic beverages. All his products were sold at the property and in the local stores of neighbouring towns. I didn't know this. I had always had a plate full of food that I knew wasn't bought in a supermarket, but I didn't think to ask who had raised the bounty we enjoyed. Darcy was always around, but I was too wrapped up in my own world to notice a man who had such a deep affinity with the land that he could make a living from it and support his extended family.

When asked about his relationship with Moya and Brannen, Darcy simply could not speak. A pall of grief settled about him, Mick remembered. He cried and had to be left alone. Only Billie could offer him any solace. Cillian turned away from his brother and sister and walked back to the lake. Mick said he and the other officers were somewhat interested by this strange divide that emerged when Darcy seemed at his most vulnerable.

"When I went out to interview the family a second time after your father killed himself, Darcy was nowhere to be seen. He avoided us like the plague. Your aunt said he was ill." Mick's tone was matter-of-fact, neither confirming nor denying his belief in Darcy's whereabouts on that day.

He continued with his assessment of the "witnesses"—his word, not mine. These people were my family and family friends who had experienced a terrible tragedy. Whether it was murder or misadventure, the loss would have reverberated throughout the community. These terrible events had always brought us together or polarized us in the blame laying. Everyone would have an opinion.

Billie, apparently, had been stoical and prepared to give lots of background information that helped give a picture of the family, but she had made few speculative comments. She was like a wall that had risen to protect her brother from suspicion of wrong doing. Despite her resolve to give little away, Mick had made notes about her assessment of Moya. The two women were not particularly close, Moya being an outsider who hadn't really found a life for herself on the lake. Moya had grown up in Canberra after coming out to Australia with her parents from London when she was only four. She had worked in a hotel for a while after she finished school, and she was musical. She played in band and sang when she met Cillian. He was attracted to her immediately; she was beautiful, in a natural way, and needy. He like that about her. She was hopeless at nearly everything, couldn't cook or mend anything, didn't like gardening, and barely ate anything, even when she was pregnant. Flighty. It was an unusual word for Billie to use, and I questioned Mick about it.

"Was that the word she used? Did she call my mother flighty?" Mick looked at a well-thumbed notepad. "Yes, and she said your mother was highly strung, more so after Brannen's birth and worse after you came along."

I was thinking that this was a clue to something. Mick thought it was more like a motive. A highly strung—these days one might say *anxious*—outsider with no family of her own about. Maybe she had some postnatal depression? Or from Mick's point of view, maybe she was troubled enough to be difficult in the home and therefore had fallen victim to an impatient man who couldn't take her behaviour any longer.

"What else did people say?"

Rudolph Chaffey, who employed Cillian, was interviewed several times both in 1975 and in 1976 when Cillian took his own life. Chaffey was a local builder who used craftsmen like Cillian to complete specialized carpentry work. It wasn't just nailing together stud frames but rather work that in the past artisans would have done. Apparently my father made furniture as well as working for Chaffey. He made specialty pieces for many people, including several Canberra politicians. Chaffey even claimed that some of O'Hara's work was in the Lodge, because John Gorton and Billy McMahon had both commissioned work from him when they each became prime minister. It made me wonder if a man who could create furniture art for the men who ran the country could really murder his wife and son.

But Chaffey also had some other things to say that might have worried the detective who already had his suspicions, from which no accolades about Cillian's talent would dissuade him. Apparently, even though he was a good man, Cillian drank too much. It had become more obvious to his employer over the last year or two of his life. Chaffey thought there might have been trouble at home.

"Isn't it the reason most men drink?" he had asked. He had gone on to say that there had been rumours about Moya. Mick stopped here in his narrative. He was reading back his notes to me, and this point pulled him up short.

"Do you want me to read this?" I was not unmoved by hearing the word *rumour* and my mother's name paired, but I nodded my assent and he continued.

Moya had been spending more time in Canberra with her friends. Chaffey couldn't really say who the friends were, but the gossips about the lake had suggested that it was those musicians she had played with before she married. She wasn't seen much about the community except at school events and was seen even less at church. Of course, she stopped going once she was obviously pregnant with her second child.

And what was my father doing while my mother was going into Canberra. He was drinking most nights at the local pub—not getting drunk, just having a few drinks with the locals and enjoying talk about the state of the world, rugby, and work. Sometimes Darcy joined him, but not often. Chaffey's comments about Cillian seemed innocuous enough, but even I could tell how this information might point to something untoward happening in the O'Hara family. I couldn't help but think of that photo that had been in the newspaper, the one where my little family seemed to be grasping on to each other and the smiles were perhaps something other than joy. Perhaps those smiles were masks hiding something that neither of them had control over. Some terrible inevitability was rising out of life, something that would not only consume them but also the child they would leave behind.

Mick shuffled a few pages of his notes past things that he obviously thought could add little to the story. He then moved onto the material provided by the Sarah and Thomas Murphy. The Murphys were a fourth generation Lake Road family. Thomas' parents and two previous generations had raised large and unruly Catholic families on a property close to the main road. It made sense that they knew my parents well, as they had children both older and younger than me. I lost count of the actual number of Murphys, but I had been good friends with Rosie and Kathleen, who were about my age. Perhaps one was a year older and the other eight months younger. Sarah had always been pregnant or had a baby at her breast for as many years as I could recall. Surely as friends of the O'Haras, they would never believe my father could ever do anyone harm. I was hopeful of hearing something positive and leaned closer to Mick as he began recalling and reading what had been said.

The Murphys, both of them, didn't have a bad word said about Moya. When they were questioned about her visits to Canberra, Sarah had a very plausible explanation for her behaviour. She said that Moya had decided that she wanted to be more than a wife and mother and decided to go to university to become a teacher. One night, when the two families were barbecuing, Moya brought up the issue about them moving to Canberra so she could study. The university had a preschool nearby and a local Catholic primary school for Brannen to attend. There would be plenty of work for Cillian, as all the suburbs both north and south of the city centre were developing. Rents were cheap, and there was little standing in the way of them moving from the lake. Thomas said that Cillian had never agreed to such a move. He was a lake man and wouldn't want to live in the city. He hadn't said no to Moya, but he was a long way from agreeing to such a thing. The second pregnancy seemed to put the idea on hold, anyway. The Murphys both confirmed that the birth of the little girl seemed to halt all future plans. Mick had then asked them two other questions: Did they know who Moya was seeing in Canberra? And was Cillian ever violent or ill-tempered about his wife spending time away and making plans that didn't suit him?

Sarah answered the first question by filling in what she knew about Moya. She confirmed that she was a musician and had friends who were still in the band scene in the city. Sarah knew that she had been born in London and had emigrated with her parents when she was four. Not surprisingly Moya's parents, Leo and Vivienne Bryant, had returned the UK after she married Cillian in 1968. She was an only child and was seemingly distanced from her parents. They were unhappy at the wedding and didn't approve of Cillian, who was not as sophisticated as the Bryants. He was a country boy with no airs or graces. They felt he had few prospects, given that he wasn't really ambitious. But it was their lack of connection to Moya that surprised Sarah most of all. When she went missing, neither parent returned for the investigation, nor did they appear for the memorial service that saw their daughter and grandson commemorated by simple headstones.

"Did you ever hear from them, Lily?" It was a reasonable question from Mick.

"I'm embarrassed to say that I had never thought of my mother having a life before she came to live, and die, out on the lake. I had never heard Billie or Darcy say anything about their own parents, let alone the Bryants." I wondered if they were still alive and did a quick calculation in my head. They would likely be in their eighties but possibly still alive. Did anyone tell them about what happened to Moya? Should I try to find them to tell them they have a granddaughter? It was an investigation for another time, perhaps. I felt strange thinking about having family and even stranger for not knowing anything about one half of my genetic make-up. I wondered briefly why I had let myself be so ignorant of such things.

As for the second question, I was more anxious to hear this answer. Thomas provided what I thought was further evidence of my father's commitment to family, but Mick saw it as deepening the motive. He was a drinker—Cillian, that is. He liked the pub because it was full of men like him. They worked hard and spent time in quiet contemplation or rowdy discussion over simple things like rugby or building materials or who had ripped off whom in certain transactions. Cillian was the quietest of all, mainly listening to the nonsense that went on. But according to Thomas, there was one night, a couple of years after Brannen was born, when one of the workers from Taylor's farm—he might have been a shearer—said something about Moya. That fired Cillian up and resulted in the man who spoke out of turn being taken to hospital to have his head stitched and his jaw wired. Thomas and a few other men who worked for Chaffey had to pull Cillian off the fellow before he murdered him. Thomas added that he was a devoted husband, defending his wife's honour. When pushed, he wouldn't say what the comment had been about and was even less forthcoming when questioned about the validity of the slight against Moya.

"Cillian defending his wife doesn't seem to support your motive, Mick," I suggested.

"Depends on what he was defending her against, doesn't it? I mean, if it was baseless, then why would your father be so outraged that he nearly killed the man? Why didn't he just let it go or, sure, thump the fool once?" It was a reasonable proposition. Mick saw it as a motive, but I was less convinced.

The final part of the file had the interview notes with Arlen Beltz. This was one witness who I still saw occasionally. I thought

Arlen must have been close to eighty, and he was still working on European cars on his property—not the new ones, but the vehicles that had been loved and nurtured by families. My, or more correctly, Billie's 1958 Mercedes had survived more than forty years through his meticulous tinkering. There was little he didn't know about that car. Surprisingly, he knew more about the O'Haras than the car they drove.

It was obvious that Mick had wanted background on the German immigrant when he first interviewed him. Arlen had arrived in Australia as a single man in 1947. He was looking for quiet life in the Australian countryside after the tumultuous years of the war. I had guessed correctly that he had been a mechanic and had trained in the big car-engineering factories prior to the terrible violence unleashed on all Europeans during those years. He didn't confirm or deny having had military experience when Mick had questioned him in 1975. He did, however, confirm that he knew the O'Haras well enough. They kept to themselves and paid their bills on time, often generously.

He had worked for the parents of Cillian, Darcy, and Billie. He remembered the three little ones coming out to his farm with their father when work had to be done on cars or farm equipment. They loved his German accent and played happily on wrecked cars and piled tyres until they were called to heel by Padraig O'Hara. They were three peas in a pod, according to Arlen—inseparable, vigorous little dark-haired rascals whose blue eyes radiated mischief. Even Billie. She was a real tomboy who gave her older and younger brothers as good as she got. They were happy. That was Arlen's assessment. The parents, Padraig and Patricia, died young. He couldn't remember why or how many years there had been between the deaths. The three kids were in their early twenties, Cillian perhaps only eighteen. Lucky for Arlen, the youngsters continued living on their family property, bringing cars to him over the years. He would never believe that any O'Hara could kill anyone. Mick's notes ended with the words *nothing to add*.

What Mick couldn't have known in 1975 was that Arlen's words would add so much to my understanding of the family that had long gone. I thought about how the three children, two of whom I knew and one I didn't, were once free and wild kids who played together with no sense of the awful future that was waiting. The thought that my father, too, was alone at the age of eighteen, except for Billie and Darcy, made me incredibly sad, but it also made me think that he would have valued family above all things. Surely he would not have wanted one of his children to be dead at the bottom of the lake and the other to grow up alone. What kind of legacy was that? How could it have gone so wrong? But life does go wrong.

"That's it, then. I don't really have much to add, Lily." Mick was bringing the session to an end, but I wanted to know a little more about him.

"How old were you, Mick, when you were investigating my father?"

I was surprised by the answer. He had been thirty-five and married with two daughters, aged nine and seven. I wondered if he had grandchildren, but a quick glance around the room revealed no evidence of such.

"No grandkids," he responded to my unspoken question. He went on to say that his wife left him the week Cillian O'Hara was about to be charged and subsequently killed himself. Apparently it was a brutal divorce, and Mick didn't get custody of his girls. His work, his obsessiveness, and his temper were cited as reasons to keep his little ones away from him. There was no self-pity in this part of the story, but it did perhaps help me realize why this case might have meant more to him than others. It was not just that he couldn't solve it but that it coincided with personal pain. His disclosure that one daughter overdosed when she was sixteen broke my heart; that the other one had disappeared when she was twenty-four was unbearable. Although I felt like he was almost my enemy in the search to absolve my father, I had begun to like this man. He was quiet yet persistent in a way that I had imagined fathers might be. Or should be. He offered two final statements; both created complex feelings for me.

"It's hard to be a copper's wife," he said. "You might like to remember that." He smiled good-naturedly. I might have blushed as I thought about the remote possibility that anyone might ask me to be his wife. The blush deepened as I thought about how much I might like it to be Phillip.

His second statement made me feel strong: "I don't pity you, Lily, or anyone like you who has had to suffer. It's those who don't or can't survive I pity. You're resilient; there's a will in you that will allow you to rise above the truth."

The truth? What might the truth be? Perhaps I would have to accept an approximation of the truth when it seemed that I would never be handed a clear and undeniable version of events. I recalled the Sherlock Holmes quotation that was the source of much debate about logic and the flaws in it. I recited it to Mick.

"Once you eliminate the impossible, whatever remains, no matter how improbable, must be the truth."

He responded, "Perhaps what you must accept is that the most probable, in the absence of certainty, is likely to be the truth."

So a search and a challenge were ahead. I would be searching for things that might approximate facts and eliminating what I might consider impossibilities. Both Mick's final warning and my reliance on a fictional detective simply pointed to the reality that truth is elusive.

CHAPTER NINE

Mick's final words would stay with me for a long time. They might even have been the most prophetic words I'd ever heard. So I drove away from the detective's home with both regret and relief. Mick had been so patient and thorough in his recounting of events and in providing some further direction for my own investigation. It was good to get to know something about him too. But I had to admit, I was rather relieved to escape his intense scrutiny. While he was talking, it was obvious that he was noting the impact his words were having on me. I wondered if this was merely the leftover professional modus operandi of a man who had spent a lifetime working with the vagaries of truth and lies, perpetrators and victims. Or was he simply a kind man who was worried about a woman who might have been like his own daughters. I wondered if he actually knew where his daughter was or if the separation had been so painful for the whole family that he didn't ever search for her. I wondered also if he thought about his girl who had overdosed on heroin at such a young age. It must have driven him crazy to think of her caught up in a world he usually prosecuted. I wish I'd been able to ask him more about himself, but my own search seemed to take up too much room in my head for me to be a generous listener. Maybe one day.

My trip back to the lake was slow and not because of traffic. I was pulled over—flashing lights on an unmarked police car in my rear-view mirror. Initially I was concerned that I had, in my distracted way, violated some road law and was now about to incur an unpleasant expense just before Christmas. But the officer who climbed out of the driver's seat was not in uniform, and he didn't make his way to my window but came to the passenger's side of the car and got in. Phillip had been lurking about the border waiting for me after Mick's second call to him.

"Hi, Lily. Big day?" It was a rather flippant question, given the number of emotional bruises I felt I was carrying.

"Yes. A big day, Detective Swan. And what are you doing using your police powers to pull over compliant drivers?" He laughed and then leaned in and held my face in his hands. He didn't actually kiss me but rather put his face close to mine and just let his breath waft over me. His face grazed my cheek, and he simply stared into my eyes. As if on cue, I felt the lack of restraint bring tears and a pathetic lip quiver.

"It's too much, Lily. You might have to let this go. Mick said he did everything he could to make you understand that your father did kill them and you stoically refused to accept the truth." There was that word again: *truth*. I couldn't answer for a while. I just wanted to enjoy—just momentarily—the feeling of his face being so close to me.

"I can't give up. Not yet. I know you can't understand why I need to know if there is an alternate truth." I tried to explain without breaking down completely that I needed to know more, to have a greater understanding that exceeded the simple question of innocence or guilt. I really needed to know myself.

Phillip listened without letting go of my face or interrupting. He simply said, "I understand, Lily. But I don't want it to break your heart." Then he kissed me ever so briefly on the lips. I stopped my tears by holding the palms of my hands to my eyes and pressing as hard as I could. By the time I'd settled again, Phillip was half out of the car. He leaned back to say that he would ring me later when I got home and that I should get my beach bag packed, as he would be picking me up on Sunday for our Christmas at the beach. I hadn't yet thought of my exit strategy, and after today's performance, I imagined that I wouldn't be trying to make one up. I was shocked to find that despite the roller coaster I'd been on with Mick, Phillip made me feel settled. I think I could even say I felt happy, but I remained cautious of using such problematic words.

He left as quickly as he turned up. A brief wave and he was gone from sight down the highway, back into the city. I tried to imagine what might have been on his mind and decided it was better to think about him focusing on his work, on real crimes that had obvious criminals and hopefully living victims. I thought he was probably very good at his job. He was physically imposing, but more importantly, there was a stealth and certainty about him that made me feel that perhaps all was well with the world. I hoped I wouldn't be stupid enough to fall in love with him, but being incautious and determined despite the odds seemed to be the motivator for all I was doing. Falling in love was probably in the cards too.

As I pulled off the shoulder and back onto the road, I began to process Mick's information again. So much had been filled in by listening to the details he had been given twenty-six years ago. Things that should have been old news to me were revelations—things like my mother's ancestry. I had no idea that she had been born in England, and, perhaps selfishly, I thought about how that would mean that I could get a UK passport. It meant I could go looking for my grandparents, Leo and Vivienne Bryant. Maybe there were other relatives who I could claim as family. Perhaps their absence from my life could be explained. I also mulled over the picture that was painted of Moya. Was she growing away from my father before she became pregnant with me? She had ambition and wanted more than the life she had, which I was pleased about, not for her possible rejection of her life with us but for striving to be more, to use her talent as a musician. Learning that she was talented in this area had been the nicest moment of the afternoon. Billie and Darcy had never told me a thing about her, and yet when my own talent became obvious, surely they would have said that I was like my mother, that I had inherited her gifts and her looks. We were possibly two peas in a pod, just as the O'Hara kids had been three kindred spirits. I had an emotional wobble at the thought of being like her and of my father being so like Darcy and Billie. A tremor of sadness started in my chest, and those unwanted tears created heat behind my eyes. I had to grip the steering wheel really hard and put the window down to let the early evening air blast away the feeling of loss. There was so much to remember, and I wanted to get home and open up the house to the summer evening air and the sounds of birds and the breeze over the lake. I wanted most of all to write down the things that had been said that were beginning to frame the story in my head. I wondered, too, if I could possibly accept the story, whatever it was, and begin a real life as a woman who knew who and what she was. Whatever remained after this would be the life I had.

The turn from the highway onto Mac's Reef Road was always tricky at this time of day and the impending holidays encouraged a steady stream of early holiday makers and Christmas shoppers to flow in all directions at the intersection. Some of them were making desperate dashes across oncoming lanes and speeding to overtake in the most improbable places. I feared for my life as I surged off the highway and onto what should have been a more sedate trip over the hills, past the wineries and hobby farms, and down Smith's Gap to Lake Road. But my wandering thoughts about the past were snapped out of my head as I approached a line of stopped traffic.

There were only about eight cars stopped on the hill near The Forest Road. The sound of an ambulance was audible through the open window. Everyone was out of their cars and running towards the place where a collision had obviously occurred. I joined them after putting my hazard lights on to warn any motorists coming up behind me that we were at a standstill. I had hoped that it was nothing but a single car that had slid off the road into the gravel. Going a bit too fast on these corners could lead to an easy exit from the bitumen. But as I got to the first stopped car, I knew that it wasn't just going to be an expensive lesson for a small mistake. Somehow, God only knows how, the accident was a head-on collision involving a small sedan and twelve-seater school bus. Thankfully the bus was empty, apart from the driver. The kids who caught this bus were all safe at home, and the driver was taking his vehicle home for the day. He was conscious but bloody at the wheel and yelling for help. The driver of the other car wasn't moving, and even to the untrained eye it was obvious the he was already dead. His head was at a peculiar angle, and the car was emitting an appalling low whine. His young face was bloody and smashed; his body crumpled and lifeless. I knew nothing could be done for him, as did my fellow drivers. Someone eventually put a towel over the front window of his car so we could drag our disbelieving eyes from the ghastly sight.

I stood beside the bus driver's window and talked as calmly as I could to him, spouting those terrible platitudes that everything was going to be all right, that the ambulance was coming, that we would stay with him. On instinct, I put my arm through the window and held his hand, which was still gripping the wheel. The young man who had placed the towel over the other driver's window and had announced what we already knew to be true about the deceased came around to the passenger side of the bus and forced the door open. He was a pharmacist on his way to the coast. He had a better understanding of first aid than the rest of us and made some assessments of the bus driver's well-being. His injuries were not life threatening but were painful. His legs were trapped and possibly broken. I simply stood by him and moved away only when the paramedics and police arrived to do what had to be done.

We went back to our cars, rattled and shocked. The police cordoned off both ends of the road, which would force other drivers to make a long trek back to the city to find alternate routes to the Kings Highway. The few of us who were stopped at the crash were allowed to snake around the mess and make our way to our destinations. It was the sort of carnage that you don't imagine you would ever see. It was a tragedy that this young life was taken and taken at Christmas, because from this day, every single December would be tarnished for the families and friends of this boy and for the driver too, despite his recovery. I wondered if this was a serendipitous reminder about the value of life and the too-permanent nature of death.

I drove the short distance to home at a snail's pace, my thoughts of Christmas tragedies never more real. I really couldn't go away to Phillip's family for the holiday. I was afraid of how I might react to all that familial happiness. Surely coming across the accident was some kind of sign that I shouldn't try to be happy.

My phone rang as turned into the driveway and turned off the engine. It was Phillip, checking that I hadn't been on the road when the accident happened. I confirmed that I did come across the smash and that I was upset but all right. It seemed to be the right time to tell him that I wouldn't go with him that the weekend, but for some reason the words wouldn't come out of my mouth. Before I could recover myself, he had rung off. I sat in the car for a few more minutes and tried to pray for the family of the dead boy, but I wasn't able to form the words either in my head or out loud. I think I was in sensory overload. Too much was happening at once. I had broken the seal on the internal container into which I had packed down my emotions, my fears, and my family. I was in danger of drowning in the uncontrolled flood of images and pain that had now been joined by the sight of a young life eradicated. I had to choose at this point whether I would simply allow myself to be consumed or find the resilience within myself to control what was happening. I knew I would never find any answer to any question if I became immersed in self-pity. Sure, I could cry for the things that been taken away or had never been. I could weep for the dead and those broken by unexpected death, but I would have to find my way back to the living. If I was going to triumph in life, I had to be prepared to feel bad, to feel angry, to despair, and, most terrifying of all, to love.

I dragged myself up the veranda steps and fell into my favourite chair with my handbag and brief case dangling from both hands. I heaved them onto the daybed beside me and stretched out in the warmth of a setting sun. Something about that kind of warmth is healing. It's as if there is a special quality in the early evening rays that has the potential to sustain us through the darkness of night. The view of the lake, now a parched paddock, was as familiar as ever. The colours of dried plants and the shapes of those that had succumbed to drought had their own kind of beauty. It was nature's tableau right before me that reflected perhaps the greatest truth: We live; we die. And somewhere between those events is an opportunity to bring something to the world.

I thought I would get changed, drink something other than tea, and walk up past Darcy's cottage, through the overgrown orchard, and up to the forest. The forest was a small ridge that formed a natural border to my property. From there, there was a view of the long expanse of the lake. The dips and curves of the once-filled depression could give perspective. I hadn't climbed up through the fruit trees for years. I remembered as a child I would play up there in all seasons, eating the ripest fruit before they fell and doing nothing to help either Darcy or Billie with picking. I didn't know this was the work they did. I had no idea that, from the berries, cherries, and stone fruit that grew prolifically on our land, all my opportunities were realized. I hadn't been up there for years.

Dressed more effectively for trudging up the hill, I left through the back door of my parents' house—my house, more correctly. From here I could see both Darcy's cottage and Billie's weatherboard home. It was as if the houses were placed far enough apart for individual privacy but close enough for safety. Within the triangle formed by the houses was a once-beautiful garden. The beds were now emptied of the flowers and shrubs that coloured my childhood. The rose beds were full of stunning plants that, despite my poor attention and the occasional vicious pruning, were bursting with scented blooms. But they looked ragged and savage, growing despite neglect. Darcy's yard was where, years ago, free-range poultry wandered in rural bliss until they were ended for the plate. I was terrified of the bigger birds, the geese and turkeys particularly, and one rather bold rooster I remembered. My favourites were the bantams, a variety of fluffy little hens that despite their gender were always called Petey or Bob. I loved them so much that I often would put one version of Petey or Bob into a bird cage by holding its wings tight against its body and folding it through the cage door. I would put the cage in the basket on my bike and take the traumatized bird for what I thought was a pleasurable sight-seeing ride along the lake. What I failed to realize, of course, was that birds wouldn't naturally contract their wings in order to be pulled back out of the cage. My many Peteys and Bobs had to be cut free of the cage by Darcy, released to the freedom of the yard. The cage was then repaired until my next chicken trip. The thought of Darcy's frustration and the bird's possible bewilderment made me actually smile despite the heaviness I felt.

These little stories came back in flashes, things that were exclusively my memories of growing up here. From the bottom of the orchard, a dozen crows flew into the air simultaneously. I remembered learning the nursery rhyme about crows. I think in its English origins it was about magpies: "One for sorrow. Two for joy. Three for a letter. Four for a boy. Five for silver. Six for gold. Seven for a secret never to be told." How many single crows must I have seen for all this sorrow to be a regular companion? Would I ever see four? I am not superstitious in any way, and neither was Billie. But she did seem to pay particular attention to the myths about birds, including counting crows. God forbid a bird die by crashing into a window, as she seemed certain it meant death would visit the house.

As I climbed a little higher into the shambles of the orchard, I could hear Billie reminding me about snakes. There were seasons when we could be careless about the dangers, but in the current season, we had to be watchful. The numerous snakes were more prevalent from spring to summer's end. They didn't, as I had it in my mind, lurk menacingly, waiting for a child's bare foot to be within striking distance, but they would rear up and wound if they were disturbed or frightened. I saw snakes about the place all the way through to my teens, but I had seen fewer since moving back into the house after Billie's death. The general build-up of local traffic and rural properties was one deterrent, the drought another. Even the snakes were looking elsewhere for water. I was sure I'd be safe making my way up to the ridge, but I kept a wary eye out all the same.

I also resolved to do something about the orchard. I'd consult one of the other growers to see if something could be done to save Darcy's trees. It might be nice to see the place productive again. Not that I had images of myself becoming a self-sufficient farmer, but I had the notion that it might be wonderful to see something grow and burst with life. I had stopped watching the seasonal changes in the land, particularly this year. I'd forgotten the joy of spring blooms and the change in the light of day. The sun being higher in the sky brought an azure blue to the heavens so sorely missed in winter. By summer, that blueness was deeper, and it resonated with the intense yellow of the sun's rays. The sky was somewhere between the two blues on this day.

The last bit of the walk involved a climb over rocky ground and a scramble to reach the top of the escarpment. But from this point the view was expansive. I wouldn't call it a beautiful view. The indigenous people call the lake *Weereewa*. It means bad water. It might as well have meant no water. Sometimes the Australian landscape looks anything but beautiful. Its ancient face looks worn and brittle. The sameness of the brown terrain and the yellowness of the flora speaks only of the rainless months and dry years, but it is so familiar to me. In the vista, my practiced eye could see the variations of colour that flow from olive green to dusty brown to the chocolate streaks of moisture and the whiteness of seed pods on the breeze seeking a place for procreation. When you take the time to look at this plainness, the beauty comes in those faint gradients of tones and topography. This was how I felt too—washed out and faded. I felt as if I was so arid that I would soon disappear and become merely a vague reminder of what it was to be human. I think this was the point of my greatest desolation. I had been told to accept what I could not bear to believe. I had seen a dead boy and had walked through the decrepit remains of my family's life. And before me was the parched view that the drought had created from what was once a lake. What was left? What really remained? Tears to be shed in sorrow and rage, unanswerable questions, and a story that had to be constructed from a smattering of clues.

The furthest point of the panorama was, ironically, the place where Moya and Brannen were discovered. From this distance I could not see the disturbance of the lake bed where they had been disentombed from the sediment that held them for all those years, but I could see that local lease holders had begun to use the lake's expanse as a place to run their sheep. The flocks milled about the intermittent oases where grasses were clinging to life in the remaining moisture. The lake had all but gone. I hadn't, for whatever reason, been out to the recovery site. I told myself I didn't need to as those long-rested bones were now secured in the family plot. What could be gained from visiting the place of misadventure? The place where a murder may have occurred.

These questions, like my prayers, remained unanswered, and I had to make some decisions if I was to move forward. Perhaps if I closed my eyes and rested here lying above the houses, above the lake, above the chaos that had to be ordered, I would find some strength and, most of all, hope.

I slept, to my surprise, despite the thronging noise in my head. My eyes shut, and the day began to close without me. The dreams were fleeting and the rest short. A single crow woke me by landing too close to my head, and its cawing brought me bolt upright. "One for sorrow." Even after shaking my head a few times, I thought I could still hear Billie's voice. She was calling me by the nickname she used when I was a tiny girl: Lil Mag. It was short for Lily Magdalena, which was a big name for such a small child. It always sounded as if she was saying little mag. The neighbours often thought she meant little magpie. "Lil Mag, come home!" I was sure I heard her call. Dreams are stubborn things at times. Their meaning refuses to be cogent or apparent, but the feelings they conjure remain long after one awakens. The day, however, was ending quickly, and even with the fuzziness of dreams about me, I knew I had to make my way down from the forest and off the ridge before darkness fully arrived. I didn't need to add a broken ankle to my woes. The ridge would be there tomorrow if I wanted to come back and attempt to gather the illusive images of an all too brief dream.

I was back in the house by eight o'clock, just as twilight was relinquishing its last pink light. The lights in the house were on, and the doors were open to the sound of a lazy breeze that could just bring itself to rustle leaves. My phone rang, and I scrabbled about to rescue it from deep inside my handbag. I'd missed seventeen calls in the time I'd been up on the ridge. This one was call number twelve from Phillip.

He opened with, "Jesus Christ, Lily, answer your phone when it rings. I was just about to send the local blues out to see if you were all right." I imagined *local blues* meant the police stationed in Bungendore.

"I'm sorry, Phillip. I went for a walk and didn't take my phone. I've just got back to the house."

"What are you doing wandering around in the dark, for God's sake, girl." His voice started to ease a bit, and it had lost its frantic edge and was almost warm again. "You had a big day, and then you weren't answering your phone and ..." He didn't finish.

I was able to assure him that all was well. *Well* was a word that could appease the worrier and give little away about what I was really feeling. And perhaps I thought it was nice that someone was worried about me. It was nice that *Phillip* was worrying about me. We spoke for a few more minutes about things that produced no tension in either of us, and by the end of the conversation, I was happy enough to concede defeat about the upcoming week away. I would go to the beach, I would survive Christmas with the Swan family, and I would continue to find evidence that help me make sense of my family.

"Goodnight, Lil."

"Goodnight, Phillip." I said it twice. Once to him and once to myself.

We had known each other six months, much of it in a professional capacity, some of it as friends, and a short stint as two people who might just fall in love. The rollercoaster I was on started to climb out of the afternoon's depths and make its way back to higher ground. Perhaps I might just get some sleep after all.

The other calls had been from Helena and Mick. Helena's first message, left on the third of five calls, enquired about my visit with Mick. The last two were in the frantic zone that reflected some of Phillip's angst. I rang her back and calmed her down. All was well, and the planning for dinner out here on the Friday night was going well. Yes, I had enough bedding for the three of them. Yes, I had the food planned. And yes, I'd do something about Christmas decorations. The latter was off the cuff, as I really didn't know if there was so much as a string of tinsel in the house, let alone anything more Christmassy. But I had two days to do some shopping before Friday's celebratory dinner, four days before going away with Phillip, and six days until Christmas. I had time.

When I rang Mick back, he was just keen to know I got home safely. He and I might not ever agree on the circumstances that ended my mother and brother, but he had a kind heart. And I liked him. It seemed impossible to believe that perhaps I had made another real friend. There was no room for secrets in friendship. Mick had laid the facts out clearly; there was no guile or hidden agenda in his approach to me. He knew I was hurting, and it wasn't his intention to make me feel bad. But at the same time, he wasn't going to sugar coat the facts. He obviously did not want to purposely hurt me. I liked the fact that he wanted to check.

With my world righted and my friends placated, I ate a little and slept a lot. "Lil Mag" still echoed about the house, the lake, and the ridge as I drifted from night to morning.

CHAPTER TEN

ednesday morning was as warm and sunny as the previous day. It was early, and I had time to open the doors and let the fresh air stir the place up. By the second cup of coffee, I was ready for the day, but I wanted to check one thing before leaving for work. I usually left the house at 7:20 to ensure I made it to work by 8:25. Some mornings I was in my office by 8:00, but other days, when the traffic was mad, I just shimmied into the building right at my unofficial start time. Some sensibly started at 8:50, which was the official time we were meant to be on deck; others wandered in at 9:00 or 9:10 or thereabouts.

I wasn't going to be late this day, but I had to have a quick look to see if anything had been kept from the Christmases of the past. My hope for some form of decoration was probably misguided. The brief search reminded me that the unearthing of the O'Hara treasures would start in earnest in the New Year, and every cupboard and box would be recovered, unpacked, and evaluated. Surely starting with Christmas was reasonable, but it was unlikely to be that easy. My house had several rooms. I lived in the main sunroom, kitchen, and front bedroom. The rest of the house was comprised of a formal sitting room and two bedrooms. There was a long, enclosed veranda at the back of the house, which still had remnants of my father's life as a carpenter. The two bedrooms I knew were actually the nursery I started life in and Brannen's bedroom. Billie and Darcy had generally cleaned out the rooms when I was moved into Billie's house, just before my first birthday. There wouldn't be much there, but the cupboards had never been opened. I imagined that there would be some things that had escaped the broad sweep of Billie's broom.

I was right. In the other rooms, the cupboards were filled with boxes. In Brannen's room the boxes were labelled with his name. In the nursery, there were two boxes: one said "baby," and the other, miraculously, said "Christmas." How logical of Billie to sort things so simply.

The morning had not been wasted, and I still had time to get to work, focus on the new exhibition that would open in February, and complete my Christmas shopping at the end of the day. Real shopping this year. It would be my first Christmas with people outside the lake, the first without the penetrating loneliness of every other December. My thoughts fleetingly manoeuvred towards yesterday's accident and the family that would have to deal with the loss of a loved one, but I didn't want to dwell on the unhappiness of strangers. It was not that I was being heartless, but rather for the first time in many months, a hopefulness was emerging. It was tenuous at best, unfamiliar and exciting. I was not prepared to give that up for immersion in feelings that would not be productive and certainly could do nothing for the dead boy. I was sure that the papers would have the story emblazoned on the front page—details about the accident, the victim, the survivor, and the suffering of loved ones. There would be enough tragedy to go around. Locals would be sobered for a few days, drivers might just slow down, and families might just remember to tell each other how much they love them. If there was any luck to be had, the road carnage would be minimized by this one terrible sacrifice.

The day progressed well. Everyone's spirits were high, given that the working days were few before the holiday break. Most of us would finish work on the twenty-first of December and not return to our offices until the seventh of January: two weeks of down time. Some people would take more of their annual leave and extend the summer break for as long as possible. I had never taken more than the stand-down period, preferring to leave my holidays for midwinter when life was quieter. Maybe one year I would take a month or more—I had plenty of holidays owed—and relive the European tours of my university years. There were plenty of good memories from those wild days of feeling free and disconnected from my past. But in a few days, I would leave for a week at the beach and then come back for a week of attempting to clear the family archives. It would be easy to feel overwhelmed by both events if I let myself, but I was determined to remain optimistic and believe that only good things would come from both events.

"Thinking too hard, Lily. You'll get wrinkles making that face," a voice said. It was Helena, who had been standing at my door watching me meander around inside my head. I've never been very good at preventing my face from revealing the internal machinations of my mind. Apparently I'd never make a good poker player. "What are you dwelling on?" Helena asked. She could read me better than most.

My first response is usually to say that I was consumed by a work problem, but because I had very little in front of me to back up such a claim, I thought I'd have to come clean.

"Christmas, mainly," I offered lamely.

"Not our Christmas dinner on Friday night, I hope." Helena knew exactly what I was referring to. "I hope you've bought us nice presents." Again she was teasing me. I had previously always bought them wine—expensive stuff—but not this year. If life was going to change, I was going to have to be a better friend, which included knowing people better. This meant avoiding giving out safe presents and beginning to let them see how much I valued them. I was inexperienced in gift giving, and quite frankly, it scared the hell out of me. But I had been busy ordering things online and had pretty much everything ready for wrapping. My gift for Phillip was the most frightening of all, but I'd made the effort to get two things for him that I hoped he might like. This afternoon I would simply be buying some small things for his vast array of nieces and nephews. Again, if I thought too much about it, I felt traumatized. They ranged in age from newly born to about eight years old.

"Stop worrying, Lil. About a billion people every year do Christmas, even if they're not Christian, and most of us survive it. Do what I did for years if it gets too much: feign an illness. It means you get to lay down for most of the day while everyone else rampages about it. It's easier, of course, if you are not the host."

I laughed despite my thoughts. I could just see the grand dame Helena Howard swooning and taking to her bed as soon as the day got going. Of course for her, Christmas without her son, Louis, was a real reason to swoon, and if I'd been her, it would have been my reason to shut the world out. Until this Christmas, I thought that the potential reminder of pain was a good reason to keep away from such things. But not Helena. She had a strength that I could only watch and admire. She embodied the power that comes from getting repeatedly knocked down and yet rising to greater heights each time. One day, perhaps on Friday night, I'd ask her about Louis and about whether she had searched for him or whether she simply had to make do with memories. Or make do with a truth that was born of probabilities.

She could tell that I'd moved away from the conversation and back inside my head. Helena brought me back by stating, "I've bought our boys Sony PlayStation games because they are still such babies." Brendan and Jimmy loved computer games, and when Sony launched PlayStation in 1995, they were hooked from the first minute. I couldn't begin to calculate how much the two of them would have spent on games since then. Luckily their habit continued to be fed by Helena, who was not beneath wasting quiet weekends having a go at *Final Fantasy IX* and *Warhammer: Dark Omen*. I couldn't think of a worse way to spend five minutes, but then I'd never played and didn't really understand how addictive the interaction with screen events could be. Sometimes I couldn't even sit through a whole film at the cinema and remain fully focused.

"Have you bought us a nice Tasmanian Pinot Noir? Or are you moving us on to something from the big island?" A little more teasing from Helena.

"You're getting nothing this year. I'm feeding you, and that's it. Count yourself lucky that I didn't give in to your nagging and buy you your own PlayStation." She laughed and hugged me. It was a real hug in which some of the air from my lungs was squeezed out.

"You scared me, little Lily. I didn't think you were going to make it out of the darkness for a while there." I was surprised to see tears running down her cheeks and truly touched that she thought of me in this maternal way. I was the same age as her son, and perhaps the need to mother someone extended beyond supervising Brendan and Jimmy. It made the day equally wonderful, sad, frightening, and hopeful. Perhaps this was real life after all. Laugh, cry, fall over, get up, and experience the freely given hug that makes it all okay in the end.

The day went on as if those revelations hadn't occurred. Lunch was eaten, coffees were swilled down at varying degrees of warmth. At the end of the day, I locked away the few items I'd been virtually ignoring when I was supposed to be cataloguing them for a new exhibition. The report I'd finished remained unedited, and the applications for a new research assistant were unopened. It was possibly my least productive day since the stinging discoveries in June. I resolved to make Thursday a proper day of work, and I would follow that up with a frenzied morning of activity on Friday. I was taking the last afternoon off to prepare for my visitors. But this afternoon was Christmas-shopping day and pick-up-Phillip's-present day.

Six days out from Christmas and the shopping centres were packed to the rafters with bustling mothers, unleashed school kids, and somewhat less-than-determined men who looked uncomfortable in the jewellery and underwear shops. My mission was to negotiate my way around the department stores to find a range of soft toys, board games, action figures, and art materials. My idea was to simply put these things in a large box and, on Christmas day, put the whole thing in the hands of Mrs. Swan to let her determine who should get what. I had gleaned from Phillip that his three sisters had six children between them. There were four boys and two girls. The eldest was a girl of eight, the youngest a second girl, who had been born in June.

In the middle were the boys, aged between two and seven—a tribe of them. I was determined not to be put off the task. Surely someone in a shop that sold toys would have some idea. Phillip's gift would be picked up last, as it was the biggest thing I would have to carry back to the car. I wasn't sure how I would conceal what it was when the time came to leave on Sunday.

As I expected, the shopping was nightmarish, but it was completed without a total loss of confidence. I was buoyed by the finished product that I'd organized in order to wish Detective Swan a merry Christmas.

I did not take my usual route on the trip home, since I didn't want to pass the spot where, on the day before, the accident had occurred. Best to avoid anything that might derail my positive disposition. I had gifts to wrap, a menu to mull over, and a box marked "Christmas" to investigate. There would be no soul-searching climbs to the ridge, no longing looks at the empty lake, and no self-pitying reflections. Just busyness—the normal busyness that everyone experiences at this time of the year. For a little while, I felt free of the vault that had been sheltering me. The storm hadn't passed by any means, but I felt confident enough to wander about in the weather and courageous enough to face the possible inclemency of what was to come.

I ate soup from a can for dinner and finished it off with another huge slab of Mrs. Swan's pound cake. It was still holding its own in the container she had sent it in. I had to remember to wash it out and put it in with the things that were going to the coast. I'd recovered last season's swimmers and beach towel and washed them. The warmth of the last days had quickly dried everything I owned that was suitable for the beach. My clothes were beginning to fit me again, most likely due to the fact that I'd eaten nearly all of the cake Phillip brought with him last Saturday. If I wasn't careful, I wouldn't fit into anything after the Christmas week if his mother's cooking was as good as the cake had proven to be.

I made tea, and while it brewed I went into Brannen's room and collected the Christmas box. It had been sealed with masking tape that had become brittle and yellow over time. The edges of the tape curled away from the cardboard, but it had remained firmly in place over the opening. Despite the feathery layer of dust on the top of the box, the tape had resolutely kept the past twenty years or so out of the contents. This was not just a box of tinsel and baubles, as I had expected. It was so much more than I could have imagined. I was not surprised that Billie had put these treasures away; to conceal them rather than dispose of them meant that she had seen the value in such beautiful things.

On the top of the pile of items that I carefully removed was brittle clutch of paintings and drawings that were immediately identifiable as the naive work of a tiny hand. My brother's little world was captured in a dozen faded images of water colour, crayon, and pencil. Each little piece was the same size and was clearly taken from a sketchbook of once-snowy-white, thick paper. The pictures had been written on by a grown up hand, and his name was printed neatly in the right corner of each. As the pictures grew more sophisticated, he had attempted to write his own name above the perfect script of, I assumed, my mother.

The first picture was a series of coloured scribbles. It seemed to have little sense of conscious creation, but a neat hand had written *Swimming with Daddy* as a record of Brannen's attempt to capture what was likely a real experience. The other pictures showed the development of his skill with colours and his growing understanding that symbols represent real things and that pictures tell stories. He was obviously a bright little boy, as his drawings improved quickly from scribbles to identifiable forms. One of the last pictures represented five human figures. They were labelled *Mummy, Daddy, Darcy, Billie,* and *Brannen.* Each figure had a very large head and a small body. The arms were extended and disconnected from the bodies. Brannen had drawn himself as the smallest of the figures and had used different colours for each person. It was ostensibly a happy picture. The little boy had captured a moment in time and the images of the most important people in his life. Each figure's wiggly arm reached out for the person next to it. It was imperfect in its execution and yet conceptually so accurate: a family, united and reaching out to one another. The last paintings in the pile were alarming, given the fate that befell the little boy. There was a scribbly image of water, and high above the blue scribble was the large head and arms of a figure identified as "Daddy." Floating above the water in a similar position was Brannen. I knew I was bringing my own emotional interpretation to the possible symbolic meaning of the image, but when I revealed the final picture of a single human figure that was described as "Mummy crying," I began to feel ill. Brannen had drawn a little figure, again floating above the blue scribble of the lake. He had placed eyes and a mouth on this figure that looked like they were sliding off the face. His intent could not have been to recreate Edvard Munch's *The Scream*, but the naive figure in the painting conveyed something of the agonized features of a character in extreme pain. I wondered what this little boy was witnessing in his life. I felt a pang of guilt that I had never bothered to think about him, my brother, being happy or sad about experiences he had during his short life. Why had Billie put these in a box marked Christmas? Was this part of some past celebration that I would never know about? Did Brannen spend some part of Christmases past drawing pictures for his parents and family?

Beneath the little bundle of childish art lay a repository of treasures. The expected Christmas symbols were few, but they were carefully wrapped in white tissue paper. There were twelve glass balls with simple etched images of wintery scenes. Two strands of plastic beads in the shape of hearts and snowflakes were wrapped around a wad of white calico, and beneath that, ensconced in more layers of undyed fabric, was an exquisitely painted plaster nativity scene. I had no recollection of this ever making into the light of day during any Christmas I'd had with Billie and Darcy. The little figures were immaculately preserved, and the careful storage away from light and moisture had protected each figure completely. I knew that at some point I would begin to research the origin of the set, but for now I was simply thrilled to have found it. It made me wonder what else might be hidden about the houses.

In the very bottom of the box was still a further surprise and delight. Unwrapped but placed cautiously between the figures was a small, carved wooden box. As I lifted it out, I could see that tiny slivers of wood had been inlayed into the lid, imbedded so perfectly that one might have assumed the timber from which the lid had been made simply grew like that. As I brought the box into the light, I could see that the darkened shards spelled the name *O'Hara*. As I gently turned it over, I could see that my father had signed the work with his initials: *CFO'H*. The reports that my father was a gifted woodworker were not exaggerated. His skill was further evidenced when I opened the box and found inside two sculpted hands, each in different types of wood and of slightly different sizes. The fingers of each hand were spread and seemed to be reaching out for something. Across the wrist of the smallest hand was etched the name *Lily* and *Brannen* was etched on the other. My father had carved two life-size artworks to celebrate the lives of his children. The work was so precise that it captured the sense of a living hand in movement. It reminded me of the marble statues in Italian museums that were so lifelike that one might expect to see a heart start beating beneath the cold stone. As I held the little wooden hands, I almost imagined that those fingers might curl around my own and hold on for dear life. How could a man who could capture life in this way so callously take life away? It seemed impossible that the hands that carved, shaped, and etched these symbols could give up on his family.

This first box had rendered such treasures. While I was disturbed by Brannen's drawings, I was elated by the decorations and the carvings. Although the yuletide decorations might be meagre to some, I felt they were so astonishing that they would outshine the garish lights of city streets and stores.

I set the little hands and the nativity scene up on a small console table in the front room. With the overhead lighting from the wall sconce above it, the little scene came to life. Beneath it I set the small dried branches I had gathered from the lake some days ago into a pot and tied them into an upright position—a makeshift Christmas tree. Around it, I wound the strings of hearts and snowflakes that had been saved by Billie. I tied the twelve baubles onto the branches in a random fashion. It was so naive in its construction that it took on an artistic life of its own. I may have invented the first bespoke Christmas tableau. More important than the artistic flair, as I chose to see it, was the intense sense of connection I felt to my lost family. One can deny the importance of material objects, but there is no denying the palpable pleasure that comes from being surrounded by things that have meaning, items that, by their mere placement in a room, forge a link between the present and the past. I have known this in my work when I've held a significant artefact and felt its powerful story and the residual sensation of those ancient lives that once held the same thing. Now for the first time, I felt that connection with the history that shaped me.

With the coming of night, I slept on the couch in front of my little display. I left the lights on and windows open and fell into a deep dream filled darkness. While I'm sure I didn't wake until the early hours of the morning, I was convinced that I had been in conversation—a dialogue that started with Billie calling me from the lake's edge. "Lil Mag!" Her voice was clear and insistent. "Come home!" she demanded. In the dream I thought it strange that she was on the lake and I was home. At some point in the dream, we talked about where I was and where I was going, but when the growing light signalled that night was nearly over and dawn was close, I awoke. The discussion with this ethereal conversationalist drifted out of consciousness.

It was very early, and I was feeling a little cold. Closing the windows and showering off the shackles of sleepiness helped waken me fully and prepared me to be one day closer to the beginning of something new.

CHAPTER ELEVEN

he work day was a breeze. I forged on through the final tasks I'd set for myself. No more daydreaming at my desk. I was driven by my pathological need for neat endings, an ironic trait in one whose past life was obviously so ragged and without conclusion. The thought of returning to work in two and half weeks and trying to pick up the threads of unfinished tasks made me feel ill. The first task was to edit my report and submit it to the various board members for their perusal in preparation for our first meeting in the new year. I knew none of them would read it until a day or two before the meeting, but I was a stickler for protocol. The applications for research assistant were easily dealt with. There were nine applicants, of which three were not suitable and possibly delusional. Two were interesting but had no qualifications, which left me four who should be interviewed. I asked Jimmy to ring the applicants and tell them that we were keen to speak to them but that given the poor timing of the advertisement for the position, we wouldn't be interviewing until mid-January. If they were still interested, we would set up times to meet them then. If they were no longer interested, I'd move the two less qualified but obviously skilled candidates into the running. I drew up plans and objectives for two possible new exhibitions for 2002 and finalized the acquisitions for the April show. All this was completed without interruption amid the strange emptiness of several of the work spaces. It was nearly Christmas, so I couldn't really complain about my colleagues taking extra-long tea breaks, shopping breaks, and lunchtime strolls or engaging in other unscheduled work activities. Some things are just more important than crossing the t's and dotting the i's.

The only interruption to the day came at 5:20 in the form of two unexpected phone calls. One was from Eddie Towell, the photographer who had found Moya and Brannen. He had rung to say Merry Christmas and to thank me for purchasing one of his photos. He asked if I'd had it framed and said that he would have given it to me if he'd known I wanted another of his works. I couldn't really tell him that I'd purchased and had framed one of his extraordinary lake photos for a special friend. I was giving it to Phillip. I liked Eddie, and despite the awfulness of what he brought to me, I didn't blame or curse him for it. I told him I'd be away and busy for a few weeks but that I would like to catch up with him later in January. I thought he might want to come and see where I had hung his second photo if he came to the house at the lake. I'd probably lie to him and say it was at work. The first one was hanging over the mantelpiece and was placed so that one could look at the photo and then out the window and see almost the same view. I thought Eddie would appreciate the symmetry of it.

The second call was a bigger surprise. The voice simply asked if I was Lily O'Hara from Lake Road and was I the daughter of Cillian and Moya O'Hara. It was impossible to deny that I was, but I felt wary about these types of calls.

"What can I help you with?" I asked. It was the best I could muster, given that my suspicions were aroused.

"I don't think it's your help I want, Miss O'Hara, but I think you might like mine." The voice was male and older, I thought. Before I could respond, he continued. "I'm Thomas West. I reported on the disappearance of your family and the death of your father back in the seventies. I heard you were trying to investigate what happened." Again before I could gather my wits to respond he went on. "I would like to write one more piece about you and the events on Lake Road."

I was astounded, as I had, after visiting Mick Flynn, put Thomas West down on my list of people to find, and here he was, finding me.

"I'm very keen to speak to you Mr. West, but I'm not so sure about follow up stories. My privacy is very important to me. However, I would like to meet and perhaps talk about the possibility." I was becoming a proficient liar these days; I had no intention of being the subject of any newspaper story ever again, but I did want to see him and talk about his impressions of my father. "When are you available, Mr. West?"

"Please call me Tom. Are you available early next month?" I thought about the big clearing-out of the houses that was scheduled, but I thought that Jimmy, Helena, and Brendan wouldn't want to spend every day working out at the lake. I could make an appointment to meet Tom during a break. We decided that Friday, January 4, would work well for both of us and that I would meet him at his house at 2:00 pm on that day.

"How did you know about me?" I asked after the details were finalized.

"I'm old, Lily, but I'm still a journalist." He laughed to himself. "Your mate Mick, actually. He contacted me about something to do with case when the bones were recovered. He spoke about you, and I read what the papers were saying last June. You weren't hard to find." And with that he gave the obligatory Merry Christmas closure to our conversation and hung up.

It was bewildering that this seemed to come out of the blue. The mention of Mick's name reminded me that I had to put his Christmas card and small gift into the post if he was to get it by next Tuesday. I had bought two key rings, and one of them was for Mick. It was a silver medallion with St. Michael etched into it. I thought both Mick and Phillip would like them, given that the archangel is the patron saint of police. And perhaps I thought the saint might offer them both a veil of protection if it was ever needed.

And so that day ended with a flurry of work, a sense of accomplishment, and a quick trip to the post office to express-post Mick's gift. Tomorrow I would host my first-ever Christmas celebration. In three days, I'd be going to meet Phillip's family, and in five days, it would be Christmas day. In the days after that, I would delve into my family's past. The months after that were mysteries that I could not begin to imagine, but I knew that the past would be unearthed, dusted off, and laid to a proper rest. I would accept what came and live with what was found. I'd accepted that a tragedy, and possibly a murder, was a part of that story. But knowing more was essential. Perhaps then I could leave Stone Orchard and commence something brighter, something unshackled from the weight of the past.

CHAPTER TWELVE

hursday night was a blur. Sleeping on the couch and being plagued by dreams the night before meant that I was tired and in no mood for unpacking any other secrets from Billie's carefully arranged hoard. I thought briefly about the strange things we humans stash away to commemorate our lives, how in the moment, we ascribe value to seemingly worthless things and etch the secrets of our private world into the mundane. I thought about the pretty, grey pebble I still carried in my handbag. This strange talisman had been secreted deep in the corner of every bag I'd owned since 1994. It would just appear to be a pretty rock to others who might see it if they were cleaning out the remnants of my life, but for me it was a reminder of the exquisite joy and agony of my first love. He gave me the pebble when he found it on Bondi Beach the day he said he loved me. He said one day he'd buy me a diamond ring the size of this rock, and we would live happily ever after. I was nineteen and inclined to believe his lies. I traded my virginity and my devotion for a rock. I didn't keep it to remind me of what a total idiot I was or to ensure I never believed a liar again but rather because I truly loved him. I sometimes held that little thing stored deep in my bag, not to be reminded of the cynicism and bitterness that comes with a broken heart but to be flooded with the memory of how extraordinary it is to fall in love. The dizzying fall into attachment, fidelity, and near obsession was worth remembering. He wasn't. But being in love was.

I spent a lot less time these days wondering what happened to James Campbell. He was very handsome and eight years older than me. I expect he went on to break other hearts and use his glib lines to live a shiny kind of life.

My memory was clear and, I was certain, accurate. I believed I could recall the sequence of events in exact order. There were surely no clouded details that were unreliably recorded. Perhaps my interpretation of James and his swaggering insincerity was tainted by negative emotions, but what I remembered was surely fact, not fiction. My recollections, of this relationship could not be proved otherwise. But what of his memories of me? How artfully would he reconstruct his interpretation of our relationship? Would he remember the gift of a stone? I thought about how he might have reacted when he read about the O'Haras of Lake Road. Did he say, "I used to go out with Lily O'Hara, and she never let on that she was an orphan"? He might tell himself that it was no wonder the relationship didn't go anywhere. Or worse, he might not remember me at all, never recall what it was like to be in love with me.

There was a question that stirred in the dark corners of my mind: who could love me? Somewhere between thinking and sleeping, I found myself hoping it could be Phillip. There were no secrets left to keep from him.

No voices called out in my dreams, so I woke feeling very refreshed. It was early, which gave me time to check my list of things to do and shopping to be bought. I would go to work mainly to tidy up minor lose ends, "merry Christmas" my colleagues, and share morning tea with my team. The shopping and cooking would take up a few hours of the afternoon, and then the party for four would begin.

In the midst of my final few hours at work, Phillip called to check on me. He was quite excited about the break and about us having time together. He had wanted to take me out for dinner before we went away, but he had several work functions to attend and a couple of cases to prepare before he had his few days off. He was one of the few in his line of work who would be on holiday until January 2. It was lucky that criminals seemed take a holiday from their line of work too during the celebratory season. There was a whole lot of goodwill going on. We decided we could wait until Sunday, when he would pick me up.

"My whole family is keen to meet you, Lily." It sounded a bit like a warning, but his tone was so light that I didn't think that there would be a problem with their expectation. They must know who I am from the publicity and would have asked Phillip how he met me. He finished with, "They don't bite very often." He laughed. "I'll protect you."

These were a very special three words. Not that I thought I needed protection from his family or from anyone, but I felt my heart beat in my chest as I thought about being in his protective arms, being shielded by his body, being held against him. I felt myself flush at the thought of him and remembered the times he had touched me. Despite the fact that he had hung up, I was still holding the phone to my ear as my imagination got away from me. It was obviously too highly distracting to think of Phillip Swan, and nothing would get done if I kept conjuring up visions of his body and mine together. I had to look about the room to make sure no one was privy to that unguarded moment. I'm sure my face had revealed all too clearly what I was thinking.

Grocery shopping, an intense burst of food preparation, and Christmas cheer would dispel all those sensory diversions. After the long morning tea of well-wishing and genuine convivial interactions with my co-workers, I stole away from the museum. My leave started at midday, and I didn't feel one bit of guilt at leaving five minutes before the official end of the year. I had a crowded supermarket and fishmongers to deal with, and this seemed to be a worthy excuse for cribbing five extra minutes.

As it turned out, the two places were quieter that I thought they would be. It seemed that everyone was having end of year lunches that day and was leaving the madness of food shopping until next week. It made me think that I should have asked Phillip what I could bring to the Swan family Christmas. I had purchased chocolates by the crate load and wine to offer as a thank you for having me, but surely I should take something substantial. I sent Phillip a short text message asking him if I should buy a ham for his parents. Or should I buy a turkey? He replied almost immediately.

"No! Unless you're thinking of eating it yourself."

I suppose I was just getting carried away in the excitement of this new experience. After all, the last few Christmases I'd spent alone I'd had toast for lunch. And those I'd spent with Billie and Darcy were understated affairs. My menu for Helena, Jimmy, and Brendan was pretty over the top, but I really wanted to show off my culinary skills and hopefully let my mini banquet reflect my gratitude to them.

The fishmonger already had my order parcelled, and I had the esky in the boot of the car filled with ice packs. I didn't think the prawns and oysters would go off in the twenty-five minutes it took me to get home, but the days were already hot and dry; I didn't want anything to spoil. The car heated up the minute it was parked, and while the old Mercedes was running like new, its air-conditioning took a long time to cool the wide interior of the car. The esky was a wise move, according to the fish seller. He gave me a small bag of ice to go with my purchases just in case.

I bought raspberries, blueberries, and cream now to ensure their freshness. Everything else I needed I'd purchased days before. I was beginning to see the wisdom in Helena's words about feigning illness that required opting out. All this running about was, no doubt, a contributing factor to the hysteria I'd heard others talk about when describing family Christmases. At least the four of us wouldn't be bringing up the old dirt that, if television movies were to be believed, occurred during family gatherings. But I was sure there would be a lot of talking.

When I got home it was still quite early in the afternoon, and I felt relaxed about the preparations. The first course was a little seafood spread of prawns, oysters, and a trout mousse. I had laid the table with Billie's treasured china. I was never allowed to eat off it as a child and was only allowed to admire it through the leadlight glass of the blackwood display case. This dinner set had been her mother's and was a complete setting for twelve. It had been bought new in the early thirties when my grandparents married. There must have been some money about, because even then a Wedgwood dinner set would have set them back quite a few dollars. I love the swag-and-rose pattern in cobalt blue and gold, and I remembered desperately wanting to drink tea from the perfect cups as child. I couldn't recall ever eating off it as an adult, either, and I hadn't thought about using it since Billie's death. It was one of the few things I had brought into my home from her place, but until I decided to throw this dinner party, I'd not unwrapped the pieces. Now as I set my Christmas table, I could truly appreciate the delicate patterning of each plate. I knew Helena would love it; the boys would probably be less interested in plates and dishes and more focused on what was on them.

There was seafood for the first course, duck and accompaniments for the main course, and two desserts that I had to get on with as soon as I got home. I'd bought lots of wine, because I knew if the food wasn't great, I could fill my guests up on excellent fluids to perhaps dull the memory of my failed culinary efforts. I hadn't cooked duck before, but I thought that it would make a nice change for those used to turkey and ham as Christmas fare. My desserts, I was sure, would be a winning course, as I'd been crowned the sweets queen during my university days. While pizza and pasta were the main course staples of all students, my friends frequently insisted on dessert first when I invited them over for meals. Tonight's rolled pavlova and summer puddings would offer an elegant completion to the meal. If the duck was dry and the orange-and-cranberry sauce went awry, the sweetness of the raspberries in the puddings and the lemony white chocolate cream of the pavlova would win my guests back.

The afternoon was eaten up by the activities of food preparation and table decorating. I had blue and gold candles to match my aunt's dishes and little shot glasses filled with single blooms from the roses in my garden. Things were going swimmingly, and I had to confess that I was excited and flushed with what could only be described as Christmas cheer. My gifts for Jimmy, Brendan and Helena were wrapped and carefully placed under my makeshift tree. I had added to the sparse decorations by buying some lights in the shape of feathery flowers. They were not particularly Christmas themed, but they were pretty and frivolous. I quite liked the thought of frivolousness at this juncture. It wasn't something I'd experienced before, and I could truly see the merit in doing something simply because one could, hence the ridiculously expensive lights in the shape of flowers.

The house looked like a real home by the time my guests roared down Lake Road and swung into my driveway. Helena was at the wheel of her recently purchased BMW, which she drove with a little too much flair and a huge disregard for road regulations. I could hear the boys uttering borderline hysterical prayers of gratitude for their safe delivery to the lake. They were all full of noise and good humour as they unpacked what looked like provisions for a week rather than a single night. I'd made up three beds and put out new towels and toiletries for my guests; the cupboards and fridge were already groaning with more food than I'd bought in six months. But still, Helena had brought a dozen grocery bags filled with everything required for a month's stay. She insisted that much of it would be consumed when they came out to stay for the week in January. She was most likely correct, although I really couldn't fathom the need for twenty rolls of toilet paper. Her response to my questioning glance was simply, "You've never lived with men have you." I didn't particularly know what the gender difference was in toilet paper use, but it seemed that dear Helena knew it was substantial enough to warrant an extraordinary purchase.

Jimmy had a tiny backpack and a huge esky. It was filled with beer, wine, champagne, and botrytis sticky wine to have with dessert. It seemed that he too was stocking up for the week of searching that would occur when I got back from the beach. If he thought that we four would consume a tenth of what he'd bought in one night, then we would most likely need hospitalizing and more than a month drying out before we could drink again. They were also trying to conceal a large and peculiarly shaped gift. Brendan walked into the house backwards and made a great show of pretending not to be carrying anything. He stopped at my Christmas tree, laughed out loud at its tiny form, and then added his large parcel to the pile of gifts I'd placed there.

They were in, suitably impressed by my efforts, appreciative of the beautiful table setting, and ready for drink number one after finding their way to the beds they intended crashing in that night.

My first Christmas party began well. We made a little toast to one another and started eating. The first course was easily a success. Who wouldn't love champagne and seafood. We decided to have a brief lull in the eating after the main course, which to my surprise was perfectly cooked. We left the table to settle ourselves around the lounge room.

"Present time," insisted Jimmy.

"Is that right? Can you do presents at halftime?" Brendan asked. I didn't have a clue what the right timing for any of these celebratory rituals was, but I was very happy to oblige. I was hopeful that my friends would appreciate the gifts I'd bought them this year, and I was a little more than curious about the present that was obviously for me.

It was decided; we would open the gifts. Helena topped off our glasses with our drinks of choice. I was already a little giddy from the two glasses of champagne. I chose a Pinot Gris to be sociable but knew I'd have to watch my intake, as I wasn't used to drinking and didn't want to fall into unconsciousness before dessert. I was in charge of giving out the presents; apparently it is a job that someone is given on Christmas day. It wasn't very difficult, in that Helena had bought the boys a combined gift, they had bought something for me as a group, and Brendan and Jimmy had bought Helena something from the two of them. It all worked very well.

The boys loved their PlayStation games and were already planning some awful marathon of playing during the Christmas week. They had bought Helena two spa packages, which included facials and body treatments. I had no idea how they could have been so aware of how much she loved such luxuries, but it was obvious that this was a hit with her. When she opened my gift, she was genuinely thrilled. I had framed a series of Francis Benjamin-Johnston photos for her.

She was a fan of women who were the first in their male-dominated fields, and Francis was one of the first female photo journalists in the early twentieth century. Helena was impressed with my choice, and her smile reflected her understanding of my first foray out of the safe zone of our friendship. The gift, I hoped, had said, "See, I do know something about you."

It was the same with Jimmy and Brendan. Jimmy was a Ned Kelly buff, and I had noticed him mulling over an art catalogue that listed ceramic wall hangings of the Kelly-gang armour. The one I got him was constructed of black matt ceramic plates linked by black leather straps. He said nothing but launched into the biggest hug and more or less wrestled me to the ground.

"Good job, Lil," he said, following this with a rather noisy, wet kiss to the top of my head.

"If I had thought I was going to be injured by gift giving, I would have stuck to handing out wine." This was my best effort at fending off further offerings of thanks.

While Jimmy carefully closed the timber box that held the piece safely, Brendan opened his gift. It was awkwardly shaped, as it contained a large quantity of Bockington tinted paper and a large set of Sennelier French water colour paints. I knew Brennan had been taking painting lessons and had produced some really beautiful pieces. He was a bit shy about his new hobby, but I had hoped that these tools would encourage him to continue pursuing his talent.

"I'll paint something for you, Lil. Maybe your lake, if you'd like." It was a lovely way of thanking me for what was really a simple gift. I felt like crying. When the tears became a little obvious, I had to admit that it was the wine, the food, the candles, and the friends.

"Well, tiddly-pooh or not, you have to open your present," Helena insisted while surreptitiously wiping a tear from her own cheek. I wasn't going to be held back. Inside the wrapping paper was a wad of bunched bubble wrap that concealed the shape of my gift. But through the plastic disguise, I could see that my friends had purchased an exquisite musical instrument. They knew I was a proficient musician who had a number of instrumental talents, but this was an extraordinary thing that must have cost a fortune. Before I could protest, Brendan confirmed that it was a second-hand instrument.

"We love you, Lil, but we didn't think you deserved a brand new one." He laughed and helped me extricate my gift from the bubble wrap. It was a mandolin. Not just any mandolin, but a Gibson F-5 Fern Cremona Sunburst. I knew it because it was one of the instruments I'd had on my wish list for years. I'd learned to play mandolin when I was at school. I was supposed to be having violin lessons with my music tutor, who was a bluegrass fan, and he introduced me to the mandolin. He knew I could already play piano, guitar, and violin, so he felt this stunning little instrument would round out my talents. I loved it. I was overwhelmed by the generosity of the gift, because even second-hand, this would have cost a fortune.

"I can't believe this. This is too much," I began to protest. But I was shouted down by the three of them. I had never gone without in my life. I was well dressed, well fed, and educated. Billie and Darcy had given me everything I needed, including a range of musical instruments to hone my skills, but I'd never really received a gift that was something I simply wanted, a thing that I had my heart set on. At some point I must have talked about it, and these wonderful friends listened and then made it happen. If I had been able to control my sense of being overjoyed and moved to happy tears before the mandolin, I certainly wasn't after. I just let the tears flow, and the hugging begin. I was blindly happy, a little drunk—tiddly-pooh, as Helena called it—and thoroughly removed from my past. At this moment, I was truly absent to my troubles. They would be there tomorrow, but tonight I would not let the cruel memories of loss and loneliness intrude. I would drink a little more and pay for it tomorrow. I would eat two desserts and fill out my clothes a little better. I would play and sing for my guests and be embarrassed at my showing off in the morning. But at this moment, I would be happy.

In that happiness, I served desserts, and Brendan poured glasses of Botrytis Semillon into Billie's tiny Waterford sherry glasses. There was way too much sweetness going on, and it all went to my head.

So I was terribly malleable when it came to being talked into singing. It took a little while to tune the eight strings—the four sets of two make for a little bit of fiddling about—but I'd learned to play the Stevie Nicks's song "Landslide" when I was at school. It was full of longing, melancholy, and hope, just perfect for a teenage girl. For a while, it became my private anthem, but the lyrics probably had more relevance to me now than they did then. "Can the child in my heart rise above? Can I sail through the changing ocean tides? Can I handle the seasons of my life?"

It had been a long time since I'd sung to an audience, albeit an audience of three, but I was emboldened by wine and joy. I thought my choice of song was perfect for my new instrument, and despite a lay-off from using my voice, I managed to hit notes effectively. I won't say the crowd went wild, but they were most effusive in their praise.

"Your voice, Lily, is stunning," Jimmy said. He was most expansive in his compliments. My voice was strong, well trained, and highly suited to ballads and folk music, but in comparison to truly stunning voices, mine singing have been rated as tuneful humming. But despite my self-deprecating commentary, Brendan and Helena added to the flood of accolades and started making mad plans for me to leave the museum and take up singing full time. In the ensuing craziness, they were congratulating themselves on promoting me to stardom. We expended so much energy over this drunken dream weaving that we had to take it down a notch or two or else we would have found ourselves having to go to bed before ten o'clock. I sang couple of bluegrass versions of Christmas carols before the next round of drinks and more serious discussions took place.

Helena, Jimmy, and Brendan had pretty much steered clear of the events that had led me to let them properly into my life. But serious topics were mandatory after eating, gifts, and singing. It was Jimmy's idea for everyone to tell a secret about themselves—truth or dare without the dare part. It was a fairly sobering concept, but I thought it might be another way of cementing this new bond between the four of us. I knew the boys well because of our contact at school, and Helena had been very open with me about her past, so I wondered what secrets might come forth. I felt as if my secrets had been well and truly exposed. My past had made the front page of the papers last June, and when that happens, there is little left to reveal. But I had time to think because Helena was going to start us off.

Helena was a natural storyteller. Her voice was warm and lilting, but her secrets were heart-breaking. The three of us knew about her violent husband and that she had lost her boy in a cruel and despicable custody battle. I already knew that the violence had put her into hospital several times during her marriage and that the judicial system could do nothing for a woman too broken to bring charges against her husband. She had a scar in her hairline where he had hit her with a cricket bat. He knocked her unconscious that time, and thankfully she couldn't remember the bat fracturing her ribs and jaw in the same assault. But her secret wasn't about the misery of domestic violence. She spoke about her son Louis. She had hired a private detective to find him six years ago.

Louis was nineteen when the London detective was able to supply her with information about her son. He had been educated in Kent at a private boarding school. He was an accomplished sportsman and was academically strong. His grades would allow him to study business at Cambridge and continue his love of rugby and rowing. He barely saw his father, who had remarried. Helena wanted no information about Toby, her ex-husband, but she wanted desperately to know her son was safe and happy. He had a gap year before university and had spent eight months in Mexico working in an orphanage. He was tall and handsome, lean and blonde. Luckily he looked more like Helena than Toby. She had attempted to reconnect with him, but Toby had done a complete hatchet job on her as both a mother and a person. Louis rejected her attempts to contact him. It was an important secret but hardly a surprising one. Her additional secret was perhaps the most telling. Every year since she lost contact with her son—that is, for twenty plus years—Helena had bought Louis both a birthday and a Christmas gift. They were never sent; he would never know that his mother loved him so much that she continued each year to place a gift under her tree for him or celebrate each birthday. It was her deepest hope that one day these gifts might be given to a grandson because somehow Louis would let her back into his life. While she would have missed all there was to being a mother, she could make it up to a grandchild, perhaps many grandchildren. I was moved by her sense of hope. It seemed that this kind of hope was not simply a wish for something else. It had a palpable existence in the human heart. It was the means by which one survives the intolerable and makes the most of what might be.

We decided not to comment on each other's secrets. We recognized that each one of us would be a little less burdened by the weight of them if we shared them. Jimmy spoke next.

His admission was pained and honest, but like Helena's, it was tinged with expectation of better things. Jimmy had been struggling with depression. His whole life, apparently. He said he was hardwired to be predisposed to the illness. When he was thirteen, he was going to kill himself with his rifle, but his father found him in the shed cradling the gun and stopped him. Despite telling his father what he intended to do, the Hall family decided that sending him to boarding school on a rugby scholarship was the curative route they'd take. They would never talk about it, never ask why this child felt so hopeless that he wanted to die as a mere teenager. They just sent him away in the vain hope that never addressing the illness would make it go away. Strangely, school saved him. He knew Brendan from the town, and the two of them had had several years of primary school together, which was enough glue to cement the friendship. Meeting me sometime soon after his arrival at the boys' boarding school was part of the reason he decided living was a reasonable course of action. He took medication off and on, usually when he was slipping back. He was feeling good now, and no, he would never forgive his father for sending him away when he was traumatized by his own disregard for life. He barely spoke to his father because of it.

Jimmy's burden should not have been a secret. Depression or any mental illness was not something to hide. Wanting to take your own life could only be dispelled by airing the thoughts to others who could help—who wanted to help. My heart felt a little broken at the thought of a little boy, no matter how proficient at rugby, so frightened and pushed away from the safety of familiarity. No wonder we became such good friends. We were both cut loose from the ties that bind. We both had to find other safe harbours, and I was so glad that Brendan and I provided that for Jimmy during those strange days of school.

I wondered briefly what Brendan's secret might be and hoped that it wasn't going to be too much for us. We were all now a little fragile from the first stories and too much wine. My eyes must have given away my thoughts as Brendan commenced with, "You ready Lil?" *Probably not* was my immediate thought, but despite whatever my face was giving away, he started.

"Do you remember Charlotte Kimson from your year, Lil?"

Well, of course I did. It was almost the most sensational event of 1991. We were in year eleven, and Charlotte Kimson was the most glamorous girl we knew. Her parents were involved with the American Embassy, and she seemed to be above us country girls. She looked at my misfit band, including Jimmy and Brendan, with disdain. I think I hated her. Her perfect, dark-brown hair was always restrained and sleek. She was buxom, and she swaggered when she walked. She had the most fabulous accent that made her seem exotic and much better than the rest of us. It was common knowledge that she was allowed out on Saturday nights with boys.

I was so wrapped up in my own memories of Charlotte that I almost missed Brendan's secret. He was halfway into describing her sudden disappearance from our lives in second term, just before exams. She had been whisked back to America without a fond farewell. The girls spread the rumour of her pregnancy. By a grammar boy no less. By Brendan no less. Yes, he confirmed, the glorious Charlotte had been pregnant and went home to have an abortion. Mr. Kimson had spoken to Brendan after Charlotte had identified him as the most likely father of her child. He threatened to have Brendan killed if he ever said anything and gave him a thousand dollars to keep his mouth shut.

I was silenced by the admission and saddened by Brendan's final comment.

"I would have looked after her, you know. I would have been happy to be a father. Even at seventeen." I hoped the opportunity would one day come again. He would make a wonderful father. The thought of it made me smile and reach out to hug him.

"Why didn't you tell us? Jimmy and I would have understood," I said. Brendan's reply made me giggle.

"I didn't really want Charlotte's father to kill me. He was serious when he said it. Scared the shit out of me." While it was truly a secret, and a terrible one at that, his genuine fear of the American hit man, made us all laugh.

Then it was my turn. I had few secrets that were not already out there. I was currently an open book, in terms of things that had been covered up. But the three pairs of eyes were on me now, and I was sufficiently lubricated by alcohol to blurt out the first thing in my head.

"I'm scared." Their faces showed they were expecting some further terrible revelations about Moya and Brannen, but what was in my head had nothing to do with my family or my past. It had everything to do with my future.

"I'm scared that I'm falling in love with Phillip." The secret seemed paltry in comparison to theirs, but I'd never confessed any emotional failing. I was, even at school, the wise one who could calm the waters of unrestrained adolescent hysteria. Many a mountain I wrangled back into molehills. At university I took care of everyone and never admitted to being broken-hearted, fearful, or, God forbid, an orphan. I just kept my game face on and never let on about a thing that was happening in my head. And now, here I was, blurting out the most inner thoughts that I'd hardly admitted to myself. I blamed the drink.

CHAPTER THIRTEEN

ever, never drink again. This was the prevailing thought I had when I woke at six the next morning. My head felt much heavier than it had yesterday, and an awful queasy tremor was happening in my stomach. I wasn't much of a drinker and rarely had more than a glass or two of wine, but last night was my first exception in many years. It was a great night, not just because of the food and drink but because of the closeness that came from the storytelling. Revelations filled in the gaps about each one of us—our brave revelations. I felt a little embarrassed at having blurted out my feelings about Phillip, but from the reactions of Jimmy, Brendan, and particularly Helena, it wasn't much of a surprise. They, as usual, had read me so well. "And who wouldn't want him," commented Helena, who had a preference for tall, sandy-haired men.

The thing they commented on in detail was my fear that I might love him. I wondered about that too, and I worried about the secrets that are kept and the burden of their weight. I knew that my upcoming search would most likely reveal the secrets of my family's past, things they believed they had taken with them to the grave, things that could show them to be so terribly human. Our frailties are as illuminating as our strengths; perhaps more so. I wondered about falling in love. A life alone seemed infinitely more manageable; safer. Loving someone means that there is always the potential for pain. Betrayal and loss came hand in hand with the joy of love. If you loved deeply, then the vulnerability was greater. What if he doesn't feel the same? What if he did and then one day stopped loving me? I fretted about what would happen if something terrible happened to him after we got married and I'd have to be alone again. I knew the thoughts were ridiculous and rather premature; after all, we had shared little more than a few dates and some delightful close moments. The thought of his beautiful face so close to mine made my heart speed up again, and my imagination ran rampant for a few minutes.

So love is terrifying, but if I learned nothing else from my friends' disclosures last night, I learned that living without hope and without courage was not much of life. Would throwing my whole self in be such a terrible thing? The trouble with that proposition was that I wouldn't know until I did. Only in retrospect would I be able to say that loving Phillip was a good idea. Maybe when I was an old woman and Phillip an old man and we were surrounded by our own family I would know the answer. That's the trouble with everything we do. The consequences are only evident after the action. The thinking made me feel queasier.

The house remained silent, and I was concerned about my guests, as they had still been opening bottles of red when I went on to water after too many glasses of wine. I suspected that there would be a hangover or two to contend with, and perhaps coffee and a big breakfast might be a cure. But the house still slumbered. I didn't think the sleepers would appreciate me clattering around the kitchen in an attempt to cure what ailed them. So instead I struggled out of my cocoon and forced my head to balance on my neck. The proportions felt all wrong, like I was balancing a watermelon on a toothpick, but getting on my feet and moving about started things flowing. I needed fluid, either juice or coffee, and air. The barely warm air of a summer dawn is a cure all of its own.

I stole into the kitchen, poured a huge mug of juice, and opened the front door. The veranda was bathed in the early morning light, and the air was still. Today would be hot, but the first hours of daylight were always exceptional at this time of the year. I felt I could drink in the sun and sky. The lake was gone, so there was no water to satiate the eye; but my imagination or my dehydrated brain provided an illusion of water in the arid depression that spread wide and long in front of me. Again I was reminded of the coming and going of time, of life and change. Water and aridity existed within the same space, separated only by seasons and climatic whims. People could, I supposed, be like the environment. If a lake could be perfected by rain and fulfil its destiny as a lake after having been dried again by misfortune, then it was possible that a person could be made whole by love, despite the wretchedness of loss.

These were big thoughts for a wounded brain, and the juice had only been partially successful in rehydrating it and settling the gut. It had to be breakfast, which meant I had to wake the sleeping. When I got inside, though, it seemed that the call of life-sustaining fluid had brought Helena and Jimmy to the kitchen. They had the coffee brewing and were downing large vessels of orange juice. Only Brendan slept on.

"Good morning, tiny diva," Jimmy said. He was way too chipper to be around in the morning. "Oh my God, your voice has just gotten better with age, Lil." He was effusive yet genuine in his compliments.

Helena agreed with less verve but as much honesty. "Seriously, Lily, you could do this professionally."

I didn't think a career change was imminent, but it did make me think of my mother. Moya was a singer, and it was conceivable that she was good at it. I wondered if it made her happy to sing. I wondered if, like me when I was younger, she dreamt of being a star. I had no desire anymore to enter the music scene, but last night's mini concert made me realize how much I had missed music. I loved my mandolin. It was an amazing gift and one that I would come to appreciate more as I practiced and developed my repertoire. It would be a New Year's resolution: play and sing every day.

The post-mortem of the evening continued between the three of us. Eventually our talking roused the very unwell Brendan.

"Thought the Kimsons had got you," Jimmy said. He was a natural tease.

"Well, surely there was a statute of limitations on keeping my mouth shut," Brendan replied in a raspy, hung-over voice. "Fluid, I must have fluid."

So breakfast commenced. While we were more subdued than the previous evening, we talked continuously while consuming my favourite Spanish breakfast. I learnt to make huevos rancheros at university and had a natural appreciation for the healing properties of chilli, eggs, potatoes, and chorizo sausage served with a dollop of guacamole. If you could keep it down, you were cured. If you ate two servings, like Jimmy did, you were likely to live forever.

By lunchtime the house was restored and silent once more. My city pals had to return to their own lives to prepare for proper Christmases. We would reconvene here at the lake, or at the ranch as Brendan now called it, after New Year's. Then the clean-out would begin. We all promised to put "drink less" on our New Year's resolutions list, though I knew full well the three amigos never would. I was a sure bet on that front though.

Helena offered me a bit of farewell advice. "Fall in love, Lily. It will be the best thing for you."

The boys packed up the car but refused to take the excess food and wine they'd brought with them, saying we'd need it come the following week. I wished them all a merry Christmas, thanked them again for my gift, and was able to say for the first time in a very long time that I'd had a wonderful night.

I had the afternoon to pack my bag and wrap the gifts for the Swan family Christmas. It was only a day, now, before I would meet them. Christmas Day was in seventy-two hours, not that I was counting. Or counting much, at least. Phillip rang me twice. The first call was to check if I'd survived the night with my pals. He was happy that I could confirm that I had indeed survived and in fact had had a great night. And yes, I could remember the whole thing. I didn't want to say "just barely" despite that being the truth. The second call was simply to say he couldn't wait to see me. I was happier than ever. On hanging up, I did something I hadn't done in a long time: I prayed. Not just that he might love me back but that I would not run away from him if it just happened that he did love me. I prayed for courage and that I wouldn't die of fright during my first family Christmas.

CHAPTER FOURTEEN

I slept for ten hours on Saturday night. I went to bed, closed my eyes, and slept without moving. I felt both refreshed and surprised when I woke at seven on Sunday morning. I had thought I would have tossed and turned all night with the nervousness of this big day, but apparently my brain had other ideas and decided that the overstimulation of Friday night meant that it had to have some down time. Phillip wasn't coming until two o'clock. He was a bit of a stickler for meeting deadlines. If he said two, then I would see the dust being thrown up as he drove along Lake Road a few minutes before the designated hour. I had everything ready at the door for a swift departure. The house was in order, clean, and prepared for the activities scheduled for the week after Christmas. I had unplugged my Christmas light display and rid the vases of their little rosebud blooms. The place looked lovely, homely almost. At 1:57 p.m. dust was apparent, and at 2:00 p.m., Phillip was at my door.

He didn't knock; he just opened the screen and strode in. He looked even younger and rangier in his shorts and t-shirt. His huge feet were enclosed in blue canvas shoes, and he looked as if he'd just stepped off the beach. The beginnings of a summer beard were apparent, as one simply doesn't shave during the holidays, according to Phillip. In a single movement, he wrapped his arms about my waist and lifted me off the ground.

"Ready?" I didn't know what I was ready for, but I didn't want him looking at me as if I was a wounded kitten. So I confirmed that I was indeed ready for everything. "Really? Everything? How bold, Ms. O'Hara! I think I like your holiday persona." And with that he kissed me. It was a big, promising kiss that simply knocked the wind out of me.

"I'm bringing my mandolin so I can practice. I hope that's okay."

"You know you'll have to play. But some of the boys play in a local band, so there will be competition. There's always embarrassing sing-alongs on holiday. Can you sing?"

I didn't answer. One night of showing off was enough. I wasn't going to be performing for the Swan troops; I was just hoping to get a few quiet moments to steal away and practice. I said nothing.

He gathered up my things, but I wouldn't let him carry the presents. "Are they for me?" he asked. He was like a child. He returned after packing the car to fulfil a supervisory role as I locked the door. He asked if I'd checked windows and the back. He commented that I needed security doors and locks on the windows.

"If someone wants to drive out here, take things of no value, and drive all the way back to town, then they are almost welcome to what's inside."

My flippancy didn't sit well the detective sergeant. Apparently stealing is not funny, and stealing from DS Swan's friends, even less funny. In a show of chivalry, he opened the car door but kissed me again before I got in. I couldn't tell if it was good manners or opportunism that prompted this show. Either way I couldn't have felt happier.

Phillip drove out of Lake Road and onto the highway quickly. He seemed eager to get where we were going. Apparently he hated holiday traffic, and he said the fools who thought overtaking and speeding most of the way were mad. He talked about the Kings Highway and the perils of the mountain pass that kept Canberrans from the sea as if it was the enemy. I was thinking that I had driven to the beach several times and had not felt challenged by it. I had not, however, driven to the coast during the peak season. Phillip was right, as it turned out. There was lots of traffic—loaded-up family cars with bikes bobbing about on the back and stuff wedged into every possible space. The big four-wheel drives towing trailers filled with jet skis, trail bikes, and barbeques made no concession for the massive loads they were pulling. It was as if we were in a race. All I could think of was the poor family of the dead boy whose accident this week would have ruined any thought of holiday cheer, possibly for years or forever. The news of the accident hadn't had the sobering effect on the driving public that I'd expected.

Phillip had a colourful and unrestrained manner of verbally chastising the worst offenders. Everyone seemed to be a dickhead or a moron. It made me wonder how anyone in this part of the country ever got a driver's license. I thought of closing my eyes, but I didn't want Phillip to think I wasn't fascinated by his critical commentary on idiotic driving decisions. I thought I might distract him by asking him about how work finished up.

Even his usually calm and carefully edited version of what he did at work was punctuated by his further evaluation of the poor driving of others, but he did have moments where he just talked about his job. I was surprised to learn that he hated carrying a gun. He wasn't comfortable with the idea that one day he might have to use it. When I asked him whether he thought that he could shoot someone if he had to, he said, "If the situation warranted it, I would shoot and most likely kill if I had too." He was terribly matter-of-fact, and I was amazed that this gentle, funny man had a precise sense of what the expectations of his job were. I hoped the little key ring of St. Michael might just afford him protection from ever having to make that choice. He was so kind; I felt that actually hurting someone else would damage him.

The two-hour trip was done and dusted easily, despite the endless number of vehicular crimes that Phillip had pointed out. We rolled through the main town and arrived at his family home in Broulee at 4:10 p.m., the exact time he told his mother to expect us. For the first time in several days, I thought that this was a terribly bad idea. I wasn't good at meeting new people. I was hopeless and predicting what they might expect of me. Panic seemed to set in as we pulled into the driveway. Phillip seemed to sense the change in my mood.

"It will be okay, Lil. Just breathe." Breathe. I wasn't sure I could. We sat in the car for a few minutes while I garnered the strength to overcome the desire to run. I told myself to make observations about where I was, to forget what I was doing and who I had to meet. Just look about. It helped take the edge of the anxiety.

Phillip had grown up here. His parents' house had been one of the first on the street. It had been built in the late 1950s and had been extended several times over the decades since the Swans had lived here. The view of the beach was stunning. The house was eclectic and rambling. The huge deck ran across the front and both sides of the original building. The extensions were generally in sympathy with the rest of the house but had a delightful "tacked on" feeling at the same time. It seemed that the house was stretched to accommodate all eventualities. Four kids and now six grandchildren, boats, surf boards, sea kayaks, and cars all had to be billeted here. Room was made, and now there was room for one more—a stranger whose life was strange and strained. Could this burgeoning home accommodate me? I was unlikely to take up much room physically, but I felt the baggage of the past made me seem obvious and ungainly. To reassure myself I walked close to Phillip, trying to hide behind his much bigger frame, but he simply took my hand and pulled me close to his side. We stopped, and he looked down at me. I thought I was going to cry and run.

"There's nowhere to run, Lily," he said. It was if he could read my mind, and I thought about the possibility of actually outrunning him, another unlikely event. I was fast, but I imagined my leggy friend would outpace me in a couple of steps. The thought of the two of us racing off before his parents could get a good look at me made me smile and then relax. What could really happen here?

And then there they were, eagerly exiting what could be the front door but was not obviously so. Phillip's parents were Margaret and Peter Swan. They were tall and sandy like their boy. They had enjoyed a life on the beach and were tanned and lined by an unrelenting sun.

They exuded a relaxed friendliness that dispelled the first surge of fight or flight. The adrenalin levels dropped a bit and then dropped even further when Margaret Swan grabbed me from Phillip, hugged me, and said, "We are so glad you were able to come and stay, Lily. Oh my God, you're so small and so pale. You need food."

That was it, the fear was gone. Margaret was going to feed me and, no doubt later in the week, interrogate me, but for now she had sensed that the fretful friend that Phillip had bought home needed to feel like she belonged. Being a stranger is hard, particularly in a world where everyone else is familiar with the landscape and its inhabitants.

Peter was quieter, but his welcome no less genuine. "Glad to meet you, Lily. Don't let Margaret bully you into eating. But she will." He politely shook my hand and went to Phillip. He embraced his son lovingly. Phillip returned his father's hug, and they spoke to each other. I couldn't hear what they said, though, as I was being ushered into the house. Phillip and his father gathered the gear from the car and happily continued talking as they made two trips to bring in the ungainly luggage I'd brought: a small suitcase, a box of gifts, a box of wine, one of groceries, despite having been told not to, and a mandolin. I was going to take up space, despite my initial desire to shrink into the sand beneath my feet.

Margaret's interrogation commenced with my first mouthful of her orange cake. I had to wash it down with tea before answering the first of numerous questions, none of which referred in any way to what she must have known about the circumstances that brought me and Phillip together. She started with a series of questions and statements about what I did for living. Margaret was genuinely interested in my work at the museum. She had been to it when it first opened, but she and Peter hadn't been back to Canberra for years to visit the tourist attractions. They had been to see Phillip several times in the past few years, more so in the last year, as Peter had to visit a specialist at the hospital. It was nothing serious, Margaret added without interrupting her flow of questions. She asked me about the Lake properties and commented that it seemed to be a huge responsibility for someone as young as me. She quickly ascertained that I had turned twenty-seven a few months ago.

I thought she must have been warned off asking anything about my family because despite asking me about how much I weighed, my religion, and where I went to school, she didn't once stray into talk about my parents or guardians. It was as if that topic simply didn't exist. I tried to test how stern a warning Phillip had given his family by creating an opportunity for Margaret to ask when she talked about how musical I was. Phillip had told her I played a number of instruments, and she had seen the mandolin being dragged in from the car. I told her that my mother had been a musician and that perhaps I had inherited her talent. Margaret deftly veered away from the obvious question about my mother and went onto another topic.

Throughout this mini-inquisition, I consumed cake, drank tea, and wondered where Phillip had disappeared to. He finally returned to the kitchen both for the late-afternoon snacking and to rescue me from more questions about what I ate, whether I had allergies, whether I could swim, whether I liked the beach, and so on.

"For God's sake, Mum, leave her alone. I'm sure I sent you her resume last week so you'd know all this stuff." Phillip laughed and hugged his mother. "Leave her alone, or she'll run away." He kissed the top of his mother's head and then sat beside me, hugging me to his side. His mouth brushed my forehead, and he smiled into my eyes. "Okay now?" It was a settling question, intended to make me feel better.

Peter sat opposite us at the grocery-laden kitchen bench and drank his tea. "You're Irish, then, Lily?" he asked.

"Well, Irish enough. It's the hair isn't it? Ginger is such a giveaway." I tried to keep my tone light. "My ancestors were as Irish as they come, but the family has been in the district for over 170 years. Hardly Irish anymore," I replied, wondering if this would be the foray into discussing my past. But the questioning stopped at that, and Phillip grabbed me off the stool I was sitting on and stated that he was taking me over to the beach for a walk. He asked his father to unpack the box of food and drink I'd bought and jokingly told them not to judge me by the amount of wine I'd brought down. His father laughed, and Margaret walked with us to the door.

"Your sisters will be dropping in later, so don't be too long," Margaret called after us.

So Phillip's sisters were going to come and check me out too. I felt like one of my own museum exhibits. The Swans had thus far been very polite to me, but I wondered if the siblings would be as restrained. I knew nothing about having siblings but could only imagine that his big sisters would be quite protective of their younger brother. Despite him being in his thirties, carrying a gun for a living, and having lived away from his home town for sixteen years, I imagined that the girls would interfere in his life as required.

The beach walk acted as a calmative. I was happy to be sandy and warmed by the late-afternoon sun. The water temperature seemed fairly cool but inviting. The long beach in front of the Swan home was a mixture of flat, shallow water at the most southern end and more vigorous waves and the northern end. At the most northern arc, a small creek ran back between the homes and provided a safe play area for families with young children. And despite the approach of evening, the families clung to the sandy banks to soak up the last of the day's rays. Surfers were out in force, those who could actually surf mixing in with beginners who had brought shiny, hardly used boards out of cobwebbed garages for the Christmas break. We walked the length of the beach, sat, and watched the better-skilled board riders; then we walked back to Phillip's house.

"What do your parents and family know about me?" I asked carefully.

"They know you are a midget." An hilarious but untruthful start. "I told them not to talk about your lack of stature, as it would be a cruel reminder that you were unable to reach things from high cupboards."

"You are a fool, Phillip. What did you really tell them?"

If nothing else, this man was completely without guile. He said he had told them the circumstances under which we had met and had said that I was yet to accept the coroner's findings about my mother

115

and brother. He had told them that I'd had a really difficult year and that despite the painful revelations, I was doing remarkably well. He told his parents that he quite liked my fighting spirit and that he thought I should let go of any further investigation because it was probably likely to hurt me.

"I told them that I couldn't bear to see you hurt, that the pain of what you were going through was heartbreaking. And by the way, I told them that I'd fallen in love with you." The conversation ended there, as we were walking back into his parents' house. I wanted to be able to respond to his final comment, but there was a commotion coming from the upstairs deck. It seemed like a dozen people had appeared from nowhere. It felt fairly confronting to have so many sets of eyes on me at once. Two of Phillip's sisters and their husbands and kids had arrived to get a look at the visitor. Lisa and Robert Hughes had brought their three children over—Carrie, who was eight; George, six; and Bobby, five. The Swan gene ran strong in this family. Robert was dark skinned and brown eyed, but his wife and children were Phillip's kin through and through. Sandy, wild hair and blue eyes. Lisa was as tan as her parents, but her sandy locks had been cut short and hugged her head. She was attractive and had a lively face, but she looked faded. *Too much sun and surf,* I thought. I had guessed from Phillip's discussion of his family that Lisa was the eldest and was probably nearly forty. Robert was apparently quite a bit older than her, but I couldn't make that distinction. His second-oldest sister, Jessica, was also peering over the banister with her husband, Lachlan Thomas. They had little boys—Danny, four, and Isaac, two. The kids and the sisters were almost indistinguishable, given the uniformity of their colouring.

The shock of the greeting made me temporarily forget Phillip's last statement. The introductions were lengthy, and there was much hand shaking and many obligatory comments about how nice it was to meet each other. There was a general consensus that the family would settle into the couches and chairs on the deck and that we would all have a drink to welcome the Christmas week. I briefly excused myself, saying I needed a jumper. Phillip pointed the way to the room my things had been put in. I was not surprised, but just a little bewildered, to find myself in what must have been Phillip's childhood bedroom. Both of our things had been put here, and there were two big single beds made up side by side. I had hoped that we would be able to sleep together, but it seemed all too strange to be in his room with his football trophies and surf-lifesaving awards. I took thirty seconds to send him a quick text message, knowing he would look at his phone whenever it pinged because of the nature of his work.

A simple "I love you too" was all I wrote. Then I walked back up the stairs and back to the waiting throng of Swans to see what kind of interrogation might take place. As I walked out on to the deck, Phillip was reading the message I'd sent. His smile was all the affirmation I needed. He quickly put his phone back in his pocket as his two sisters flew into him about turning his phone off for the holidays.

"You know, Swanny, you're not the only detective in the country. Let someone else have a go," Lisa chided him.

The family all started muttering about Phillip's work and how it had taken him away from them. It was a good-humoured stirring about him being a city boy now. It went on for a few minutes, and then Lachlan, referred to as Thomo, and Robert, called Bertie, cornered Swanny and started talking about fishing and other surf activities that were to take place in the week ahead. Thomo and Bertie were not only Phillip's brothers-in-law, they were boys he'd grown up with in the town. They were older than him, but it seemed that as beach brats they had bonded over surf lore. I smiled, as I could hardly see how Detective Sergeant Phillips could fill the shoes of Swanny the surfer.

As the men got deeper into their planning, it gave the Swan women a chance to check me out. By the time the questions started, some of which Margaret answered for me, a small child had worked his way onto my knee. Little Isaac was as sandy and tan as his family, and I could almost image that this was what Phillip must have looked like as a two-year-old. The little boy, apparently called Zacko, was fascinated by my hair and spent his time pulling it out from the band that held in tightly in check. He was apparently telling me something important when Jessica launched her first big question.

"How are you coping with all the publicity about your family?"

Margaret Swan looked as if she was going to curtail the conversation, but I thought it best to answer the question like an adult. After all, I was not a child, nor was I in need of protection from the candid inquisitiveness of Phillip's sisters.

"I was very distressed at first, Jessica, but I'm fine now. I think trying to put the pieces together for myself has helped a great deal. And Phillip has been wonderful." I had hoped mentioning her brother might deter further questions and lead her to asking more difficult questions about my intentions towards her brother. But she was dogged in her desire to check my suitability as her brother's girlfriend. She obviously didn't want some flaky weakling leaning too heavily on him.

She went on. "I mean, your father killed your mother and brother, so it must have brought up terrible memories for you?"

It was confrontational for sure to be so blatantly quizzed in this way, but I was surprisingly not rattled by her. Phillip heard the word *killed* and was on alert immediately. I saw him break off the conversation with his mates and shoot his mother a warning look, a look that she heeded but that Jessica and Lisa both ignored.

"Memories are things you recall experiencing. I was only a few weeks old when my mother and brother disappeared." I was deliberate in avoiding the word *murdered*. "I knew nothing of the three of them. What you have read, or what Phillip has told you, is virtually all that I know. The difference is that I don't subscribe to the public interpretation of these alleged facts." I knew I sounded a little pompous, and to my horror, a little tear betrayed me. But it wasn't Phillip who launched in to end the questioning, it was Peter. Phillip's dad simply stated that there'd be no more talk about Lily's private business. His tone spoke volumes, and the two women seamlessly transitioned from talk of the past to talk of the immediate future. They asked if I swam, if I could surf, if I liked to cook, and a few other innocuous questions. By the time they got to questions about music, the atmosphere had righted itself and calm prevailed. Apparently Bertie had a band that played at parties and at the surf club. They would play on New Year's Eve, and the girls were encouraging me to join in.

"They can play okay," Lisa explained, "but none of them can sing. You might be able to make them sound like musicians if you perform with them next Monday."

I wasn't sure that that would happen, but I was happy enough to nod some kind of consent. As the long summer twilight began, the two families decided they should take the children home. Isaac was almost asleep on my knee by this time. I'd read Bobby four or five books, and several bottles of wine had been consumed. Food appeared and was eaten. This was apparently not dinner, it was the five o'clock drinks that occurred every weekend, and more frequently when the family was together for celebrations.

As I handed Isaac over to his father to carry the two blocks to their own home, I felt reluctant to give over the trusting little boy who had taken such a shine to me. He had no questions for me, he was just happy to colonize a soft lap for a little snooze. I'd had very little to do with children ever, but I quite liked this. Carrie, Bobby, and George wandered by a few times during the afternoon to check out what was happening with this new person Uncle Phillip had brought home. And Carrie, as little girls sometimes like to do, attempted to repair the damage to my ponytail that Isaac had wrought upon it. Danny kept his distance, preferring Phillip's company rather than the women's.

When the nine of them left the Swan home, the volume dropped appreciably. Peter and Margaret bid a hasty retreat inside saying they would prepare dinner. Before I could protest that more food was surely not needed, Phillip had taken up Isaac's spot beside me on the couch. He kissed me without asking any questions or making any comment. It was a lovely moment. It was a perfect moment. Nothing about the past mattered, and the future seemed to be a rather splendid thing. When finally his mouth stopped, I questioned him about our sleeping arrangements.

"My room is virtually unchanged from when I left it at eighteen. The sheets are cleaner though."

Great, I had fallen in love with a comedian. I didn't want to clarify anything else about the beds and who would sleep where. I would be happy on the floor, as long as I could be near this man. Our smooching was interrupted by Peter, who insisted that we come in and eat dinner. I couldn't believe that we were going to consume more food. I'd had a glass of wine and some cheese and crackers with everyone, but I wasn't sure I could follow it up with another course, or should I say, two courses. Margaret had made a wonderful garlic prawn linguine. It was a mound of creamy, saffron-coloured pasta served with cheese and fresh white bread cut into slices the size of doorstops. Dessert was a fruit salad piled high into a glass bowl big enough to bathe in. It was a glorious meal but not one I could do justice. My lack of appetite was nervously attributed to my worries and sadness.

Phillip tried to soothe his mother's worries by eating all of his pasta and most of mine. I was happy with a small spoonful of fruit without ice cream or cream. Luckily Phillip had a mountain of fruit with both cream and ice cream. It placated Margaret somewhat, but she still eyed me with either consternation or suspicion. I couldn't tell which. Phillip had consumed a few beers and wine with his repast and decided to go to bed early. I stayed with Margaret and Peter to clean up. I thought if I was with them, they could ask questions about whatever they thought necessary without Phillip interrupting or censoring them. But they were a little gun shy after Jessica's early interrogation and seemed content to tell me about the town and what life was like in the beachside community. By ten thirty, I was tired enough to make my excuses, thank them so much for their hospitality, and tease Margaret about her concerns that I would fade away before her eyes if she didn't feed me to the gills.

"I was a lot thinner a few months ago," I consoled her. "I'm virtually pudgy in comparison." In a swift movement, she was out of the chair to hug me. It was, I'm sure, this thing mothers did. It was the same hug Helena had given me when she thought I'd never make it out of the darkness I was in. It was a rescue hug, a "lean on me" hug, and an "it'll be all right in the end" hug. It was the type of embrace that I hoped one day to master and give out freely to my own children. One day—I'd been saying that a lot lately. It had been a term that had never been in my lexicon until I was shaken out of my denial, was forced into accepting a dreadful past, and then met Phillip. One day. I quite liked it.

The bedroom where we were sleeping was dark and cool. Phillip had taken up one of the singles, so assumed the other was mine. I was mindful of not waking him when I stretched out between the clean sheets of my bed, but I did turn on my side to watch him sleep. He was confident and at peace even in sleep. He was on his back with his arms and legs stretched out wide beneath the top sheet of his bed. He chest was bare and was rising and falling with each snoring breath. He looked like a big version of Isaac. I fell asleep easily. The sound of Phillip's breath, along with the constancy of the waves across the road, lulled me into a happy sleep in which no haunting voices called me, no sadness clawed at me, and restorative sleep claimed me.

I was woken early in the morning by a sense of warmth that engulfed me. Sometime during the deep sleep, Phillip had made his way from his bed to mine. He was taking up all the room, and I was almost off the edge. I would most likely have fallen out except for his long arm wrapped around my waist. He was still emitting the sounds of sleep, and with his face so close to mine, I could study every little feature. His sandy eyelashes were long and fanned out over the dark circles under his eyes. I hadn't noticed that he looked weary. His job, I suspected, was the cause of some stress and nocturnal restlessness. But here beside me, he looked like a sleeping boy, careless and free from the harrowing events of life. At this distance, I could even see a smattering of freckles on his nose and the fullness of his lips. There was a tiny, almost imperceptible scar on his top lip that extended a centimetre towards his nose. Another silvery line was evident above his eyebrow. These tiny imperfections were evidence of an active life spent in this beautiful place.

I closed my eyes for a moment and attempted, in the tiny space I had left, to roll onto my back and stare at the walls around Phillip's bedroom. They had recently been painted but still looked like a boy's retreat. With all those sisters, no wonder he selected the bedroom at the bottom of the house. He could bound out the door and virtually onto the beach. What a life. I looked back at him and felt surprised to see him awake and staring at me.

"Good morning. Hope you didn't mind me taking up some room in your bed?" How could I mind? "I hope I didn't snore too much." Well, he did earlier in the night, but all the food and the sea air knocked me out like a light. I failed to notice him taking over my bed. To answer him, I just turned back on my side and wrapped myself around him.

"Can we stay here all day?" I asked.

His answer was a resounding no as he dragged himself and me out of the bed and onto the floor. It was 6:30 am and time for the first swim. It was high tide, and the bay was as flat as a millpond. We were on the beach in twelve minutes. I was trying to put clothes on over my bathing top and board shorts, but all I was given time to grab was a towel and shoes for my feet.

"Should I take my rash vest?" Phillip gave me the once over.

"Well, you are the palest person I've ever met, but not even you could get burnt by the early morning sun." I was quite sure that I could prove him wrong on that count. I had been known to get burnt by candle light in the middle of winter.

The water was cool. I think it was actually cold. But my body adjusted quickly, and I found I could just about outswim Phillip. At university I'd swum nearly every day at the beach. Sydney water temperature and daytime highs were fairly mild in comparison to Canberra. I loved the sea, and despite my family's history with water, I never felt fear or second guessed myself when it came to tackling waves or swimming out beyond where waves were breaking. I suppose I occasionally worried about sharks; most Australians who swim in the sea occasionally consider the possibility. But the lovely bay that stretched between Broulee Island and Candlagan Creek seem innocuous enough.

By the time we had raced each other and made more and more ridiculous challenges, it was nearly seven thirty, and Phillip decided he was starving. Food was obviously going to be a theme of this week, and being in love another theme. As we were drying off, Phillip pulled me into his arms and kissed me.

"This love thing is pretty serious," he said in solemn tone. "We should think about living together."

I was a tiny bit bemused. We had really only been seeing each other since August, after our rather awful introduction in June. Perhaps that was long enough to know that you had to be with someone. I had little practical experience with the course of relationships. I had fallen in love and fallen in lust a few times, but since I moved back to the lake, I'd been quite celibate. Living cloistered out on my property, I didn't get to meet many men, and I spent most of my time working or, in the last few years, dealing with Darcy and Billie's deaths. I wanted to stop myself from over thinking things, particularly with Phillip.

"You look grim. Is that a no then?" he asked. But it wasn't a no.

"It's yes, but only after I sort out the issues with the property." And more honestly, "When I've explored all the possibilities concerning Moya and Brannen, then we can talk about the future. I promise." It was not a promise I made lightly. I wanted a life like the ones his sisters had. Kids and extended family all jostling for a place in the clan. I wanted to have memories of the best and worst times, to be in on the family jokes, to be the subject of some of them. I wanted to give support and be supported because we all shared something incredibly important. Phillip was that important thing. I didn't want to be the subject no one could talk about. I was currently the "don't mention the war" visitor that everyone had to be wary of. I couldn't effectively tell him how much I wanted to spend every day of the next millennium with him without sounding desperate or giddy. It was more than seeking the protection of this big, capable man; I wanted to be the one to protect him from the hurts life might hurl in his direction. But standing in a sandy, salty embrace on the beach in front of his parents' house wasn't the place for such enormous declarations.

Phillip broke the silence and the solemnity by announcing his need for more sustenance. The man could eat; no doubt about that. I'd have to sell the lake properties to keep him nourished. We wandered back across the road under the watchful eyes of Margaret and Peter. They seemed happy enough that I'd become a part of Phillip's world, but they were understandably worried too. I did not seem to be the most robust of candidates for their son, and I'm sure they couldn't help but worry about my past and the impact it might have on his future happiness. They were sensible people though. If they had doubts and fears, they never conveyed them to me in that happy week I spent with them. And if they spoke to Phillip about it, they certainly did it out of my earshot.

The day was filled with eating and preparing for the feast of Christmas Day. Phillip and I were dispatched to pick up the seafood that had been ordered at one of the local suppliers. A giant ham was basted and studded with cloves and then sat waiting in one of the many fridges the Swans seemed to have. I learned that there was a fish fridge, a beer fridge, and sundry others for what seemed like masses of varied delights. I thought of the meagre pickings in my own fridge, which included coffee beans, cheese, and a few vegetables. Margaret would have had a fit if she could see how little food was in it, and Phillip would expect to starve to death.

The day and evening were filled with preparatory jobs, which were punctuated by several more swims and a few glorious moments alone on the beach lying side by side on our towels. By this time, I'd found my rash vest, sun block, and hat. I lay beside Phillip, fully covered by a light-weight Turkish towel and half an inch of 50-plus lotion. I was not getting burnt on day one. Occasionally he would look over at me and laugh, but he was kind enough to adjust the towel over the backs of my legs when I turned to lie on my stomach. Only about twenty times did his parents comment on how untouched by the sun my skin was. I felt like a novelty for a while. I was a little bemused when I heard Peter ask Phillip how "Casper" was holding up. That was me, I presumed—Casper the friendly ghost! I could have been insulted, but I couldn't deny the reality of the situation. I was translucent in comparison to the whole family. It was the first time in my life that I'd ever considered a spray tan to be a good idea.

I didn't consume as much food as Margaret would have liked me to have consumed, but by the time Phillip and I decided we would go to bed, I'd consumed more calories in a day than I had possibly ever consumed in a week. I was pleased that Phillip had pushed the beds together while I was in the bathroom brushing my teeth. I felt a little juvenile in my boxer shorts and t-shirt, but he was pretty happy with the way the evening appeared to be unfolding. It was our first real night together. It was wonderful and weird all at once. I felt it was strange to be making love for the first time in his boyhood bed in his parents' house. Phillip could have cared less about the venue.

When Christmas morning arrived, I felt that I had celebrated Christmas well and truly. I was terribly happy and even enthusiastic about our dawn swim. I just hoped the day would be easy. I had one more sister to meet—Sophie, who at thirty-five was just a year older than Phillip. She and her husband, Max Fraser, had a new baby called Sarah. So ten adults and six little ones would sit down at some point on this day and begin not only to celebrate the special things of Christmas but also to rejoice truly in the power of togetherness and the delight of familiarity.

Present giving preceded eating. The children were ecstatic with the tearing of paper and giving and receiving of parcels. The adults had a more staid approach to the gifts, but their interest was immediately spiked when Phillip and I tried to quietly exchange gifts. He opened his and was genuinely pleased by the framed photo of Lake George. It didn't really need any explanation, but his family was keen for some details. Despite commenting on its beauty, they obviously wanted to know what it meant. He also loved the key ring of St. Michael. I felt shy about opening the gift he had for me in front of the assembled masses, who were now not even trying to mask their collective interest. The first part of the gift was extraordinary, and I knew exactly how expensive it had been. I also couldn't help being amused by the underlying meaning of his choice. It was a first edition of Sir Arthur Conan Doyle's 1915 novel *The Valley of Fear*. It would have cost him a fortune, and I would have words with him in private about spending so much money.

"How romantic, Phil. An old book. You have much to learn, my son." Bertie's comment drew support from the watching crowd. I laughed too but was incredibly touched by the depth of meaning of such a gift. He had also bought a beautiful bangle made of two leafy strands of silver and rose gold that entwined. He had had it made by a local silversmith. He wanted it to be unique and special. It was delicate and fitted perfectly. It seemed too lavish to receive two beautiful things, and I wanted to simply tell him that his presence in my life was enough and that he didn't need to buy such extravagant things. My silence and teary eyes probably told him more about my gratitude and love than words might have. The family seemed to realize that something else was happening between us and that they should turn their attention back to their own gifts. Only Margaret continued to watch her son and the teary woman who was clearly moved by these gifts. She watched Phillip wrap his arms around me and hold me quietly for a moment. She heard him say "Cheer up, Sherlock" and heard me respond "Does that make you Doctor Watson?" His light kiss on the top of my head finally made her look away. I began to worry that she was concerned about the life he might have with me, if in fact there was to be a life together.

Christmas lunch was a noisy and lavish event. Prawns, oysters, and several lobsters that had been caught that morning by Bertie and Thomo formed the opening gambit. This was followed by the baked ham, roast pork, and, I estimated, twenty side dishes. Each of the girls had brought vegetable or salad dishes to round out a menu that could have fed ninety. The food was one thing, but the talk was another. Initially I couldn't properly focus on any one conversation. There seemed to be a dozen going on at once, punctuated by interjections from the children, requests for dishes to be passed around, and the general questions and answers about who had made what. Reminiscences of Christmases past would come during dessert, and the storytelling about Phillip as a child after that. I was seated between his eldest sister, Jessica, and his mother, Margaret. Phillip sat opposite me, and despite the width of the table, he could still stretch his long legs out and gently kick my shins. I think it was his way of checking that all was okay and that I wasn't completely overwhelmed by the hubbub of the Swans. I would look up occasionally and find him either shovelling mouthfuls of food in his mouth or simply staring at me. He stared as if he'd never seen me before, and only when our eyes met did he smile ever so slightly and move his head in a small sideways nod, which I took to be him saying "Let me know if you need rescuing."

But I didn't need to be rescued, except from Margaret, who was insisting that my plate should contain the entire contents of the table. The conversation died down a little, as we all were reaching our stomachs' capacities. Some of the diners were a little giddy on wine, which was poured generously into Margaret's best glasses. After my awful hangover on the Saturday morning that followed that Friday night of unrestrained drinking, I was pretty gun-shy. I had a glass of white wine that I'd barely touched, and it had warmed as the afternoon temperature climbed. As the bellies swelled and the tongues loosened, I sensed some questions were about to be asked. It was Sophie's husband Max who kicked off the interrogation.

"So Lily, what the hell do you see in Swanny?" I didn't get to answer, as there was general input from everyone else, the gist of which was that there was little to recommend him as a partner. Max had gone to school with Phillip. He was in the same year as him and had fallen in love with Sophie Swan, despite her being older and his best friend's sister. When the shouting—the apparent standard convivial mode of conversation in this family—ended, I was called upon to answer a more difficult question from Sophie. There were no other respondents this time. In fact, the entire table fell silent; even baby Sarah stopped her happy burbling. I felt myself blush a little and become a little breathless. A quick slug of warm wine delayed my answer for ten seconds.

"I know you must all be wondering about my past and the discovery of my mother and brother this year. I realize that you believe, as the police and coroner do, that my father was responsible. As I said to Jessica and Lisa yesterday, I simply believe that something else might have happened."

"That's enough, Soph," Phillip interjected, and he pushed his chair back as if he was about to stand up to make his point more emphatic. But I interrupted him before he could get any further into his angry defence of me.

"I grew up happy, Sophie. I knew nothing about my family and, to answer your question, no, I don't believe children can inherit a gene that makes them murderers. I know this is difficult for you all, and I am happy to answer any questions if it makes you feel better about who I am." I tried to lighten the mood. "I guarantee you're all safe from me. I've never committed a crime; haven't even got a parking ticket. I'm sure Phillip's already done a police check."

Max intervened before Sophie could defend her question. I'm sure it was because she loved her brother and had a new baby sitting at the table that she was the most suspicious of my pedigree.

"You don't look like you could do much damage anyway, Lil," Max said. His comment seemed to get universal agreement. The tone of the conversation changed, but Sophie's dark mood did not. And for the rest of the meal, I could feel her eyeing me closely. She seemed to resent being cut off in the midst of her questioning. I wish she'd asked me about being the child of an alleged killer in private so I could have told her about the propensity for criminal activity being more about learned behaviour than about DNA, but the chat had moved on to Phillip. Despite being a little hurt, and a lot humiliated, I started to laugh with the others as the world according to Swanny got going.

He was obviously a boy who had a thirst for adventure. Despite being only a few metres' walk from the beach, it seemed the young Phillip had tried to circumvent the walking part. He had attempted to build a zip line or flying fox so that he could jump from the veranda and fly across the road to land on the beach. Without his father's knowledge, he had strung a nylon cord from the veranda roof to a reasonably tall tree beachside. He fashioned a handle out of a piece of hard plastic and, without testing the tension, threw himself off the balcony and rode the zip line straight into the side of a car that just happened to be on the road at the same time as Phillip's leap. He hadn't quite gotten the tension right, and just eight metres from his launch point, he had collided with Danny House's work ute. Luckily Danny had his windows down, as Phillip's legs powered through the opening, and he landed, somewhat surprisingly, on the builder's lap. He was lucky not to have broken his neck, and despite having scraped the skin from his back as he shot through the car window, he survived to be given a bit of a flogging by the disgruntled neighbour, who had simply been driving slowly off to work. When Peter got home that day, Danny was around to shout about how he hadn't appreciated Phillip landing on his knee and causing him to wet his pants in fear. Needless to say, the zip line was dismantled, and Phillip was banned from further aerial feats.

The beating and the parental disappointment did not stop him from trying other exploits. According to Bertie and Thomo, his best effort was with the BMX bike jump he made at the end of the driveway. Swanny, apparently, was convinced that he could jump his bike across the road from the front yard and land safely on the beach. He obviously had little appreciation for physics at this stage. It was another disaster, resulting in a few broken bones and more disgruntled neighbours. Other attempts included a surf board launcher, something with roller skates, and a series of trampolines, two of which had been stolen.

"They weren't stolen; they were borrowed," both Phillip and Max interjected.

The scar on Phillip's forehead was the result of this particular attempt. The scar on his lip was from some trick he had tried to teach one of the family dogs. The more the stories grew, the greater the interest the little boys, George, Bobby, and Danny, had in their uncle. Phillip was obviously now even a bigger hero to his nephews. Carrie had little interest in anything her father or uncles had done, and Isaac was sound asleep in his chair. I loved the idea of being filled in about

Phillip's childhood. His parents participated in the mocking and exclamations of horror at their wild son's antics, but it was expressed with such love and admiration. I learned that he was the leader of all Broulee misadventures but was also an exceptional student. He didn't fall by the wayside, like some of his mates, and he kept away from the destructive habits that often befell youth who lacked ambition and hope. He left home at eighteen for university and now sixteen years later was the champion of his family. He took the tale-telling well; he laughed with his co-conspirators, teased his sisters, denied some of the alleged facts, and insisted that if they could not present evidence, he'd have to conclude an alternative truth. It seemed that these were my words exactly. Somewhere there was always an alternative truth.

Lunch ended. The late afternoon malaise began. The kids settled in to naps or to play with new toys. Several members of the Swan clan slept on a number of surfaces, couches, spare beds, and pieces of outdoor furniture. Phillip had stretched out on the front lawn on a deck chair. I took my mandolin out of the bedroom and settle by myself on the back deck, so as to not disturb the groggy sleepers. I'd helped Margaret, Lisa, and Bertie clean up and stack the dishwasher with its first load. Leftovers were wrapped in plastic and sent to various fridges, where they could easily be retrieved when hunger roused the house again.

Max joined me with his guitar and asked about my musical abilities. He was suitably impressed with my repertoire and asked if I would play with them on New Year's Eve. I didn't really want to, but I also didn't want to be rude. So I thought no answer might be my best response. I just started playing and, without much encouragement, started singing "Flame Trees." It was one of my favourites, and I thought it lent itself well to an acoustic version. Max knew it well, and between the guitar and mandolin, we managed to sound like we were ready for a public performance. We played a few more tunes, and I taught him my long-term favourite, "Landslide." At this the sleepers woke from their light sleeps and made their way to where the music was emanating. We had a little concert out on the deck, and when joined by Thomo and Bertie, we cranked up the volume and enthusiasm.

Phillip had joined us as well, but just as a spectator. He had allegedly played drums as a teen, but his kit had long ago been sold. The family enjoyed music, and there were some passable voices joining in the choruses of a number of songs.

"Well, that's it. We've got a singer for New Year's." Max said. He was convinced. I wasn't so sure, but I again, in my usual fashion, thought about having a few days to enact the escape clause. The day was ending, and Phillip and I decided to have a swim. We were the only pair who hadn't been drinking, so we could safely have a dip. The others had, and it was clear they were happy to be rid of us for a bit so they could talk about me. I was so happy at that point that I didn't mind.

After Phillip and I swam and talked about the extravagance of his gifts, we returned to the house, showered, and dressed for what I thought would be a cup of tea and an early night. But the Swans don't finish Christmas with lunch and a quiet afternoon. They continue eating. So a light dinner of ham, salad, bread, and leftover prawns was laid out on the veranda table. People sat and picked at the food, drank a little more wine, and let the day become an evening filled not only with food but with a gentle happiness. This must be what mellow feels like, I decided. Contentment and the joy of simply being must feel like this. I thought I might learn to like this state of existence. I caused further tiny ructions when I refused all temptations, including anything from the dessert menu. Phillip obliged and ate my share. He is such a good man. I rested my head on his chest as he finished off the last bit of something that his mother insisted someone had to eat.

The day seemed to be a success. Most of us got through unscathed. There would be some prices to pay when Boxing Day began. The sisters and their families made their way home, again on foot, somehow juggling and balancing kids, presents, and platters of food. Thomo borrowed Peter's wheelbarrow to transport the family bounty home. They looked like a small but noisy parade as they left the front yard. Margaret and Peter said goodnight, as they were exhausted by the labours of the day. Phillip and I sat outside for a little while longer. There was something truly magical about watching the sun disappear and the stars simultaneously appear over a silent sea. I was grateful for this day. I was actually looking forward to six more days together. I decided not think about the pressure I was under to perform with the family band. I would not think about the mysteries I might discover when I return to the lake. I would simply attempt to go with the flow and continue to discover the wonders of contentment.

CHAPTER FIFTEEN

The days leading up to New Year's Eve were wonderful. I wouldn't say they were idyllic, but they were close to it. Phillip got out several surf boards to find one I might be able to manage, and the lessons were hilarious. By the end of the second day of lessons, I had the rudimentary skills to tackle little waves close to the shore. It was great fun, and I was confident enough to send him off with the rest of the town, who all seemed to surf effortlessly at whatever beach had the best waves. They trundled off in convoys to MacKenzies, Malua, or out to the Heads—places I hadn't heard of and other unnamed places that seemed to be an enormous secret, a bit like Bertie and Thomo's secret fishing spots. I was sure that the seafood they provided was all legal; after all, their brother-in-law was indeed the law. I made Phillip go on these surfing sorties and made do with walking around the little town, walking up and down the beach, and swimming happily alone.

A few days before the thirty-first, Phillip went off with another group of men who had called in firstly to get a look at me and secondly to spirit him away to some surf mecca that only they knew about. Sophie had brought the baby around for Margaret to look after while she went with her friends to have haircuts or manicures. I wasn't really listening, as I felt she still hadn't warmed to me. I wandered down to the bedroom to gather my beach things and inadvertently overheard her conversation with Margaret. The general gist was that

133

Sophie didn't want to ask me to go with her. I had rightly sensed she didn't like me, and I had suspected it was because she thought it was likely that I could spontaneously turn into a serial killer. It hurt only when she told her mother not to let me hold Sarah. Sarah was a fat little baby of six months. She was a Swan too in colouring, and despite her mother's mean streak, the little girl seemed incredibly placid and happy. Before I could get back to the two women, Sophie had stomped out of the house.

I went back up to tell Margaret that I was going over to the beach and to check if she needed me for anything. She was sitting holding her sixth grandchild, humming a little tune, and bouncing the wee one on her knee. Margaret had this mothering caper all worked out.

"Oh Lily, I thought you'd already gone to the beach." She reddened, obviously thinking I'd heard Sophie's comments. I thought I should put her out of her embarrassment.

"It's all right, Margaret. I'm not offended by Sophie's caution when it comes to me. But I can assure you once again, everyone is safe." I laughed a little, and she smiled.

"Would you like to hold her?" It was Margaret's peace offering, I thought, chancing the safety of Sophie's baby with me.

"Better not. I'm terribly unpopular as it is. If we are caught conspiring, it will just make matters worse." I waited a second and added, "You can ask me anything, you know, and I'll tell you. I just don't want you to discuss Sophie's comments with Phillip. It just hurts him, and there's no need for that."

Margaret looked like she was about to add something, but I was really ready just to be alone. It was what I knew how to do, and I was just a little worried that she might ask me about my relationship with her son. I had no idea how to discuss things such as love with the mother of the man who was the object of my affections. I wondered if mothers and daughters did talk about such things. I had never spoken to Billie about my boyfriends, particularly not when they had broken my heart or when I was head over heels and making all sorts of poor decisions. And what would Billie know about love anyway? Was she ever in love? Was there ever a man like Phillip in her life, and if so, why didn't she marry him? So many questions and still no closer to answers.

The surf was a little rougher by the time I'd walked the length of the beach, but I was determined to get in to cool off and exercise away some of the millions of calories I'd ingested. A number of the holidaymakers had retreated to the calmer bay near the island or the little beach on the creek. Most of the people in the water were new surfers like me or big kids with boogie boards. Both were dangers to the lone swimmer. I remember a newbie surfer falling awkwardly into a group of swimmers once at Maroubra. I was the one whose face caught his foot across the bridge of my nose. I was dazed and bloody and, luckily, was plucked from the water by a fairly burly surf lifesaver. He was stunning, and I laugh now at the terrible image I must have presented with a face covered in blood. I survived but felt too embarrassed to ever swim there again.

To make sure I didn't have to return to Phillip's family injured, I entered the water well away from the boards. The water temperature was low enough to make me breathe a bit deeper as I dove under the first set of waves. They were rolling in fairly strongly, and the key to a good swim was to get away from the place where they were breaking. When you were just out the back, you could be lifted by the swell or dive through the wave without a problem. I was relaxed and felt I could simply float about on these watery rollers forever. I shouldn't have closed my eyes, but I did. I wasn't going to sleep; I just needed to shut out the brilliant brightness of the sun. In combination with the salty water, the intensity of the light was stinging my eyes badly. I had stopped paying attention to what the sea was doing, which I know was a stupid and dangerous thing to do.

I appreciated the change too late and only opened my eyes when a wave was breaking directly on top of me. Without preparing myself to take the blow, I was tossed about dramatically. It was like being in a washing machine. The water was relentless in driving me into the sand and flipping my legs over my head. Everything was confused. Other than my mouth and eyes filling with sand, it was impossible to tell which way was up. Then panic joined the party. I thought I was drowning. My lungs were hot and tight from holding my breath, and my body felt sore from the pummelling. I was able to get my bearings after a few seconds that seemed a lifetime, and I could look up to the surface of the water. I was momentarily struck by how beautiful it was to see the world through watery lenses. Refracted light and swirling sand made this underwater world seem safe, peaceful. I was thinking in my now-oxygen-deprived way how Moya would have seen this as she fell beneath the cloudy waters of Lake George, how she might have looked up and seen a similar view.

I knew I would have to stop thinking and kick myself to the surface if I was ever going to survive this, but before I had the chance to surface under my own recognizance, a large pair of hands grabbed my waist from behind and forced me upwards. I was startled to find that I was in Max's arms. Sophie's husband had been surfing when he saw me go in. He was on his way to talk to me when he saw me hit.

"Fucking hell, Lily. Jesus, were you trying to drown." He was quite rattled and refused to let go of me until we were both out of the water. He was carrying me, or rather dragging me, as if I was a child who seriously infringed the rules. I was too filled with sand and water to comment or complain. "What the fuck were you doing?" Max seemed to have a limited vocabulary when concerned. My continued silence seemed to worry him more. He sort of shook me by the shoulders and then pulled me into his arms and continued to where I'd left my bag and towel. He sat me down and unfurled the towel. He wrapped my upper body tightly, keeping his arms about me. I was too shocked by his closeness and anger to analyse how this might look to anyone who might be close by.

"I'm sorry I yelled," he said more quietly. "I was just thinking about Swanny and how he'd feel if you washed up on his favourite beach. You looked like you were in real trouble." I didn't think I was in trouble, but I might have been if I'd stayed under the water for much longer.

"Don't tell him. Don't tell Sophie." Max didn't seem to think these requests were unreasonable, and he nodded knowingly. He had let me go by this stage but was sitting very close beside me. I put my head down on my knees and for some ridiculous reason began to cry. It wasn't that I felt that I nearly drowned, nor was it entirely the fact that Sophie seemed to hate me. It may have been a little bit about my mother's death, but it was most certainly the thought of Phillip having to deal with my drowning. The sudden realization that there was now someone who might care if died was a huge responsibility. To actively participate in one's demise, knowing that it might hurt others, seemed unbearably selfish. That's certainly how it seemed curled up on the beach with a man I'd only met a few days ago. I didn't think he cared a great deal about me, but his love for Phillip made him, by default, have to care about my safety.

After a minute, I was able to sit up and turn my sand-scrapped face to Max. He sort of winced when he looked at me, so I could imagine I wasn't looking my best.

"It's only on your forehead and bit beside your eye," he said, trying to be clinical in his assessment of my injuries. It would look like a rash; no flesh actually had been removed, even though it felt raw and hot. "Did you take in any water?" An important question, given the fact that liquid in the lungs can be deadly well after the time a near drowning victim is pulled out of the sea. I hadn't. I could reassure him of that at least.

"Why is Sophie angry with me?" I thought a distracting question might stop Max looking at me as if he'd have to start CPR to bring me back into coherence.

He thought for a bit and then said, "She's a bit overwhelmed with Sarah. We had been trying for a while to have a baby. She's IVF. Sophie's a bit jealous of her sisters who had their kids easily. She super protective of Sarah. Even I can't get a look in most days." That might explain why she was generally uptight but not why she had taken such a set against me. I looked at Max to see if he had more of an answer. "She really liked Samantha, Swanny's ex," he continued. "You are nothing like her. Sam was a big, strong girl and just a bit older than Phil. You, on the other hand, look like you need a bit of looking after." He laughed.

"It's odd that I look like a good wind might tip me over, but I've managed my life and had my own property to contend with, not to mention the publicity earlier in the year. I'm still standing." It was hard not to sound a bit put out. I wasn't in love with Phillip because I thought he could look after me. I could go back to my life of solitude and crawl back inside my head if things didn't work out with Phillip. It would break my heart, but I was not a stranger to loneliness. I felt angry that Sophie or Max, in fact that any of the Swan clan, thought I needed to be sheltered and indulged. Indeed the more I thought about it, the angrier I got.

"Just don't tell anyone about this, Max. Please," I said. I would, however, have to make up something about my face. "I'll tell them I got dumped by a sneaky breaker. It should amuse them all for a bit."

Max helped me to my feet and suggested that he drive me back to Margaret and Peter's. I begrudgingly agreed that walking might put a bit of a strain on my already sore body. In the tumble dryer of the sea, I'd been thumped into the ground quite hard, so I'd not only been scraped by the sand but bruised as well.

Max's car was his work ute. It was messy and filled with tools, fishing rods, an esky, and a couple of surf boards. On closer inspection, it had clothes, towels, and discarded take away wrappers on most surfaces.

"I take it that this isn't the family car?" I was trying to keep the critical tone out of my voice.

"I have it like this to keep Soph out of it. She wouldn't be seen dead in it." I wondered for a moment if the strain of conceiving Sarah and the years of disappointment might have put a strain on their marriage. Max was a very affable man, manly and a bit rough around the edges, but that added a certain appeal. I imagined that when he was younger he would have been chased mercilessly by the local girls. Perhaps a few might still hanker after him. He had a natural smile and a rather disconcerting way of letting his eyes run over your body before starting any conversation. I noticed it when we first met, not that I was much to look at. I thought about how lucky Sophie was to have such a good-looking husband and now a truly beautiful baby. I felt she should be a little more generous, given that she had so much good in her life.

The drive from the beach to the Swans' was only a couple of minutes by car. I was grateful to Max for his rescue and his candid discussion. I asked him again not to tell anyone about the near miss, and he assured me he would keep quiet.

"It's sort of fun to have a secret to share," he said in a mock whisper. "It means you might owe me a favour one day, Lily." His tone was light, but I sensed he was a tiny bit serious with this final comment. I got out of the mess of his car and grabbed my bag, hat, and towel.

Margaret was surprised that I was back and called to me down the stairs that she had put the kettle on if I wanted a cup of tea. The baby was asleep, and it seemed like a good opportunity to find out some things about the family.

"Dear God, what happened to you?" Margaret said when she saw my scratched face.

"Got tumbled by a sneaky wave. Face planted rather indelicately. It's just a bit of a rash. It'll calm down." I tried to downplay my injuries. I didn't want her getting all concerned about it. Her cure was an immediate cup of tea, a sandwich, and some locally made balm that would heal any hurt. The two of us installed ourselves within earshot of the baby in case she should wake up. Then Margaret began.

"I can tell you and Phil are getting on really well. He was pretty upset over his last girlfriend cheating on him." This sounded like a mother warning off someone who might see her boy as prey. "You have a lot to sort out, don't you, Lily?" I knew that this had nothing to do with my relationship with Phillip; she was alluding to my past. I was hesitant at first, but I realized that she was the mother of the man I loved. She had to be a good person, given the exceptional qualities evident in her son. I thought I could try to let her in, just a little.

I began by telling her how Phillip had come down to the lake to tell me about the findings after the bones had been examined. These were findings, I reminded her, not actual conclusive facts. These were the probable events according to the coroner. I knew I sounded defensive, but I was trying to justify the course of action I'd decided to take. She nodded a few times but didn't stare directly at me while I talked. She looked out to sea and sipped her tea. I went on to tell her about Billie and Darcy and the role they had played in my life. I confessed my ignorance of their past lives and stated that it was my intention to right the situation by clearing out their homes and learning all I could by chasing down people who had known them. She listened closely, both to me and to any little noise that might come from Sarah. I explained how it felt to be without family. It wasn't about self-pity or the need to be comforted. I just thought she should know what it was like to stand in that cemetery and look at the grave stones of all the people who, by rights, should still be alive.

"I can't live in ignorance about my past, Margaret. I have to do something to get a sense of what happened in the lives of my parents. It's not enough to say he killed them and then killed himself." The more I thought about telling her that, the more committed I was to the notion that it just wasn't good enough. I'd avoided the question "why?" my whole life. It was exhausting to keep running away from that very question, or maybe running away from the answer. If Cillian was simply an evil man who wanted something else in his life and thought he could achieve it my killing Moya, then that was an answer. But why kill Brannen? Why a little boy who was too innocent to have done anything to deserve his fate?

During this diatribe Margaret turned to face me. She put her hand out and held my arm but didn't interrupt. When I finally stopped I looked at her. Tears had run down her cheeks. "Please don't feel sorry for me, Margaret. I'm strong and determined to find some of the answers. I will be even stronger when I work through this."

"I think you are wonderful, Lily. You look so young and tiny sitting there with your scratched-up face and wild hair, but I believe that you are strong. You're intelligent and passionate, too. You might just be the right woman for my Phillip." She leaned over and gave me another one of those mother hugs. At that point, Sarah woke and let out a slightly disgruntled cry. Nothing was wrong; she just wanted company. Margaret left to get the baby, and to my surprise Phillip, took her place. He had been waiting in the kitchen, listening to what I'd been saying. He was about to say something important, and then he saw my face.

"What happened to your head, Sherlock?"

I gave him a brief version of events: just hit by a wave and surfed the bottom of the sea on my face for a bit. I said nothing about Max's rescue—unnecessary rescue, that is—and certainly didn't mention thinking about my mother when I was under the water. I thought it might freak him out, and I didn't want him to think that I was wavering in my recovery. His response was simply to insist that I shouldn't swim alone again, as for some reason I couldn't be relied upon to be sensible.

"A few more surfing lessons then, dear Lil, to ensure you learn how to keep your face off the sea floor." He kissed me with a bit too much determination, but I didn't have the heart to say that he was hurting my face. I hoped Margaret's secret salve would ease some of the redness and promote a bit of healing, given that I was supposed to sing in front of the New Year's revellers in a couple of days.

True to his word, Phillip didn't leave me alone again. He refused to go fishing with Thomo and Bertie the next day until I said I would go too. I wasn't keen to go fishing as such, but I was happy enough to be aboard as we went out in the Swans' boat. I had to be sworn to secrecy about the location of the fishing spot, as it was their spot. Surprisingly, there were no other boats in the area. I took up residence in the forward part of the boat with my usual sun protection, which ensured no skin was bared to the now fairly brutal rays. The men, including Max, who had decided at the last minute to come too, readied themselves to catch a week's worth of dinners. I had bought a book to read and some papers from work that I really should have looked at in that frantic last week. To further my comfort, Max appeared by my side with a bottle of water and bag of grapes. He knelt down beside me and had a good look at my face.

"Not too bad. You're obviously a good healer. Still a secret, then?" Max's face was full of mock seriousness. I confirmed that it was and that I was grateful for his support.

We stopped whispering as Phillip's voice boomed out. "Max! Get away from my girl." There was a bit of hooting and laughing from the other two, and Max gave as good as he was getting.

"Just offering her a better alternative, Swanny."

They settled down to the serious business of fishing, and I lay back with my eyes closed to think about the way life had changed so suddenly. I was in the midst of a family and group of friends that had generally embraced me as one of their own. In a short time, I'd moved from social isolate to part of a group, not to mention being in a proper relationship with a man I was now sure I loved. It seemed I could add Max to my short list of friends, and despite his wife's unreasonable loathing of me, the two of us already shared a secret. I'd always imagined that life was simple, that people were somehow fairly uncomplicated. What was on the surface was what lay beneath. I know this came from a childhood of taking everything at face value. Billie and Darcy were, through my child's eyes, one-dimensional characters. They were, for the most part, silent observers who hovered at the periphery of my vision, always there and kind to a fault, but the life beyond that was invisible. A veil while living, and a shroud in death, covered the people I thought I knew.

As was made clear by the truths we revealed to each other during the Friday-night dinner party, Brendan, Helena, and Jimmy were not cardboard cut-outs but people with pasts and hopes for the future. They were not living some utopian life that I had prescribed for them. All of them were hurting from some unresolved incident or heaving about some terrible baggage that had shaped them and would continue to do so until they could finally let it go. And at the back of the boat were four men who, despite the idyllic nature of their beach lives, were also chiselled into shape by things inside and outside their control. Phillip had his heart broken by the robust Samantha and worked in a job that must have provided moments where he would doubt the decency of humankind. Even the happy fishermen must have experienced some dark moments. I felt Max might be mentally traversing some miles, given the tension with Sophie. He seemed not unhappy but uncertain about the near future. And Peter and Margaret could not have always found it easy raising four children, particularly their youngest son, who must have broken their hearts a few times with his raucous behaviour. No one gets through unscathed. If you are pristine at the end of your days, then you have failed to live. If risks were not taken, then you never stepped out of the shadows. Damage allows us all to make the best of ourselves. We can find out how strong we really are when we face the challenges of life. The alternative to taking on the challenge was not a pretty one: give up, lay down, and die or live cloistered away from people in a world that you refuse to discover. I know I had taken the latter path.

My deep thoughts were interrupted by the noise of success. Thomo had pulled in a big snapper at the same time that Bertie reeled in a trevally. Both were great eating fish. I ceased my ruminating to turn and watch them bring in a dozen more trevallies, a few flatheads, and two more snappers. There would be fish for dinner for a week. I was amazed at how these men, all in their thirties and forties, became boys again in each other's company. The serious business of fishing was accompanied by the antics of adolescent boys who, despite what had happened and what might happen, certainly knew how to make the most of the present. I was offered the chance to join in the fishing using a rod that Max had baited for me. I thought I'd give it a go, but on my first effort to cast my line, the hook got caught on the back of my shirt, which led to an immediate, self-imposed disqualification. The boys, however, persuaded me to keep trying. In the end, Phillip cast for me and then handed me the rod. Within the hour, I had also caught a couple of fish.

"You're a natural, Lily," Max said, overstating the facts. But it was fun to be included.

The eskies full of fish and the desire for lunch brought the expedition to an end. We'd been out on the water for a few hours, and the fishing had been successful. I hoped I wouldn't be called upon to do any of the gutting and cleaning of the fish. I was planning to run a mile away if that was part of the deal, but neither Phillip nor I were needed for that. When the boat was back on the trailer, we left in Phillip's car to have lunch at a local café. I'd promised to rehearse with the in-laws later in the day so that when we played the next night, we wouldn't embarrass ourselves. To my relief, I was finally told that we wouldn't be the only group called out to entertain the town. It was more of a jam session, and lots of local artists would be performing. It seemed that everyone could surf, strum a tune on a guitar, and fish. It was the rule of living here. Well, I'd been able to fish, I was musical, and given a few more months of learning, I'd master basic surfing. I smiled at the thought of belonging and at what that might mean for Phillip and me.

Days came and went in an easy rhythm. Every day followed a lovely pattern: swim, drive about, eat, rest in each other's arms on the beach or on the veranda, and sleep deeply after making love at night. Could life get better? But holidays end, and reality doesn't always include such depths of serenity and unblemished joy. The New Year's concert was not as daunting as I thought, and after fortifying myself with a couple of glasses of wine, I was nearly as bold as the rest of the band. We had rehearsed a few times and could belt out a couple of tunes. My voice surprised everyone. I think they were expecting a little tinny sound, but the one thing I knew I could do well was hit every note with precise and forceful accuracy. After a few Cold Chisel songs, my finale was a bit of Joni Mitchell. Can't beat those lyrics of "Both Sides Now," "Big Yellow Taxi," and "Circle Game." We were followed by a troupe of local banjo players who filled the makeshift stage in the surf club. The noise was sensational, and the extraordinary vision of these bearded, dreadlocked musicians was nothing short of inspirational.

I was elated by my success and enjoyed the attention I was getting. The wine, the noise, and the gentle summer evening made me feel more relaxed than I had all week. Phillip watched me closely as I clapped along with the banjo extravaganza, and when the second piece was over, he grabbed me by the hand led me out of the club and down to the beach. It was cooler down there, and the volume of the music was dampened by the dunes and breeze. Phillip had been drinking more than he ever had in my company. I think he was quite drunk, really, as his first kiss was wet and messy. He was slurring a little when he finally spoke. His opening gambit was to tell me he loved me. It was easy to return these words to him. His second statement was to reiterate his belief that we should live together. And his third was unexpected and sobered me up pretty quickly. Damn Max! He had obviously blabbed to Phillip about how I hadn't surfaced, possibly deliberately, when I got hit by that wave.

"Please don't do anything to hurt yourself, Lily. I couldn't bear it. If you are sad, I'll fix it." I wondered how he might do that, and I wondered how I might tell him that he made me so happy that I didn't want to go anywhere without him. I held him tightly and let his head rest against my breasts. I'd sort of wrapped my whole self around his body as we lay in the sand and watched the night.

"My resolution is to finish looking at the past by the end of January this coming year," I said. "I just want thirty-one days to clear out the ancient history of my family's lives. Then I'll be ready to start my life with you. I promise."

Phillip hardly responded. He mumbled something about never letting anything hurt me and promptly fell to sleep. I was aware of the weight of his body on mine and the increasing chill of the sand beneath me, but I was fixated on the starry sky. The blackness was punctuated by millions of tiny lights and a sliver of moon, a new moon that heralded the beginning of a new cycle of life. At some point I'd have to wake him and help him back to his parents' house, but for now I was content to feel his breath against my neck and listen to the party goers at the club count down the end of 2001 and cheer in 2002. What would the year bring? What would I know by this time next year? Would I ever be this happy again?

CHAPTER SIXTEEN

I didn't let Phillip drive the next day. He was fairly worse for the wear. We said farewell to his family on the morning of New Year's Day, despite them wanting us to stay for another meal. Everyone was in the hugging mood and said politely how nice it was to meet me. Only Sophie didn't show for the goodbyes. Max's hug was a little too warm, but he was holding the baby, so he couldn't quite sweep me up with two arms.

"You told our secret," I quietly berated him.

"I didn't. I said I wouldn't, and I didn't tell anyone." He was a little defensive and, in typical male fashion, couldn't quite manage a whisper. I wondered then what it was that Phillip was alluding to in his less-than-sober discussion last night. I thought I could ask him on the trip home. It would take two hours or just a little more depending on the traffic. It was lovely to see him hug his parents. It wasn't just a perfunctory action of a dutiful son but a comprehensive sign of his admiration for them. Looking at Peter, I could see just what Phillip would look like as he aged. I imagined momentarily the two of us being in our sixties and wondered if it could actually be possible. Margaret did the mother thing again with me, saying that I really needed to look after myself. She insisted I take her balm to keep my scraped face healing. She desperately tried to give us food to take back, and in the end, Phillip acquiesced and put a box of bits and pieces on the back seat. I carefully backed out of the drive with Phillip waving to his assembled family from the passenger window.

"Thanks for driving, Lil. I think I'd be over the limit still if I was pulled over, and it's likely that the boys will have the booze bus out on New Year's Day." Ever the pragmatist. Ever the copper.

The drive was quiet. The traffic into and out of the bay had ceased, at least for a week or so. We were able to enjoy an uninterrupted journey back over Clyde Mountain and through the countryside from Braidwood to Lake Road. Phillip slept most of the way, his head lolling about and his breathing easy. We talked for a little while as the trip started, and I thanked him for taking me away. I told him that initially I hadn't wanted to go and I had been trying to think of a way out. He laughed at me for thinking I was going to get away with saying no to him. Our discussion briefly touched on his sisters and brothers-in-law. He jokingly said I'd have to watch Max. He was a bit of a flirt. I questioned him about Sophie and her reaction to me.

"Sophie's just mean," he said. "Always was. Wanted everything everyone else had; couldn't be happy with her lot." Phillip yawned and began to drift away. I desperately wanted to talk about Samantha and why Sophie liked her so much, but he was no longer listening. And I really didn't need to know.

Phillip woke as I slowed to drive through Bungendore. As I always did, I gave a long look at the roadside cemetery that safeguarded my family's remains. I would take flowers to the graves later in the week and tend the little plots to ensure that everyone was neat and tidy. All country towns had their graveyards, usually set out on the edge of town, sometimes near the churches—one Anglican and one Catholic. This graveyard was built right beside the railway close to the station. The irony made me smile. No one was really going, but over the years many had come to this dusty place. Any attempts at beautifying the place with arbores and plantings seemed to be at the mercy of the weather. The whole country, even the burial grounds, was ravaged by drought or threatened by flood. This cemetery was a dry as I'd ever seen it.

"You think about them a lot, don't you?" Phillip asked. He was awake and noticed my line of vision. His hand reached out and rubbed my tummy, and then it rested on my sore hip. I could feel him staring at me.

"A bit. Usually when I'm passing here. It doesn't make me miserable, Phillip. I don't go spiralling into despair, but it's a bit like my bruised hip: I only notice it when it's touched." With that, he moved his hand to the top of my thigh and cheekily between my legs. "If I crash your car, I'll be telling the police that I lost concentration when my boyfriend decided to feel me up."

He removed his hand but continued to lean close to me. "You must have been speeding to make it here by this time. I really can't be consorting with criminals."

"Well, you know the car is registered in your name, Detective Sergeant Swan, so if you haven't got a job tomorrow, you'll know why."

It only took a few minutes for us to make our way sedately through the town and make the turn onto my road and a few more to make the dust rise and to pull up outside my home. Another week without rain had dried things out even more, and I would need to check the tanks to see if I had any water left for the gardens I'd intended bringing back to life. Phillip helped me inside with my bags and the food his mother insisted we take. I tried to get him to put it back in his car, but after he'd had a quick look in my fridge and pantry, he refused stoically to take it with him. The only way it was leaving my house was if I was leaving with it and going to stay with him. It was most tempting. The thought of packing clean clothes and leaving the whole sorry mess of the O'Haras behind had great appeal. The thought of giving Phillip up even for a day or two seemed impossible, but we both knew he had to work tomorrow. And I would be inundated with the party of three from the museum for the great clean up.

Before he left he did that thing where he simply held my head in his hands and brushed his lips over my face, finishing with a tiny kiss between my eyes. As he strode back to his car, now hopefully leached of alcohol, I was just able to restrain myself from calling out "don't go."

It sounded weak and adolescent, but I was suddenly afraid of being alone, even for a day—afraid of the thoughts I would have about what might be discovered, or worse, the fear that nothing would be uncovered and that I would have to accept the legal interpretation of the events of 1975. Being with Phillip and his family had distracted me from such. As his car turned, before he accelerated back down the dirt road, he waved and shouted, "Love you, Sherlock." The noise of the car and the swirl of dust brought several crows from their roosts. I childishly counted them. Seven. I was hoping it might be four; four for a boy. But perhaps seven was more prophetic: secrets that should not be told. Are there really secrets that should remain concealed forever? I watched the black birds settle back into their positions where they eagerly waited for some carrion to feast upon.

I had a day and night to myself, so I began putting Margaret's food parcel away into the pantry and the fridge. I'd asked Helena to get milk and fresh bread before coming down with the boys. No doubt they would bring excessive amounts of food with them. On top of a huge slab of Christmas pudding wrapped in layers of cling film, Phillip had left me a little note.

"Not even you can change the past, Lily. But you can make the future whatever you want it to be. Love you. PS." PS? Postscript? Phillip Swan. I smiled at the thought of a lifetime with PS, thinking he was always right. I must one day correct him on the first point. I didn't want to change the past; I just wanted the facts of it laid bare and fairly examined. Perhaps Mick's assumption was correct and I would have to come to live with that. But at least for the next five days, I would live in hope that an alternative was possible.

After I had a shower and put a load of washing out on the clothes line, I set to making sure I had enough garbage bags and plastic storage containers. I'd purchased acid-free tissue paper for any documents that needed special care, as well as a few dozen document wallets. The rubbish skip would turn up tomorrow, and the sorting would begin. We would start with Darcy's house. All papers and small items would be sorted by me. Clothes and kitchen utensils would either be donated or binned and therefore were to be piled up on the front porch of his house. Helena, Jimmy, and Brendan had a good eye for knowing what had value and what didn't, and junk would be sent straight to the skip. In our planning session, I asked them to be mindful of anything concealed within folded items. Everything would need a good shake. I wasn't optimistic that anything would show up in Darcy's meagre possessions, but I did think I might get to know him a little better by handling the items he retained. I knew the story of my uncle would only come to life with some careful reconstruction and perhaps a tiny bit of creative license, but knowing something of his journey would be better than knowing nothing.

Darcy. Dear Darcy. So quiet and introspective. Or was it sadness? I tried to put a sequence of memories together that gave me a chronological pathway of his life as I experienced it, but the few things I remembered were only vague images. These memories were like sepia photographs that had started life out of focus, blurry figures engaged in indistinguishable actions that were nonetheless recorded. Other than his love of music and his unrestrained amusement when he told the story of Billie's lipstick, little came to mind. He was almost a shadow in every event I tried to recall: learning to drive, shopping in the city, picking me up from school and taking me back, helping me move to Sydney. Darcy was always there, but he was not able to make his presence felt. I was straining to remember the sound of his voice or any snippet of wisdom he might have passed on, but I came up blank. It would be different with Billie's house.

I'd already been surprised by the newspaper cache I'd discovered in my old bedroom and the music room at Billie's. I was still quite baffled that her interest in global catastrophes and royal weddings had led her to save dozens of papers from those years. I thought about my own interests and realized that the only newspapers I'd ever kept were those from June last year. And even those I'd throw away in this clean up.

The final house would be mine, my parents' home, where they had Brannen and me. I didn't think there would be many secrets to uncover, but it was time to do something with my father's tools and the furniture he made. There were two or three big wardrobes that needed to be divested of the remnants of Moya and Cillian's lives. Then would come the final assessment of furniture, deciding what I would keep and what things would go. The houses could then go on the market as one property. Then it would be over, the last O'Hara would leave the lake and make her way somewhere else.

I felt melancholy and was not without fear. But I was set on this course, and nothing could stop the inevitability of change. It was like being on a runaway train. There would be chaos, maybe some hysteria, bruises, and wounds, but it was inescapable that either the train would come to a stop of its own accord and peace would be restored or it would leave the rails at some point in its journey and crash, throwing all occupants free of the carnage. Not all would survive in that latter scenario. But in either case, the train would be stopped, and what was left would be the beginning of something else. I wasn't really committed to praying, but at this point I felt like an appeal to a benevolent god might not do any harm. In the end, all I could muster was "God help me."

Sleep was not easy. I missed Phillip and had not realized that in the past week I'd become so used to the sound of him, the scent of him, and the sex. I felt very alone in my bed, and despite the warmth of the night, I couldn't get comfortable. I shivered and curled into a ball, trying to insulate my body from the cooling air. Most nights like this I could have slept under a sheet, but restlessness and a busy mind played havoc with my comfort switch. When I did sleep, dreams rolled in like storm clouds. I was under the water; Max saved me and then told me I had to run away. We were being chased down the beach, and when I looked back it was Phillip. He was in a police uniform and he had his gun in his hand. Somewhere else in the dream, his parents were standing out in the middle of the lake when suddenly crows in the thousands fell upon them. I was trying to count them, but they were too numerous. I couldn't get past *one for sorrow*, and I repeated the line over and over. Then I heard Billie's voice, which kept calling me to come home. I hated these confusing dreams. I wanted my subconscious mind to leave me alone. There was enough in the here and now to deal with.

At dawn the light and the yellow rays of the sun woke me. I was unrested and restless, but this day was the first day of an inexorable expedition into the past. I had to remember that I would not be alone.

The first hours of the day I cleaned the house, showered, and put away my paltry Christmas display. I kept the two little carved hands out so that I could carefully wrap them and put them into a box labelled *Treasures*. By ten o'clock the team had arrived, this time in two cars, as Brendan wasn't going to sleep over.

"It's a woman," Jimmy informed me. "Apparently he can't be parted from her for a single night, lest she wander off, seeking other nocturnal pleasures." In response, Brendan swung a backpack at Jimmy's head, just missing him. Helena ignored the two, simply rolling her eyes, and squeezed me conspiratorial.

"You look well, if you know what I mean." She was never one for subtlety. "Good week?" My blushing face said it all. It had been a very good week.

We decided to have coffee before launching into the task of unpacking the past. Jimmy wanted further clarification about what could go straight to the skip and wanted to know whether if he found a million dollars he would have to share it. My confidence that the O'Haras had never amassed that kind of sum made me magnanimous.

"If you find a million, Jimmy, it's all yours."

And then we began.

Darcy's home had been mostly shut up since his death three years before. I'd been up there with Billie to find clothes to bury him in and occasionally since she died to check for damage after storms and do a little cursory cleaning, such as vacuuming floors. But I'd never really roamed about Darcy's cottage. With the doors open and the windows wide, I saw what a lovely little place it was. Obviously sometime just before he died, the bathroom had been upgraded and the walls painted. The polished boards were in good condition too. Dust mites and significant cobwebs revealed my lack of attention to housekeeping, but in general, the place was habitable and, according to Helena, marketable as a separate property.

Darcy was not man who had a lot of possessions, so I was sure things would be easily sorted here. As we performed a kind of reconnaissance and delegated jobs, the noise of a truck arriving took me back to the main house. The driver had manoeuvred between the cars and had found a flat spot to swing the skip into. He was an affable chap and was happy to chat about the lake while he gathered the paper work that had to be signed. Like a number of people who knew a bit about the lake, he wanted to share his expert opinion about the water's appearance and disappearance.

"Haunted. Like bad magic happened here. Not just those bones they dug up last year but hundreds of years of bad things." He was keen to share further mad theories and hadn't made the connection that the bones were explicitly linked to me and my need for this super-sized garbage bin he'd just delivered. I gave him five minutes and then said I really had to get on with filling the skip.

"You moving out?" he asked. A reasonable question.

"Moving on," I responded. A reasonable answer.

Back at Darcy's, the rooms had been divided. Helena was in Darcy's bedroom, Jimmy had the kitchen, Brendan had the lounge and sitting room, and I would tackle what looked like a study and storage room that would have been a second bedroom.

Within an hour, Helena had put all Darcy's clothes and shoes into the skip. Nothing was salvageable, according to her. She had stacked several piles of books on the veranda after checking each one for tucked-away items. She found only two old receipts, hand written and faded. In his chest of drawers, she found an old Walkman cassette player. I couldn't remember ever having seen Darcy with it, but I knew he loved music and was at his happiest when I gave little concerts at home—an audience of two and a solo performer. What a funny little life. I was, however, interested in what Darcy might have been listening to and asked Helena to put the devise into the keep-and-check box now located in the middle of the sitting room floor. I didn't think I'd need a whole box for Darcy's treasures, but

I didn't want to throw away his whole life and have nothing left. In the two books she found on his bedside table, she found a photo that was acting as a book mark. He had been reading *Cities of the Plain* by Cormac McCarthy. The photo was one I'd never seen, and I would certainly keep it as a treasure. It must have been taken in the early autumn of 1975. Moya was obviously pregnant in this photo of her, Darcy, Billie, and Brannen. It was a faded colour print, but the image was sharp and well framed. I thought my father must have taken the picture, because he wasn't in it. The four of them were standing in the rose garden, which was devoid of greenery, but the orchard could be seen thriving in the background. Billie was holding Brannen on her hip—that dear little boy with his big smile and hopeful eyes. I had to swallow the sadness of what might have been before it got in the way of the job at hand. Billie was looking at Brannen and laughing, her mouth open as if a giggle must just escape. I thought my brother must have done something to make her laugh in this way. In the middle of the photo was Moya, her hair a tangle of curls, her belly beginning to round out with me, and her eyes looking beyond the photographer. She was not looking into the camera's lens but looking off into the distance, over the shoulder of whoever was calling them to "look this way." She smiled with her mouth but not her eyes. Darcy had his arm around my mother's shoulders. He too was not looking at the camera. He was looking sideways at Brannen, his face bathed in the delight of a little boy who was loving the limelight. What a lovely few months they must have had before I was born in the October of that year, before everything ended. Moya's protruding belly should have been a sign of the wonders of life to come, but my birth ended any happiness this little family was experiencing on this day. Was there any sign that in five months two would be gone, the third in a year, and less than three decades later only one would be left? Not more questions! I had to stop asking so many questions and focus on any sort of fact that could be gleaned from this photo. Fact one: Brannen was the darling of his family. Fact two: Billie and Darcy obviously loved this sunny little boy. And fact three: Moya was cared about. Darcy's easy embrace of his sister-in-law reflected that he was at ease with her and she with him. She did not look unhappy; maybe she even looked contented.

The photo was one of many artefacts that we would uncover. The second came from my unpacking of the Darcy's study. The things we learn from what is left behind. Beneath a carefully covered sheet was a well-kept but somewhat dusty butler's desk. It was the kind of desk that had a number of shelves and compartments for storing household bills and documents. I thought that if money was ever an issue, this lovely piece would probably fetch several thousand dollars. I would not have thought this was Darcy's taste, but it probably came to him through another long-forgotten member of the O'Hara clan. I wondered if anything inside might render a secret not to be told.

The first set of compartments was filled with car repair receipts from Arlen Beltz. Darcy had them all arranged in date order. They were stamped "paid in full." Cash. It was the way things were done. No one used credit cards, and the O'Haras certainly didn't borrow money. Billie mistrusted banks, and when I went away to university, she only begrudgingly put money into an account for me, although she really wanted me to take a wad of cash. I remember having to argue that I'd be mugged the minute I turned up with thousands of dollars tucked into my shoes.

The second set of compartments was more interesting. Darcy had, of course, had a real life. His marriage certificate and decree nisi were neatly bundled with four photos and two letters. Either this was a secret, or I had simply failed to ask questions. Darcy O'Hara had been married, albeit briefly. The marriage certificate was dated April 16, 1960, and the bride was Lidia Anne Harris. Darcy was twenty-three years old, and his new wife was twenty. She was the same age as my father. I wondered if she was still alive; it was most likely that she would be, as she would only be sixty-two. Another possible lead to investigate; another voice to add its story to the general pool of knowledge about my family. The divorce papers were dated 1968. It must have been a short period of wedded bliss. One of the four photos was of the wedding. Lidia was a sturdy girl with long dark hair and olive skin. Her dress was a very simple white-lace frock that did little to disguise her curves. She looked happy as she stared into the camera lens. The background looked familiar, but I couldn't immediately place it. In the photo with the couple were two unhappy-looking bridesmaids, my father, and another man. My father and Darcy were so alike. Cillian was looking at Darcy, who was grinning like a man who knew a thing or two. He actually looked rakish and bold. At twenty-three he was a man who seemed to believe he had it all. It didn't match the silent man I'd lived with or the beaten man who died alone except for his loyal sister and niece. Where did this Darcy go?

The other photos were taken a few years later. Darcy's hair was long, and he had certainly embraced the fashion of the 1960s. His beard and wild hair spoke volumes about the direction his life took after marriage. The others in the photo were named. Someone had taken the time to write across the photo. It was a band; the name was inscribed on the bottom of the photo. They called themselves Wayfarer. The date was January 1968. Their instruments were about them or held casually. In the centre of the photo was an unmistakable waif: Moya Bryant. My mother was in this band with Darcy, Paddy Lock, Stephen Doddy, Carl Blackberry, and Sean Page. I couldn't help but stare at each musician in turn. This was the life my mother had before she married Cillian and had Brannen. It must have been Darcy who introduced my parents to each other. I thought about the images of my father in the photo printed in the paper and in Darcy's wedding photo. He was so conservative looking in contrast to this wild lot. Moya was dressed in flared denim jeans and a skin-tight t-shirt, obviously without a bra. Her hair, like mine on its worst days, was splayed out from her head in a wild afro of red curls. And Darcy had his arm around her again. I wondered about the friendship between them and about the other men in the band. Would they remember Moya and Darcy? Did any of them know about her disappearance? Why didn't Mick have any notes about what any of these men might have added to the mystery? I was beginning to loathe the number of questions that kept welling up with every new thing I found.

As for the letters, one was from Lidia to Darcy. He had obviously gone to Queensland to work in the mine at Mt. Isa soon after they were married. I imagined that young girl being left out here at the lake with only Billie and Cillian for company. The money was obviously good enough to take the young groom away from his bride but not good enough to make her wait. The letter didn't even start with "dear Darcy." It just started with "I hate to tell you this." Lidia continued briefly, without softening the blow, to state why she was leaving him. It seemed she didn't want to be responsible for the O'Hara property and in-laws in the absence of her husband. She hated living on the lake and wanted a life in the city. She had been to secretarial school, and she could support herself. Her friends had confirmed that her life on the lake was without merit, and she would move back to her family home. The letter was dated one year after the marriage—a failure, one might say. Poor Darcy.

The second letter was perhaps even stranger. It was from Moya and dated the same year as the Wayfarer photo. Darcy had been separated from Lidia for seven years, and they had just divorced. It read "Dear Darce, don't leave the band. Please don't leave on account of me. We'll never be able to replace you. I've written a song about you, and I want you to there to hear it." On the back of this neatly penned note was what I took to be the song lyrics. It was titled "Darcy's Song." Unfortunately the lyrics had been written in pencil, and much of them were faded and indecipherable. There was something that looked like *out of storms ride heroes, from the tempest comes the calm*, and then several grey blurs followed by *something light always comes in the wake of deepest darkness.* There were other snatches of words and phrases, but for all intents and purposes, this seemed to be a song honouring a special person in Moya's life. I wondered if Darcy had loved Moya and then wanted to leave the band after she fell in love with Cillian. How awful must it have been for her to then live several metres away from him in the main house on Lake Road?

I returned to the desk to sort the rest of the papers and evidence of Darcy's past. Other than bills and a few photos of the property, only a yellowed envelope caught my attention. The photo inside both shocked and slightly appalled me, but it did confirm the issue about who Moya might have loved before my father. It was a picture of

Darcy and Moya sans clothes. They had set up camp by a river, and she was laying back against Darcy's bare chest. His hands were linked beneath her breasts, and their eyes were locked on each other. If it had been anyone but my uncle and mother, I might have been able to appreciate the beauty of their bodies and the love reflected by the way they looked at each other, but all I could think of was how she ended up with my father and who was there taking this photo. A tangled web of hurt feelings and broken hearts followed this happy snap of a carefree couple. It might have been the last time Darcy was happy.

Part of me wanted to rip the photo up into a million pieces. Most of me wondered if this was evidence that might explain the events of 1975. Moya was only twenty-two in this photo with Darcy; he would have been thirty-one. She was just a girl. She looked like a child. I didn't want to be angry with her, but I couldn't help feeling that her relationship with Darcy was something that made everyone unhappy at some point. Despite partially crushing the photo, I looked again at the two of them. She was the woman who would become a wife, a mother, and a victim of something reprehensible. How can we ever know what will be our last happy memories?

This desk had offered up all it was going to—shocking and somewhat troubling revelations provided by several simple pieces of paper, kept undercover, only viewed in clandestine moments, and now revealed by the necessity of time. They were never meant for my eyes.

I put the letters, the certificates, and, somewhat reluctantly, the photos into the box to keep. Darcy's keepsakes were few but important. I shifted his ancient Walkman to make room for the thin bundle that I'd wrap in acid-free tissue. I'd didn't want to document these just yet. Later I would make copies and store them in the archives I'd create in my new life. The tape in the player caught my eye; it had a single word written on it: Wayfarer. It was the band in the photo, and there was every possibility that my mother might be singing on it. I'd never heard her voice. The thought of making some connection to her through something other than the photos I'd found and the tragedy that befell her was compelling. Somewhere in this house or Billie's would be a cassette player. I would be happy to share this with Helena, Jimmy, and Brendan, but not the photos and not Darcy's secrets.

As I had thought, we cleared out Darcy's place within the day. We stopped for lunch and worked together to drag things out to the skip and onto the veranda. Over a sandwich made with Margaret's leftover ham and salad, I told them about the cassette. They wanted to listen immediately, but I asked them to wait until the day was over. I wanted to clear Darcy's house and clear my mind before what might be an assault on the senses if what I believed to be my mother's voice found its way into my head.

Darcy's cottage looked better emptied than filled and neglected. It looked ready to take on new occupants, now that it had been divested of its dusty past. A few items of furniture remained. The desk, of course, which I'd have moved to the main house, and a few of the heavier things, such as the two oak beds and matching wardrobes, stayed in place. We took the mattresses and heaved them into the skip. It took the four of us to lift and carry them. Other things were waiting to be loaded into a trailer I'd have to hire and then donated to local charities. The old couch was tossed, but the Formica table and chairs could be reused. Little tables and few knick-knacks might bring a dollar or two from charity-shop sales. Darcy's meagre belongings spoke little about his life. From looking at what was left, minus the things in the box, he seemed to be a man who read, listened to an eclectic range of music, and dressed badly. It was a simple life that hadn't amounted to much. I looked beyond the sad collection and looked at his beautiful garden and orchard. Perhaps more than the motley possessions and a few photos, the land was Darcy's legacy, not just to me but to the world in which he lived. Whatever his mistakes had been and whatever sadness he had contributed to, his greatest work was in the land that provided both beauty and bounty. Darcy's hands had tended this lonely little plot of land, and perhaps just a little of him was left here. He had loved and was loved. Mick Flynn's notes had recorded the terrible state he was in when Moya and Brannen disappeared. Now it made sense. He wasn't grieving for Cillian's loss but his own, silently bearing what was undoubtedly more painful than losing her to his younger brother.

Showering off the dust of the day felt great. I had time to call Phillip before Helena and the boys located a grimy cassette player. They'd found it in Cillian's workroom. He must have listened to music when he was working. I had serious doubts about its ability to play anything, but with the cord unwound and checked, Jimmy got it going.

"I'm not sure what we are going to hear on this, and I'm not sure how I'm going to feel if it's my mother's voice." I said. I was a bit shaky already. Phillip had asked me twice if I was okay when we spoke. I was getting into the habit of lying to him when I said I was just weary from dragging and heaving furniture. I would show him all the documents once I'd cleared the three houses. Perhaps everything together would make sense.

"That's why we're here," Helena said, reminding me of the conversation we had in the museum office some months ago when it was decided that they would help me. So with that, the cassette was released from the portable player and put into Cillian's. I hadn't played a cassette for years and worried about the integrity of the tape, but Jimmy's technical skills had the tape rewound and the music beginning. The opening of the first song was a simple guitar strum, perhaps a few piano chords, and a male voice singing "People Got To Be Free." It was quite good and musically better than proficient. It had obviously been recorded using professional equipment, and therefore much of the sound was of reasonable quality. In the chorus I could hear a woman's voice. I assumed it was Moya.

The second track floored me. There was a brief introductory statement; a woman, my mother, said she'd sing "without the band." The girl said, "Put your instruments down, boys; this is my show." She laughed a little giggle, just like a teenager. It was the first time I'd ever heard her voice. What followed both lifted and crushed me. She sang in a strong voice that belied her tiny stature the song "Tears of Rage." It was a faultless rendition, perfectly executed in the style of the song as it had been intended. Her flighty comment at the beginning of the song bore no resemblance to the woman's tone and vocal tenacity in the rendering of the lyrics. There were tears in that sound that were both sweet and demanding. The words *come to me, now you know we are so alone and life is brief* were more poignant than she could ever have imagined. How could she ever have known that her daughter would listen to her mother's voice for the first time more than thirty years later, a voice that sang about life's brevity? It was Helena who pressed stop before we could listen to more. She could tell the profound impact it was having on me, and my pain was felt by my three friends perched on various chairs around the tape player. I wanted to cry out for my mother. I wanted to say a word I'd never uttered in naming her—*Mum*. It was all that came to mind, or more correctly, to heart. In the minutes I listened to her sing, I lived an imagined childhood in which all my fears were soothed by that voice. We would have sung together, and she would have revelled in a child made in her image and sound.

This, along with the disturbing discoveries of her relationship with Darcy, brought bed time around rapidly. I was silent, and my face was strained. Helena was concerned for me, thinking I'd returned to the dark days of last year, Jimmy was up making tea and putting food together, and Brendan beat a hasty retreat out of the house back to his new girlfriend. I just wanted the comfort of sleep and the obscurity of night. I wanted Phillip, but knew I couldn't ring him with more gloomy thoughts. Instead I drank tea, said little, and allowed Helena to run me a bath. When I went to bed, she sat with me a while and simply reiterated her mantra.

"It'll be all right, Lily. You have to expect to fall occasionally through this process." I knew she was right, but I'd not even gone half way through the procedure of separating the past from the present. What else would be waiting to wound me?

CHAPTER SEVENTEEN

I was awake and as fretful as I had been the day before. Surprisingly, the night had passed, and I had slept. The day was hotter than the previous ones, and January was obviously going to be rain free and sun rich. The prediction of bush fires was a summer reality, and this time of year was rarely free of blazes somewhere in the country. But the big ones, the fires we remember as being catastrophic, hadn't happened seen since 1983, Ash Wednesday. Nineteen years ago seventy-five people died in Victoria and South Australia. These types of fires are called firestorms because they roar down upon communities and bushland with the ferocity of tornados; burning hot gale-force winds eradicate everything in their path. As a terrifying force of nature, fire is unforgiving in its violence and impossible to contain once it has gained velocity. It wasn't the happiest of thoughts, but concentrating on the power of nature to destroy life was almost a welcome relief from agonizing over the trail of destruction human beings bring about.

My phone rang; it was Phillip checking on me. He was simply happy to hear my voice and told me how lonely he was. We had been apart for less than two days but it felt longer. I gave him a brief introduction to what I'd discovered in Darcy's house and he was, I could tell from the change of tone, working out how this new information might have been seen as evidence.

"So others knew about the relationship?" he asked. It was a reasonable question. I could only assume that everyone knew—Billie and Cillian, the band, the neighbours, everyone but me. I couldn't keep the hurt and the fear out of my voice when I tried to tell him about hearing my mother's voice, how it was the most wonderful sound and yet was also just so harrowing. My mother was not the innocent she appeared to be in photos. Her waiflike face concealed the truth about her behaviour.

"Lily, life is imperfect; people are imperfect. We can't change that. We have to cope with the fact that parents, sisters, and lovers are not faultless. We are simply human."

Phillip's wisdom was hard to argue against. It was my fault that I had such a naive view of what a parent should be. I was chastising myself for having worn rose-coloured glasses for so long and then applying blinkers to ensure my view was completely obscured.

"Lily, why do you have to make this about faults and blame and then find a way to make it all your responsibility?" Phillip's voice was sterner. "You can wrap yourself up in all this past misery, which happened before you were born. You can let it weigh you down and take you back to square one. Or you can be more objective in your thinking." I wasn't sure I had the capacity to be forensic in my examination of my family. "You're not responsible for their choices, Lil. You are for your own." He finished the conversation more gently. "I love you, Sherlock, but you are going to have to toughen up. I could come out tonight." I wanted him to be here and it would be nice for him to meet Helena and Jimmy, perhaps even Brendan if he could be persuaded to leave his lady-love for a night.

Getting up took some effort, but the others had breakfast ready and were insisting I eat before we tackled Billie's house. Brendan had called to say he wouldn't be down until lunchtime and that he'd bring food and stay the night. All was well with the new relationship, but he thought we could have another night to celebrate being close to the end of the process. I was happy thinking that we would be a full house. No matter what was discovered today, I would have friends to help with the burden or perhaps acclaim the successes.

Maybe after today I would know something that would exonerate my father. I wasn't convinced that the revelations of the previous day had done anything other than give more credence to the theory that his jealousy had led him to kill them.

After food the three of us walked over to Billie's house and opened her front door. It was a familiar and homey place. She was orderly, yet the place was filled with things she obviously loved. The house was dotted with little *objets d'art* that she had collected over her life or had inherited from her mother, things I'd seen my whole life but had taken no notice of. It seemed that anything from relatives beyond my grandparents were lost or perhaps, given the O'Haras less-than-auspicious beginnings, never existed. Whatever existed in this house that was either Billie's or Patricia's was now mine. It had been mine since Billie died and I was all that was left of the family. The enormity of the task made me think, momentarily, that one of those bush fires that roar down hills could just come and claim all of this—the houses, the orchards, and the belongings. Everything could just go in one fiery gulp. Then I'd never have to look for further secrets. The treasures and pains of the past would just be gone, and all I'd have to deal with would be the blackened residue of the tangible things. The mystery would be gone. Then perhaps I would lose the longing to know, because knowing would be utterly impossible. This was a totally irresponsible thought, of course. If a fire came, others would lose their properties, animals both wild and domestic would perish, and the firestorms would ultimately claim human lives too. To want such a thing was terribly irresponsible and cruel. I liked to think I was more courageous than to want an act of God to annihilate my obligations. I had to search, reconstruct, and live with the conclusions that I would draw from what was within Billie's world and inside the carefully labelled boxes of my own house. And the conclusions others might come to as well.

I don't know how long I stood staring at Billie's front door, but I was shaken back to the task at hand by Jimmy asking if I was all right. He was laden with boxes, marker pens, and garbage bags for the easy clean up. Helena was waiting at the door, just watching the hundreds of thoughts that were obviously evident on my face—not the details, but the feelings, the trepidation about the investigation and the memories that might be uncovered. My own memories. They are sketchy at best and buried deep. I imagined a psychologist might have enormous interest in my capacity to draw a veil over the events of my life. The disquiet of the past is silenced by my inordinate ability to ignore what I don't want to see.

But the job had to be done.

I remembered seeing some unlabelled boxes in Billie's bedroom when I had gone to search for the newspapers before Christmas. It seemed like months ago that I was in the house just searching for simple answers, believing that answers would magically reveal themselves to me. This morning I would not refer to the unknown as boxes of treasures. Despite the value of what might be inside each one, I thought calling them treasures was inappropriate. These boxes of secrets were beyond monetary value. They were laden with both emotional and historical weight. Somewhere in Billie's house were the burdens she had carried, the joys she had had, and the life she had lived.

I didn't know at that moment what a bombshell I'd uncover. If I thought I'd learned it all in Darcy's house, I was sadly mistaken. What was to come was more tragic and more regrettable than affairs, unrequited love, and other decadent sexual misadventures. Billie's secret life carried the kind of weight that was made even more unwieldy by the end of hope, by loneliness, by lost love, and by shame. Billie, my Billie, had lived an unrequited life that surely my own selfish existence had made worse.

Helena and Jimmy tackled the easy bits again—the clothes, the things, the art, and the books. Helena was immensely impressed by the library Billie had amassed and insisted I keep it in tact. She drove back to Canberra to pick up preservation supplies for some of the rarer books. She was no longer interested in what I was doing but focused fully on saving some of the first editions and beautiful art books that were crammed onto shelves with Billie's romance novels. Billie had been eclectic in all things.

The clothes, shoes, kitchen items, and an extensive range of toiletries were easily dispatched. I kept Billie's coat and what was called a dressing table set. I remember playing with it as a little girl. Occasionally I was allowed to brush Billie's hair and pin it up with a range of hairpins that were decorated with diamantes, pearls, and glass beads fashioned into butterflies and flowers. I wondered where those lovely things had gone to. I hoped I'd find them in the clearing out and asked Jimmy to look closely in the chest of drawers and bathroom. Perhaps they were boxed somewhere among the hundreds of soaps and little bottles of moisturizer that had been saved. I'd never seen Billie take much care of her skin and her looks. This rather girlish collection of toiletries spoke to me more about who she might have been if she hadn't been burdened by a child who wasn't hers. Before I could get too bogged down in these miserable thoughts, Helena arrived back and started sorting and packing books, and Jimmy's careful search for hairpins turned up a find. For once it might have been truly a treasure. In a satin-lined box that once held a pair of crystal sherry glasses, Billie had stored the O'Hara women's jewellery. It was a pleasure to see how she had lovingly preserved each piece and conveniently labelled them. Perhaps my occupation was no accident. Billie was a natural archivist and preservation expert. Inside each wrapped parcel was a ring, each with a name of the wearer printed in neat capital letters. The rings of my grandmother, great-grandmother, and two great aunts had been stowed carefully and left to be found or used by the O'Hara girls to come. The wedding rings were all platinum bands of varying sizes and widths. The engagement rings were beautiful round-cut diamonds on platinum bands. In each a single solitaire was held in place by intricate filigree. The last ring was unlabelled and was perhaps my favourite. It was an art deco design of diamonds and sapphires. It was obviously an engagement ring that, unlike the others, had no signs of wear. It had been bought but remained unworn by its owner.

After Jimmy insisted I try all of the rings on and I found them all too big except the sapphire one, I carefully rewrapped them and took them back to my own home. I put them beside the little carved wooden hands I'd found before Christmas and marvelled at what I'd been living with. Secrets and treasures. I wondered how long I'd have gone on not knowing if Moya and Brannen had remained unfound. Their discovery was the catalyst for change. Things could not have remained as they were, and at some point in my life, I would have had to unpick the threads of the past. For my whole life, the tapestry of my family seemed merely to be a sepia impression of indiscernible patches of faded colours. Now as I got closer, I could see that these people were not merely confined to a few words on a tombstone; they were real and had lived lives full of complications, pain, and joy. Someone wore each of these rings and perhaps stood right here looking out at the lake wondering about its coming and going. They were in love, they raised children, they worked and farmed, and some moved away to start new lives in places unknown to me. The past was not just a vague notion in the lives of descendants; it was a force that sculpted the lives we were given. Those rings, these things, and the puzzles yet to be revealed and solved were all part of the preceding lives, part of my history.

My somewhat fanciful thoughts were broken by the sound of Helena calling to me. There wasn't anything she particularly needed me for, but she was prompted by her concern for me. When I went missing or silent, she began to worry. I reappeared with a smile and an attempt at a spring in my step.

"Sorry got lost in thought," I said—my excuse for most mental absences. It was better than being lost in an absence of thought.

Back in Billie's room, Jimmy had been hard at work removing smaller items of furniture and the mattress from her bed. He had the wooden frame disassembled and ready to put out for donation. It was a grand bed and would no doubt make some money for one of the charities that would benefit from these household pieces. He had unpacked all the drawers but had left the boxes on the floor for me to go through. The room seemed cavernous and echoed strangely as I dragged a fold-up chair in and rearranged the boxes so I could sort more comfortably.

"Well, here we go Billie." I made a verbal apology for delving into her life, or more correctly, for failing to do so while she lived.

The first box rendered another delightful find: photos. Billie's now-famous tendency for labelling and sorting made things so much easier. She had some photos dating back to the early 1900s inscribed with the names and places caught in brown tones and in black and white. The scenes were posed to capture the events of the day, holidays at the beach, Sydney landmarks, the Lake Road property, of course, and the lake itself. The second neatly tied pile of photos documented a more carefree time for my grandparents. It was obviously a time between the wars, and despite an economic global crisis in the 1930s, life was thriving on the lake. The houses were all featured in the photos, and a happy couple, my grandparents Padraig and Patricia, looked like teenagers. The land was thriving, and the photos reflected the hard work of running an orchard, farming sheep, and keeping the property running. Names, other than Paddy and Pat, meant nothing to me, but from the looks of the women, they were related to the O'Haras in some way. That look that Cillian, Darcy, and Billie all had was evident in the people who posed on front porches, sat in row boats on the lake, or were working the land. Family.

Then one by one, the photos included one chubby baby after another. Three little peas in a pod: Darcy, the eldest, Billie, and then my father. They were beautiful children and so sturdy. Their skin was brown and perfect, and they had the same mischievous expression in their eyes. How could they know what was to come? Why would we want their happy world to be invaded by visions of what was to come? They were born as the Second World War began and continued. They were immune from the impact it had on the world and even on Australia. They lived an isolated and insulated life on the lake. Whatever was happening in Europe had little impact on the O'Hara children. Thank God there were happy years. I wasn't sure who the family photographer was, but he or she did a great job of documenting the life led by my father, aunt, and uncle.

The last of the photos was a melancholy one. Billie would have been about fifteen, making my father thirteen and Darcy sixteen or so. They were posed on the front veranda of my house. A similar photo had been taken when they were much younger, but it was a very different picture. In the later photo, they were incredibly attractive, but not one looked happy or carefree. The three looked past the camera and were staring into the distance; I could tell they were looking out at the lake. It was the early 1950s, and they would have seen the water lap against the road at their front door. Billie was a stunner. Her long, dark hair was brushed over her shoulders, and her body was lean. She was not much shorter than her brothers. Both Darcy and Cillian had their hair parted on the side, and the pomade that had been used to slick down the unruly curls had failed in its job. They were dressed for church; perhaps that was what caused such wistful expressions. They might have wanted to be free to roughhouse along the lake's shore or row out for fishing or swimming. I would never really know, but I could imagine.

Then came the photos I'd never imagined existed. Two piles, neatly labelled *Lily 0–6* and *Lily 6–12*. I had had photos taken by friends and at school as I grew up. These were part of my own little archive. But I'd never known that there were photos of me from these years. I was engrossed in the task of admiring myself as a baby when I heard Brendan arrive. Someone was shouting something about lunch and my name was being called. I took two photos out of the bunch to show them. The first was me as a very new baby, days old probably. It was the four of us. A normal family—two kids and mum and dad. Of course, it was anything but normal. Approximately five weeks from this moment, Moya and Brannen would be gone. Dead, as I now know. They were looking at me so lovingly. Brannen was holding my bare foot. I was not happy; crying, I thought. But that seemed to be going unnoticed by my parents, who were just staring into my strained face. The second photo showed the beginning of the next phase of my life. I was a few months old in this one, and Billie was holding me. She had her face pressed against my satiny head. I was pretty bald, except for a few ginger ringlets clinging to the back of my skull. I was a sullen baby, but I was staring at the camera intensely. I thought everyone would be able to tell it was me. And I could tell that Billie was holding me tightly to her. I couldn't help but wonder what was going through her head.

Over lunch, which Brendan had generously provided, we discussed the finds of the morning. Helena was talking non-stop about the book cache and was suggesting that I donate some of them to the University of Canberra library, which archives children's literature. I couldn't help but agree. I knew they wouldn't fit into the world I was hoping to inhabit after this was all packed up and sold. Phillip was renovating his house, and if I was to live with him, then it would be a bit steep to ask him to build me a library and a humidity-controlled archive. Better to send things to places where they could be housed properly.

The photos were handed around, and appropriate and less-appropriate comments were made about how I looked like a baby possessed in both photos, hysterical in one and weirdly intense in the other. But they were making light of how important they knew these to be. My first family photo had been found, and the second provided evidence that maybe I wasn't Billie's burden but rather a little baby she cared for dearly. I was happy. These simple pleasures that most take for granted gave me a sense of my childhood that went beyond mysterious disappearances and chaos. I think it showed that despite the awfulness, my life offered a moment of light.

After eating enormous sandwiches and drinking too many cups of coffee, I felt ready to tackle the rest of the boxes. There were only two, a bigger one that seemed fairly light and a smaller one that was heavier. The boys started removing the substantial furniture using trolleys that Brendan had brought from the museum warehouse. They were industrial and made moving the wood wardrobes and chests of drawers easier. Luckily everything in all three houses was on one level. The removal truck Brendan had hired to get things back to Canberra to deliver them to the Salvation Army would be picked up later in the week. A couple of Brendan's rugby teammates would drive it down and help load the furniture into it. The rubbish skip was filling up as well, and the company would come to remove it the following week. What I thought was an impossible task was unfolding easily. It appears that you can divest yourself of things almost effortlessly once you begin. My initial, ill-founded hope for a bush fire was unnecessary.

I returned to my chair in Billie's room and opened the bigger of the boxes. It was light because it contained a carefully wrapped layette. These things were not store bought but rather handcrafted by an expert seamstress. The linen was beginning to discolour, but the exquisite embroidery remained intact. In yellow and pale-green silk, little rabbits and other creatures dotted the fringes of sheets and pillow cases. Little blankets were etched with the same colours and flower motifs. Tiny knitted singlets and matinee jackets lay wrapped in tissue. My favourite things were the booties, again hand-knitted in a multitude of pastel tones. These things were made for a baby whose sex was unknown. The muted shades gave no hint of the gender, and it seemed that these lovely items had been unworn by the wee baby they were made for. I wondered if these things had been put aside for either Brannen or myself. We were both summer babies, so many of the woollen items would have been a little redundant but would nonetheless have been tried on. At the bottom of the box, wrapped more tightly in tissue and calico, was another of those finds. It was a christening gown, handmade and embroidered with cotton lace panels. It would be something for Helena to date and preserve. I thought it was Edwardian, but this was not my field of expertise. It had been worn, but probably not by either Brannen or myself. We were baptized at St. Mary's church; those certificates I'd seen. Mine had to have been produced for my First Holy Communion. The photo bundle I'd found had evidence of both ceremonies, and I was certainly not dressed in this gown.

I laid the gown down on the calico wrapper I'd spread out. Perhaps it had been worn by Darcy, Billie, and Cillian and one of their parents before them. These were lovely reminders of the hopes and traditions babies bring to families. Maybe my own child might be baptized in this gown. I had to stop myself thinking this way, as it was too distracting. The other box might hold some clue as to the reason why these lovely things had been put away and not unpacked.

And so I went to the last box in Billie's house. Looking back, I almost wish this box had been swept away by a flood or consumed by those flames I'd momentarily wished upon the O'Hara museum. It was not unlike opening Pandora's Box, not that pestilence flew from its constraints to consume the world, but rather what emanated were several simple sadnesses that, once known, could not be unknown, things that were written down, read, internalized, and then hidden away in order that they could no longer do harm. Billie had squashed down into the box not treasures but secrets, which must have been at the time a great shame. Billie had had a baby. A wee girl.

The box of secrets had all the elements to make conclusive evidence. There didn't needed to be forensic audit of the contents to make sense of the world at that time. There were letters, trinkets, and medical documents. The story was clear.

In 1956, just before Billie was eighteen, she had fallen in love with a boy called Roland Devine. He had written her a letter in which he succinctly said that his parents had forbidden him to see her again and that marriage was utterly out of the question. He was going to Sydney to study law, and a country wife and baby would impinge on his parents' hope for him. The fact that he used the word *impinge* made me furious. Billie, just a teenager, a good Catholic girl from a strong Irish rural family, was pregnant with Roland Devine's baby. I wondered what her parents thought of that. It might have been easy to conceal the pregnancy out here at the lake. She would simply have been invisible for several months, and then the little one might have been adopted out through one of the Catholic organizations that did these things. Or maybe my grandmother would raise the baby as her own. It wouldn't be the first time that something like that happened. Roland's letter went on to tell Billie that he had loved her very much but that it was impossible to think that they could be a couple. He said more about his parents' opinions of a girl who had slept with her boyfriend, but he finished the letter by saying they would give her some money once the child was born if she wrote "father unknown" on the birth certificate.

That arse. That total bastard! If he was alive, I'd find him and punch him right in the face and tell everyone on the planet who knew him that he was a coward. I didn't care that he was probably in his mid-sixties, he was going to get both barrels of pent up rage, for Billie and for the baby. In my anger, I'd lost sight momentarily of the baby. It meant that I had a cousin who would be nearing fifty. My fleeting excitement was almost immediately squelched by common sense and the next few documents.

Billie's little baby had been born early—not too early, but six weeks before her due date. According to the midwife's report and both the birth and death certificates, the little girl didn't live long. Nurse Murphy had been called to the O'Hara house in the middle of a July night. It would have been below freezing when the midwife made her way from Bungendore to Lake Road in her car. She had written in her report that it took her an hour to drive here, as the night was foggy and ice had formed on the road. She was quite a chronicler. Every detail was meticulously recorded. She made note that on her arrival she was met by Mrs. Patricia O'Hara, the patient's mother. The men of the house were nowhere to be seen, but the room in which Billie Evelyn O'Hara was going to birth her premature baby was well lit and warm. The fire had been lit, and the mother had provided a number of clean, freshly laundered linens for the birth. Nurse Murphy recorded that she knew the family well, as she had attended Patricia's three births.

Details such as Billie's age and marital status were given without commentary. It was not unusual for single mothers to birth their children at home. In fact, it was pretty much the norm for country women to have their babies at home. Billie, according to Nurse Murphy, was well into her labour by the time she got there. She was only hours from being fully dilated and ready to push. The few hours were marked by the nurse's brief notes about how the labour was progressing and discussions about what would need to happen, since the baby was coming early. Inevitably she recorded what would happen to the infant should it live. She stated simply that the baby would be raised by her mother. Billie would raise the little one with the help of family. He or she would want for nothing in terms of love, and to hell with Roland Devine and his vile money. These were of course my thoughts, not Nurse Murphy's.

At 6:24 a.m., a tiny girl was delivered to Billie. She was very small; the nurse recorded her as being 3 pounds and 3 ounces, about 1.4 kilograms. She would have struggled even if she'd been born in a hospital in those days. Her little lungs would not have been developed, and all Nurse Murphy had at her disposal was her skill in encouraging the littlest O'Hara to begin breathing. The little thing gave life her best shot and struggled on for exactly two hours and twelve minutes. She died in her mother's arms after a hasty makeshift baptism by Patricia. The tiny, defeated infant was wrapped in layers of the nurse's cotton wool in an attempt to keep her warm while she fought on. The report ended with her completing the official paperwork, checking the mother's health, and washing the body in preparation for the funeral home. The O'Haras had a phone; the nurse called a doctor in Queanbeyan and called the O'Rourke Funeral Home to arrange the pickup of the little one.

Billie would need to be seen by the doctor for a check-up and to immediately stop the production of milk. There would be no child requiring nourishment from her mother's breasts. The report and Roland's letter seemed so clinical and so devoid of any understanding of the teenager who had been abandoned and then left to bury her baby girl. The girl remained unnamed on both her birth certificate and her gravestone. Baby O'Hara was not some distant ancestor's pain; she was Billie's. In a little white box lay a tiny lock of fine strands of hair. They were dark against the whiteness of the satin. The little girl had the dark hair of the O'Haras, and the few flimsy strands lay as a delicate reminder that she was ever here at all. The unused layette had been tucked away so Billie would not be reminded of what had been and what might have been. She had crushed the memories into two boxes. She had wrapped but not labelled the items that essentially did not need cataloguing. Billie would take her secret to the grave where, if I could believe all I'd been told in church, she would be reunited with her sorrowful little one.

How could I tell anyone about this? Would it be betraying Billie to reveal to my friends what I'd found? Should this be a secret that had to be kept? I wanted to make the baby known but did not want to reveal anything that Billie would have been ashamed to admit. I felt that she had been hurt enough by losing her baby, but the thought of her having to raise her brother's child, another girl not her own, seemed to be the cruellest punishment of all. Poor Billie was truly burdened by her dutiful acceptance of me into her life. She could have met someone and had another child, or children, but she was saddled with a miserable stray that had destroyed her youngest brother. She must have hated me. She must have looked at me with abhorrence, and yet she did everything she could to raise me well. I wondered again what she was thinking in the photo when she held me tightly and laid her face upon mine. I hoped it was not loathing or ambivalence. Possibly she was simply overwhelmed by the memory of a little girl born twenty years previous, and in this moment she was making a commitment to bring me up as her own but never to let me call her mother. This was the distance between us. She would do the mothering but would not be given the honour of being called mum. Another thing to regret.

I was a bit of a wreck and really needed to be alone for a little while. I left the documents and the clothes out where I knew the others would find them. It was best they make their own deductions at this point, because I could neither conceal the truth nor speak it. If I had to utter the words that Baby O'Hara was Billie's, I'd never stop crying. Running away was the best option. In the box were two other letters, both had been opened and resealed. I would read them, but not until I reached the ridge. The forest would afford me privacy, and in seclusion I could investigate what further agonies might be revealed by the letters. Both were addressed to Billie.

The climb up was hot, and I was again aware of the possibility of snakes. The afternoon was reaching its peak, and the temperature was in the low thirties. The air was dry. We never had humid summers up here, and only occasionally did it rain in midsummer. There would be no moisture about, and that made the presence of snakes even more probable. They would be looking for water and soon for mates.

But I reached my perch above the houses and felt for the first time all day the breeze that wafted over the mountain ridge between the beach, 120 kilometres away, and the lake. It was cooling and took the edge off the biting sun. I had no hat and no sun block, and the likelihood of being burnt was high. But the shady fringes of the trees protected me from the worst of the day. Flies buzzed, and things rustled in the grass, most likely hapless lizards looking for insects busy under the trees. The crows from the orchard had once again been roused by my movement but had quickly settled back to roosting nearby. Too many to count. The letters were taking on the sweat from my palms, so to preserve their readability, I put them down on the rock beside me. Before taking the plunge back into Billie's privacy, I took a few deep breaths. It was three o'clock, and the others would begin to miss me if I hid here too long.

I thought about just ripping the unread letters up into tiny pieces and releasing them into the breeze. The secrets within could just be scattered about this unused place. The words would just meld with earth and plants. Little scraps might make their way to damp spots in the forest and melt into the humus. The past could become part of the organic matter than was made up of leaf litter and animal decay. These secret words could then do good by growing new life in the dark, rich dirt instead of bringing hurt. Again, I had to remind myself that this was not some fantasy fiction I was trying to reconstruct and that such fanciful ideas had no place in this investigation. I had to be more like Sherlock in my process and less like one of the Bronte sisters in fictionalizing the findings. I was here to look, examine closely, and draw conclusions. The letters might help, and tearing them to shreds unread was both childish and irresponsible. As an adult, I had a duty to act appropriately.

The first letter was brief and tender. Patricia had written to Billie to remind her of the love of her family. The date was six months after the baby's birth and death. It was addressed to Billie at a Sydney address. The salutation filled me with hope of a better revelation. It started, "My darling Billie." My grandmother had not been an educated woman in the formal sense, but she was eloquent and passionate. She urged Billie to return home and to stop running away from what was not something to feel ashamed of. She had been in love with Roland, and if he had been a better man, there would have been no humiliation in her having a baby. She was not the first young woman to make a poor judgement about a boy. The fact that the little girl died was a source of pain for them all, and it was a pain best shared with a family who loved her. She completed her letter with words that, sadly, would not come to fruition. "There will be other loves and a good man with whom you will have another child. Love, Mummy."

Patricia's letter must have helped Billie see sense. The love and lack of condemnation healed her, and she of course returned to the lake and to her family. She waited for this other love, and then her parents died. She waited for this other child, and her brothers fell in love with a selfish girl. She waited some more, and then there was me.

The second letter was not as eloquent and did not bring me any of the pleasure that the first had. It was from my father. Cillian had written to Billie before he took his own life. If I had been looking for evidence of who my father was, it was clearly explained in this letter. It read:

> Billie, I'm sorry that the last nine months have been terrible for you. I'm sorry that all I've done has created sadness. You are the only person I know who believes that I didn't do anything to hurt Moya and Brannen. Despite her actions, I love her and my babies very much. Brannen was the dearest little boy in the world, and not a day goes by that I don't miss him. I used to dream that he would just come wandering home and tell me all about the adventure he had. You know I could never hurt him. And Lily, that dear little baby, did not deserve to be born into this turmoil. She deserves to have a mother who loves her and a father who is not consumed by the cruelty of his wife. Moya left me, took my son, and left Lily to grow up

without either of them. Now it seems that I'm going to be arrested for killing them. I would never do anything like that. No matter how bad things got, I would never hurt my family. She doesn't need a father in jail as well.

Billie you are the bravest person I know, and I think Darcy will help you. He didn't mean to be hurtful when Moya left him and married me; he was just angry that things didn't work out as he had expected. I haven't been innocent in all this. I made a mess of the life we could have had. It is my fault that Moya and Brannen are gone. I was not a good husband, probably not even a good man. I should have taken her threats to kill herself more seriously. If nothing else, I could have saved my precious boy. Please look after Lily. Make her your own daughter. Tell her nothing about the madness of this year or of her mother.

I love you Billie, and I'm sorry.

Your brother CF O'H.

His voice was as clear to me in this letter as my mother's was on the tape. From the past both of them unintentionally reaching out to the child they left behind. Could either of them have imagined what it would be like for me to find them so long after their deaths? I hoped that they may have given me some thought and considered the future I might have if they both disappeared. I hoped I might have meant something to them. Or was I easily abandoned, too new for them to have cared much for me? Yet Cillian's letter asked Billie to make me her own daughter. Maybe it was the closest to expressing his love for me that he was able to give.

The letter was dated the day of his suicide. His handwriting was untidy but legible, and the letter was written without error. I felt that it was impossible for this letter to fall so easily into my hands. It seemed ridiculously coincidental that what I needed would be extracted so easily out of the unremarkable belongings of my aunt. Surely if he had killed my mother and brother, his final letter would have been his confession. I thought this would be the undoing of me, but it wasn't. It was the making of me. If Phillip and Mick needed evidence to clear Cillian, surely this letter would be it. He had confessed that he was not a good husband and that he had wronged others, but he hadn't killed her. He really believed that she had left with Brannen and possibly one day could come back. He loved his sister enough to trust her to raise me.

The importance of the day's discoveries had exhausted me. I felt like I'd climbed several mountains. The revelations had tired me so much that I thought I would simply close my eyes and rest in the shade of the forest. As it had some weeks ago, the quiet shadows of the ridge encouraged sleep. The afternoon went on without me, and I woke only to the sound of something frantically scrabbling in the rocks and plants just beneath my feet.

"For fuck's sake, Lily, are you trying to kill me?" Phillip's enraged face was fast approaching as he reached my legs, knelt down, and scooped his arms under my body. His crushing hug thumped the air out of my lungs. I was still a little delirious from sleep and emotion. Before I could say anything, he was on the phone making terse statements. "She's here. Safe."

Then his obvious relief turned into a rather disparaging rant about my degree of inconsiderate behaviour. What the hell was everyone to think when they found me gone and the contents of Billie's past spread out on the floor of her bedroom. While pandemonium broke out down at the house, I was happily sleeping away the day, out where God knows what could happen to me. The growling went on for a while; he mentioned snakes, falling, hurting myself, selfishness, disregard for others feelings, bedlam, madness, and so on. When he gets angry, he really gets angry. I made the rather foolish mistake of smiling as he was nearing the end of the tirade.

"It's not funny, Lily. You've had your friends demented with worry, I've called Mick, who was just about to arrange a search party, and you're sunning yourself." I was not smiling at the blustering and what seemed to be real fear in this man.

"I love you, Phillip," I interjected. These are most disarming words, apparently. The kissing started as soon as I said them. The ferocity had gone out of him, and he was back to himself.

"What you found must have hurt you?" His gentleness was much more profound than the yelling.

"I'm okay. Sad but fine now that I've read my father's suicide letter."

Phillip sat down beside me and listened to all I'd found that day. I gave him the letter and let him read it, which he did several times. I was so convinced it was proof of innocence that I was really hurt when Phillip didn't exactly share my enthusiasm.

"But he says it right there," I argued. "He didn't do it. He was shocked by her leaving."

When Phillip has to give bad news, he does this thing with his body. He breathes in and holds it for a second, and then when exhaling, he looks straight into the eyes of the person he is talking to. He has done this do me several times.

"It's still not evidence of his innocence, Lil." It was a gentle but weighty statement.

I lost it totally. I'd never been one to swear or rage. Even in the midst of the tantrum, I felt terrible because I was saying awful things to the man I loved. It started badly—"You're a fucking idiot if you can't see that"—and ended worse. I was stomping down the hill, yelling all kinds of intense things about Phillip's lack of the capacity to see any logical conclusions. This diatribe was heavily punctuated with invective. And then I fell over, or more correctly, down. Tripping on a nest of weeds that had intermingled to form a trap, I virtually cartwheeled in an undignified manner and rolled several metres, taking significant blows to my body and head from concealed rocks. The conversation ended abruptly. The blood and tears flowed simultaneously. There were no broken bones, a few bruised ribs, a concussion, and multiple contusions. Luckily the overeating at Christmas had not made me too fat to carry, which Phillip did effortlessly. Brendan rushed up to help him as we approached the orchard, and Jimmy and Helena arrived with towels and disinfectant.

At some point I was ferried to Canberra and the emergency room. I was not an emergency, but there were concerns about the head injury. In the fog I thought the doctors had thought Phillip had beaten me, but after he flashed his police credentials, they backed off that idea. At another point after I had been cleaned and bandaged, I told Phillip that I really didn't think he was an idiot.

"You said 'fucking idiot,' I believe." His good humour had returned. I tried to reopen the conversation about the letter, but he shut me down by suggesting that this wasn't the time to discuss it. The next voice I heard was the doctor telling Phillip to take me home and to keep me quiet for a day or two. With pain killers on board and a strong arm to lean on, I was back at the house for a late dinner. Helena, Jimmy, and Brendan had stayed on to keep cleaning. They had rewrapped the baby clothes and carefully filed Billie's collection into a document box. The letters I'd taken to the ridge were open on the table and under discussion.

"Jesus, Mary, and Joseph," Brendan exclaimed. "Spectacular black eye, Lil, and you've lost some bark on your head." He was referring to the massive graze on the side of my head. Stones can be very unforgiving when you brutalize them with your face.

"Yes, well, apparently I can't swear and walk at the same time." Laughter and hugging ensued.

There was sympathy all round. I was presented with a cup of tea, and we sat down to a barbeque dinner that I was unable to consume. Luckily, Phillip had gotten over both his anger and shock and was able to consume for us both. I ate a little but began to feel sick. I wanted to discuss the letters. Well, my father's letter.

Phillip looked like he was about to stop me, but I looked pathetic and teary. He gave in immediately. Helena opened the discussion by posing the question to Phillip, the one he'd already shot down.

"Does it point to his innocence?" Phillip hadn't met the three amigos before, and his introduction to them had come when he arrived at the property and was met with their panicked observations that I'd gone missing after finding things in Billie's room. Phillip was not inclined to panic, but I suspect he summed up the situation pretty quickly. After I had been supposedly missing the last time, he had learned of my siestas on the ridge. I'd forgotten I'd asked him to come out and stay the night to meet everyone and to share my bed. It wasn't exactly the evening I was hoping for.

Phillip's response to Helena's question was measured and quantifiable. "It's not really proof of anything, and it could be used against Lily's father. It's circumstantial at best."

"How could it be used against him?" Jimmy asked.

"He says things about not being innocent and making a mess of his life. He even says that it was his fault that they were gone. The mention of Darcy's relationship with Moya might even point to a motive."

There was energy in the discussion after this. There was a sense that we all wanted the letter to be conclusive and for Phillip to agree, but he simply wouldn't. Or more correctly, couldn't.

"Besides anyone could have written this letter," Phillip added. "There's no way of proving Mr. O'Hara even wrote the letter."

To say I was disappointed would understate the degree of despair I felt. I was injured and overwhelmed, and I felt abandoned by Phillip. Of course, he hadn't meant to hurt me, but his common sense was quite a stumbling block. The evening felt flat, and I went to bed soon after the discussion. I couldn't shower, as I'd been instructed not to get the abrasions wet for at least twenty-four hours, so I just washed the parts of my face that were not painful to touch. The hospital had cleaned the dirt from legs and arms, so I wasn't too grubby when I fell into bed. From the relative comfort of the bed, I heard Helena gently chastising Phillip.

"Couldn't you just give her that small win? Why is it so important to keep reminding her that she will never clear her father's name?"

Phillip's answer was patient, and he was unruffled by Helena's terse approach. "Because she has to find a way to live with the truth—not that he was innocent or guilty but that she will never really know. She is in danger of immersing herself in the misery of the past traumas and, for some unknown reason, making it all her responsibility."

"Well, that's Lily. She's sensitive, but she's tougher than you give her credit for," Helena said, coming to my rescue again like a mother tiger.

"I know she's tough, Helena, but it's hurting her. I can't bear it. I'm not tough enough to see her go through this." Phillip's admission was met with what I called a Helena hug. She had given him the seal of approval. He wasn't just being bloody minded and obstructionist; he loved me.

When he finished in the bathroom, he came into my room and peeled back the cotton blanket and sheet. He lay close but without touching. We spent a minute staring at each other. He did that thing where he just put his lips on my forehead and breathed me in. I didn't care about my hurts and wounds; I just wrapped myself around him. He spoke so quietly in my ear.

"Give it up, Lil, or at least try to be more objective. When we first met, you said that the discovery hadn't hurt you because you didn't know these people. Go back to that point. Stay with it, at least while you are so immersed in uncovering of their lives." It was good advice but totally impossible to do. I was already so full of the hurt that had been my family's lot. The soreness of my body was nothing in comparison to the discomfort of my heart. I could not in good conscience, however, let Phillip worry about me. So I lied a little.

"I'll be more objective; I'll let it go a bit." I suspected he knew that those statements were not true, but for that moment and that night, we allowed them to be the truth. Sleep came and then went. It must have been about one o'clock in the morning when I woke for no apparent reason. Phillip was lying on his side, sighing the deep breaths of sleep. He had moved away from me to escape the warmth of my body, and it gave me the opportunity to sit up, albeit somewhat painfully. The window was open to the silent night, and I could see the stars clearly in the blue-black sky. Away from the city, the night sky feels closer. The stars are more evident, or at least seem so. I reminded myself of high school science classes where I learned that the light of a star reaches Earth long after the star has gone. Its trail of shimmering luminosity is just a token of its past, still providing a sense of its place in the universe. It's just like my family. Like stars, they had vanished but only now was some sense of their existence becoming apparent. The findings of the day were just like the light of those stars—something to wonder about, to admire or condemn but whose source was most certainly gone. The light of those lives was just now reaching me, and I had to remember that what happened was not happening to me. Discoveries were just events to be interpreted in the absence of tangible evidence. We did it all the time when dating and archiving the things from history. I had put my fingers in the bullet holes of Ned Kelly's armour and did not feel the pain of these blows. I'd held implements of war and torture but had been unscathed. I could respond compassionately to the suffering of others without suffering myself. These strengths could be employed to help me weather this storm. The man sleeping beside me, who had now rolled onto his back and commenced a nasal chorus of his own, the life we might have together, my work, my dreams, and right now, my battered body were the things that could touch me. In the dark of the night, despite the desperation of the previous day and the enormity of the universe around me, I resolved to be shaped no longer by the mistakes of others. Even if the world condemned Cillian as a murderer, my mother as a whore, and Billie and Darcy as some kind of failures, I could have my own version of events. I did not have to prove anything to anyone. I could simply believe.

CHAPTER EIGHTEEN

P hillip woke very early—probably about five o'clock—and his movement woke me too.

"Sleep okay?" he asked.

I had to tell him I didn't because of the pain of my bruises. My eye had blackened more and was a little swollen but not closed. He suggested that he should help me shower and dress because he didn't want either Jimmy or Brendan getting an eyeful of me naked. He smiled when he said it, but I couldn't deny the wisdom of needing help. We showered together, and he gave a fairly dispassionate assessment of my injuries.

"You'll live. I quite like blue and white together." The translucent skin on my body contrasted dramatically with the deep purple of the bruising. Again with the comedy routine. But his hilarity was stifled by his ardour. It was a very nice way to start the day.

Phillip left before the others were awake, and I was testing the limits of my injuries by stretching a little before making breakfast. I'd been given a lifetime ban on going the ridge alone and a few other bits of advice before Phillip left. They included eating properly, taking painkillers as I needed them, not being on my own, and taking it easy. By the time he had finished the catalogue of instructions, I'd forgotten the details of them, but I'd promised him this morning that I'd be careful and promised myself in the wee hours of the morning to be more impartial.

It was about nine o'clock before the others woke. A truck was coming tomorrow to remove all the items that were going to charities. That meant making decisions about what was in my own house. I would be living here for a while, but ultimately I'd be moving. I'd list the property for sale by February, and depending on the market, and Phillip, I'd move by May, before the winter set in. It helped me to have clear goals. It was one way I could move through the tasks at hand and have demonstrable targets. This piddling around in misery was not the way to a solution.

Thankfully everyone was in good spirits, and there was enough work to do about the place. Breakfast was convivial, and I did as I'd been told and ate, despite the slight pain chewing created in my jaw. Helena was going to return to cataloguing Billie's books. The boys were doing more furniture deconstruction and heavy lifting. Boxes were packed, with the items carefully wrapped and tagged. Working with skilled artefact conservators and curators was a genuine bonus. I knew that they would be using systems of classification that would help me locate the documents and items that would come with me when I moved. I knew that the precious things that had been discovered would be preserved and itemized. Since they were busy and occupied with the tasks they'd taken on, I had time to begin looking about my house with a more neutral eye. I was also able to think about the next step in my investigation. I thought I'd leave Phillip out of the plan that was gradually taking shape in my head. Mick Flynn, however, might be available to help me. If I turned up on his door step bruised and a tiny bit incapacitated, he might be sympathetic to my plight. I liked him and wouldn't play the pathetic orphan card too hard, but the ever-darkening black eye would no doubt be of use if he needed persuading.

I was meeting with the journalist Thomas West the next day. Brendan would organize the removal of furniture, Helena would take the books back to Canberra, and Jimmy would get most of the rubbish into the skip by the end of the day. They would return to their homes and no doubt be grateful to be in their own beds. But I wanted to track down a few other players in the mystery. Roland

Devine was on the list, as were the members of Wayfarer. The band, which both Darcy and Moya had played with before I was born, had played some part in the story. I wanted Mick to help me track them down so I could ask them what they remembered about 1975 and the preceding years. They might not offer much in the way of evidence, but I was sure one or all of them could at least fill out the sketchy parts and even tell me something about my mother. Maybe there were even more recordings of her voice.

Also on the list, not for immediate contact, were my grandparents, Moya's parents. If they were living, surely they would be interested in me. It's not that I was expecting them to have been pining for their only grandchild, but surely they would have wondered what happened to me and, more importantly, what happened to Moya.

I'd written my list, and I was certain there would be people to add. I thought about the Murphys and Arlen and what they had said to Mick back in the seventies. I didn't even know if Sarah and Thomas were alive. They had moved away from Lake Road while I was still at school. Their farm had gone to ruin years before they moved. I had no idea where any of the Murphy children had gone either. They could have been living locally, and I would never have known. Again I was hoping Mick might know a way of tracking people down. There were other names on his list of interviewees, and if I was lucky they might be firstly alive and secondly willing to speak about what they remembered of the O'Haras. These leads, or potential leads, gave me a renewed vigour for tackling the things that might be stashed away in this house.

Phillip could hardly believe that I had lived here for three years and never emptied the place and cleared out the past. I'd been dutiful in updating the amenities and décor but had never really unpacked my parents' lives. While Billie had gone through a lot of the superficial things, such as clothes and the knick-knacks one gathers over a lifetime, clearing out the domain of her brother and sister-in-law did not take precedence in the eighteen years I lived with her, nor in the five years between then and her death. It was just too much, I expect. Looking after me, looking after Darcy, running the property, and keeping on top of her own secrets left little time for searching through the things she had respectfully packed into boxes. I'd unpacked the Christmas box and made discoveries of happier times, but I'd not unpacked the others that had been labelled *Brannen, M, C,* and finally *Baby.* Nor had I been through the workroom where my father's tools were. These would have to go to a good home. I thought that Phillip's father or brothers-in-law might like them, or even Phillip, for that matter, as he was still renovating his own home.

Starting with what I assumed would be the easiest thing, I opened the boxes belonging to my brother and me. These were unremarkable containers that held toys, vestiges of special events, and a couple of photos. In Brannen's little collection were a couple of handmade wooden toys, again created by Cillian, his initials precisely etched into an inconspicuous spot on each one. The little trains and circus animals were a testament to his skill with woodwork. These were definitely treasures. In a brief flight of fancy, I could see a future child playing with these, happy simply because they were beautiful. The previous owner would be irrelevant to the child who would play with them, the maker not even a thought. A framed certificate of baptism and photos of a happy celebration were also cradled in the newspaper wrappings. At the bottom of the box was a little pair of leather shoes suitable for a boy of four or five. It seemed to be an odd thing to include, and I questioned why Billie would dispose of all the little boy's clothes but keep one pair of slightly worn shoes. Again I was reminded of how fruitless *why* is as a question under these circumstances, for there could be no answer. They were just there, quietly waiting at the bottom of a box for someone to make sense of them. It felt strange to hold something so mundane and insignificant and yet so moving. I felt a tenderness for my brother that I'd never experienced before. Not even when his little skeleton was buried beside his mother's or when I went through his little drawings that I'd reclaimed from the Christmas box did I feel the depth of connection with this real boy as I did now holding his little shoes. Too often in this saga I'd been engrossed in my own losses, but the reality was and always had been that a boy, my brother, died for reasons beyond understanding.

Stars. Think of stars. Far away and already gone. I attempted to bring myself back to a more cautious analytical place but held the little boots protectively to my chest, despite my resolve. I would think of a better way to honour this little boy and a better way to honour Billie's baby. Cillian too. Something must be added to their gravestones to make more of the lives that had been lived all too briefly. It was an action for a future day.

In the box labelled *baby* were the few things that had belonged to the first few months of my life. There was a knitted layette similar to the one I had found in Billie's house, used this time. There was also a single, framed photo of my baptism in which Cillian held me proudly outside St. Mary's Church. In the background were unknown people milling at the door. There were some trinkets but no toys made by a hopeful father. By the time I was ready to play with toys, everyone was gone. Cillian was too exhausted by grief to make anything for his daughter. Was he too overwhelmed by guilt?

The third box was, once again, a trap unwittingly set by Billie. I'm sure she hadn't sorted the papers and letters that she swept into this carton. Unlike her fastidious tagging and sorting in other boxes, this box was simply a jumble of things that had been unceremoniously plonked into a receptacle to get it all out of sight. I wondered if this had not been packed by Billie at all but possibly by Cillian. And perhaps she, in frustration or hysteria, had just sealed it after her brother's body was found.

I needed the time to open each letter and bundle. I suspected that much of it would be household bills, bank statements, and the like, but the careless arrangement meant that the things that had the greatest meaning were obscured by the least important things. At least that must have been the case for whoever did this. As I'd come to believe in the past few days, nothing can truly remain hidden if there is some physical record. Letters had been instrumental in the uncovering of important details not only in my own history but in history in general. In the past, the written word in letters and diaries recorded the special events, the mundane happenings, the plans, the dreams, and the things of consequence in the lives of people. And now such documents found their way to me via the rash actions of either Billie or Cillian.

For an hour I'd sorted through the inconsequential bits and pieces that meant nothing. These were disposed of after I rendered them roughly unreadable with a cursory rip. But folded neatly between the bank statements were two things—one a letter from a doctor to Moya and the other, in a postbag, a filled prescription. The contents of the letter were, at the very least, more circumstantial evidence, but the more I read, the more I came to believe that this may be the indicator I'd been looking for.

In essence the letter outlined Moya's condition and the doctor's recommendation for treatment. In the 1970s, Moya's condition was referred to as *manic depression*. It was characterized by tremendous and destabilizing mood swings. In the manic phases, people were euphoric, and in the depressive stages, they became so demotivated that they rarely got out of bed. The doctor, Vincent Smith, explained clearly in his letter that Moya's condition required treatment. The drugs would not be harmful to the unborn child, but it was essential that she stopped drinking while taking Valium. He had also suggested some psychotherapy to help manage the extreme behaviours and sleeplessness she had described to him. Dr. Smith had asked her to make an appointment and to bring her husband with her. He was emphatic that this was a serious health issue and one that would be made worse by a second child.

It was dated March 1975. She must have been just pregnant with me. The box containing the Valium was almost empty. There was a second prescription bottle that had been emptied but that was retained in the box. I didn't recognize the name of the drug. Both scripts were dated October 1975.

So there it was. Moya was ill. It was the kind of illness that, in the 1970s, might have been treated with a social contempt we rarely see now, something to remain hidden and not spoken of. Mentally ill, mad, manic, crazy, irresponsible Moya. *Flighty* was Billie's word.

Cruelly I'd begun to suspect my mother was immoral, sleeping around, falling in and out of love with two brothers and God knows who else, having nude photos taken, singing in a band, desiring an escape from rural isolation, and resisting the responsibility of parenthood. But she was sick, and my father would not have been equipped to handle such things. Billie and Darcy had been caught up in the maelstrom, and two children ended up paying a price.

I sat back for a while to take in what this might mean in exonerating my father. I'd been influenced more than I wanted to be by Phillip and began to see how this might be viewed more as a motive and less as an indication of innocence. But it still didn't explain why Brannen was not exempt from the misadventure. There were, of course, several possibilities now that Moya's mental state was clearer. Having two children took her further away from realizing her hopes for living in the city and going to university. It made it less likely that she would rejoin the band and live some kind of rock-and-roll life. Perhaps she might have seen drowning herself as a way of escape. Or perhaps her erratic behaviour made my father so furious that he thought killing her was the only way out. I thought about his letter to Billie and the line where he said he would be consumed by his wife's cruelty. Moya may very well have been behaving very badly. She might have been hurting Cillian by threatening to leave him, or she might have been a bad mother and was hurting her babies. This speculation led me closer to believing the official findings: a jealous husband kills wife. But the illness had to have been at least a thread in the story. I wanted a second opinion, and I didn't want to interrupt Phillip at work. Helena, Jimmy, and Brendan were all preparing to go home, now that their arduous responsibilities had been fulfilled. I didn't want to hold them up any longer. I offered them rewards in the near future for being such excellent friends. They were all weary and dusty, and after checking that I would stay off obstacle courses and remain safe in the house, they were happy to leave. I kept my latest find to myself.

Brendan was shouting about arriving with the truck the next day and asking if I was sure there was nothing else that needed to come out of my house, but the words were all a bit of a blur. I nodded in acquiescence where appropriate and indicated resistance as needed. No, nothing else. Yes, everything outside Billie and Darcy's. Please don't take my outdoor furniture. Thank you. Love you too. Goodbye.

And just as they arrived three days ago in a flurry of dust so they were gone. I would reward them with all kinds of wonders once I'd settled this latest finding. I would also share the fact contained in the doctor's letter. But now I needed to engage my newest friend in unearthing the real witnesses who knew Moya, Darcy, and Cillian. If they were not dead, they would soon be talking. People love to tell stories—their side of the stories.

CHAPTER NINETEEN

I rang Mick. The seemingly imperturbable Detective Flynn would hopefully become the partner I needed to put the pieces together. Phillip called me Sherlock and had bought me a beautiful Conan Doyle first edition to cement his point. I thought of Mick as my Dr. Watson, but it was a role he was not very willing to take on. My conversation waxed and waned in its lucidity. I tried to fill him in on everything I'd found in the great unpacking. He had heard some of this from Phillip, who had obviously been in contact with him more regularly than I'd realized.

"Lily, is this part of your last concussion talking, or have you fallen on your head again?" Mick was restraining his laughter as he encouraged me to slow down, try to put the thoughts in order, and get to the question that involved him.

I assured him that I'd never been thinking more clearly and sarcastically thanked him for his concern for my well-being. I offered him the wisdom of my new theory and the substantial evidence of my mother's diagnosis. He interrupted my enthusiasm with common sense questions about the letters. I felt he was taking notes, as he reiterated some points to make sure he had heard me correctly.

I had been talking for several minutes, answering all his questions, when he finally asked, "What do you want me to do?"

I was silent for a moment while I thought about how dependent I'd become on the support of others. I wasn't sure I liked needing people to help me. I had been independent and self-reliant most of my life, and I was fighting hard against the ingrained belief that asking for help was some kind of terrible weakness. In the seconds of silence, I also realized how isolating autonomy can be.

"Lily?" Mick brought my attention back to the conversation.

"I need you to help me find some people who were involved in Moya's life. I want to talk to them myself to try and fill in some details of this story."

"You mean people I didn't speak to at the time of the investigation?" It wasn't ego that drove Mick's question; it was genuine interest.

"It's more or less those who you would never have thought of. It's the band members that Moya and Darcy played with before she married my father, the doctor who diagnosed her, and a man called Roland Devine."

"Who is Roland Devine?" Mick asked. He just wanted to place him in the storyline.

"He's a man I have to punch in the face." It wasn't elegant, it wasn't pretty, and it certainly wasn't ladylike, but it was going to happen. Mick said little about that final comment, putting it down to my head injury.

"Can you email me the list of names and any details you have about them? Give me a couple of days to see what I can find out. And don't go about punching anyone." Salient advice, which was duly noted and was eventually going to be ignored.

I finished by telling him I had an appointment with Thomas West, the journalist, the following day. He wanted to come with me, but I asked him to work on the list I was about to send him. I promised to keep my fists to myself.

I rang Phillip then but gave him no details about my conversation with Mick. I felt he would try to intervene and stop me before I got going. I did tell him about Moya's diagnosis, and he asked what I was going to do about it. I lied—a terrible habit was forming—and said I just wanted to think about it for a while before doing anything. I did tell him that I was meeting with Thomas the next day. He too wanted to come, but I suggested that we could have lunch after the appointment and I would tell him everything then. He asked me to come and stay with him so he could make sure I was watered and fed. It was an invitation I couldn't resist. I knew he would nag at me about the interview and squeeze more out of me than I wanted to tell, but being with Phillip was more important than any secret I was trying to keep.

He was waiting for me when I got to his place. He was horrified by the blackened eye and the ever-increasing purpleness of my side. He jokingly asked me who I was, as he was unable to identify me in the disguise I was wearing. We had a lovely night of talking about everything other than the O'Haras.

When we were close to sleep, he whispered into my ear, "Please don't make me have to arrest you for assaulting people by punching them in the face." Bloody Mick. Couldn't keep a thing to himself.

CHAPTER TWENTY

homas West's apartment was small but in a very trendy area of town. He had been retired for several years, but he still wrote freelance for journals and had written several books on a range of subjects. He was surprised by my face and obvious limp.

"You should see the other guy." My opening line was an oldie, but it made him laugh.

"I can't imagine a little thing like you in a fight. Should I be worried?"

I assured him that I was simply a victim of my own clumsiness and that I would remind myself not to attempt walking downhill whilst fuming next time. He had made coffee and arranged some cakes on a plate. I told Thomas that I was really grateful for his call and that I'd read the articles he wrote back in 1975 and '76.

"Different kind of journalism in those days," he said. I couldn't help but agree.

"I've managed to track down a few other people who were around in those days. I hope to see them soon so I can get some background information about my parents." It seemed a pretty lame reason to be waking up the past and the people who had probably long forgotten any connection with them.

"Oh, I thought your main interest was in proving your father's innocence." Thomas was certainly on the ball and not interested in playing games.

It was hard to explain why I thought it was so important. Nothing could come of the things I found out. But the past had risen, and the conclusions were not clear in my mind. I just imagined that when I exhausted all possible avenues of investigation, the truth would be evident. I would just live easier knowing why things went so wrong all those years ago.

Thomas nodded as if he thought my rationale was sound. "I don't know if what I discovered will do anything to help you, but I'm happy to share."

Thomas commenced his revelation by pulling out several old notebooks and a printed summary of his findings. The old-school notebooks had proved invaluable so far. The day of the disappearance, the paper was informed that there was a story that had to be covered out on Lake Road. Thomas and a photographer were given the job because they'd both worked homicides and deaths by misadventure before. They were given the brief that a woman and child had gone missing, possibly drowned, more than likely murdered by the husband.

"That was the brief? Without any knowledge of the case, you went out believing my father had killed them?" A little bit of wild was rising in me. Something primal stirred and brought me immediately to the defence of Cillian.

"It was how the police framed it." Thomas said, not rising to the tinge of anger in my voice. He spent a few seconds shuffling papers and waited for me to settle back into my chair. Then he started again. By the time he had arrived, it was late in the day, and police divers had already been assembled at the water's edge. The O'Haras' side was filled with people, locals and police. He explained how my father seemed frozen and expressionless. In his career, Thomas had been to other scenes like this, and the suspects were often more animated, frequently demonstrating the hysteria of one who would benefit from putting on a show. But Cillian O'Hara was frighteningly still and could only mumble responses to the questions put to him by the lead detective, Michael Flynn. Thomas had friends on the force and was able to ask a few questions of them. They insisted the husband was drunk or on drugs. No one believed that a man could sleep through his wife and child exiting the boat, either plunging into the water or swimming away. It was impossible to understand unless he was on something, and then it was possible he was dead to the world. But this was an unlikely scenario; for the police it was just too far-fetched. He said the lack of bodies was a complication for the police. Thomas had a quick look at me, realizing that he was talking about my mother and brother.

"Did you only talk to the police?" I asked. I knew he wouldn't have if he was any kind of journalist.

Of course he had followed in Mick's footsteps and tried to speak to the family, including Cillian. But in the days after the disappearance, he was shut out of the community, which had closed ranks after the initial shock. It was fairly typical of rural communities who, no matter what they thought privately, would not betray one of their own. The O'Haras were one of the oldest families on the lake and it seemed that Cillian was generally liked. Billie was the most popular in the community. She had immediately come to her brother's aid by taking care of the baby and trying to keep everything running. Some of the locals eventually talked about Moya. From what Thomas could gather, it seemed that Moya was seen as an outsider—and too wild for Cillian.

Off the record, people said more, and Rudolph Chaffey was one who was happy to give Thomas details over a few beers in the pub a month or so after the commotion had settled. He had been my father's boss on a number of building projects. According to Chaffey, Cillian was a gentle soul. He was more an artisan than a carpenter. He was a perfectionist who would have been happier just making his furniture and carving wood, but he had to make money. In those days it was all about building. He drank too much, but never on the job. And he was rarely drunk. He just spent more time in the pub after the little boy was born. Chaffey remembered the night of the fight as a reasonable thing. A farm worker who spent more time socializing than shearing had called Moya a mad bitch and a screaming drunk. Cillian went silent, and before the first punch, the bloke filled him in on the story. Two nights before, Moya had been drinking with some long-haired stranger that no one knew. She had called him Carl and was all over him. One of Cillian's friends went over to her to remind her she was married. Apparently she went crazy—upended a table, threw glasses at the bar, and threatened to come back with a rifle and kill the lot of them. According to Chaffey's version of events, this Carl fellow dragged Moya out of the pub, and the two of them didn't ever reappear. The fight began the second time the shearer called Moya a crazy bitch; Cillian leapt on him. It was frequently repeated that the fight was about Moya's honour, but if these details were correct, there was little honour to defend. How did it help Cillian's case? Well, it made him seem less calculated perhaps and certainly pointed to the instability the doctor had been talking about.

I asked Thomas why Detective Flynn wasn't told at the time about Moya's behaviour.

"By the time I had all the ducks lined up, the story went cold. People weren't interested, and other things had taken the place of speculation. Accusations about your family disappeared. By the time I learned that Flynn was going to charge your father, it was too late." Of course it was too late. Cillian had killed himself, and anything relevant had died too.

"Did you think that I might have wanted to know when I grew up?"

Thomas was genuinely sad when he responded. He talked about how tragic it was that a little girl was alone in the world. Moya and Brannen were gone, either dead or disinterested. He asked what could be gained from bringing up all this pain again.

"You were a baby, Lily. I thought you could grow up and grow away from the tragedy. Did you need to know how badly people had behaved?"

I believed he was motivated by a misguided kindness. After the bones were found, though, he thought that the past should be aired.

"Did you contact Detective Flynn after they were found?"

"Of course I did. And I told that young detective who was involved in the recovery and coronial enquiry. Swan, Detective Swan." Phillip had been told about my mother's behaviour. He knew in July. "Both of them said it was no more than hearsay at best, unreliable memory at worst."

I couldn't listen to anything else Thomas had to say. I remained with him for about thirty more minutes while he tried to convince me to help him co-author a story about the events, but I was merely present in the room; my mind was honing in on Phillip Swan's omission. Why didn't he tell me? Why didn't Mick tell me? They hadn't held back anything else, but the fact that my mother was crazy and was seen with another man simply slipped their minds.

Lunch was interesting. Phillip was already seated at the little pasta and pizza place close to the central police-station where he worked. He smiled and stood up to hug me as I arrived. I thought I would punish him by avoiding his affection, but I was too weak to resist him. And my fury at his non-disclosure had mellowed to searing frustration.

"I don't need your protection, Phillip," I began. Given my physical state, it seemed just short of ludicrous. He had the look of a guilty man and was clearly aware of what Thomas had told me. No wonder he and Mick both wanted to attend the interview, both thinking they could prevent the truth from coming out. "Why didn't you just tell me about my mother?"

Of course he had his reasons. They were judicious and practical reasons in the eyes of a policeman. Hearsay was no more useful than gossip. It simply pointed an investigation in a direction; it allowed for few conclusions. Moreover, he said thought of me learning about my mother's less-than-appropriate behaviour at that time just seemed unwise. I questioned what he meant by *unwise* and then wished I hadn't. Phillip drew a very compelling picture of my state at the time the skeletons were uncovered. He couldn't have been clearer in his description of how vulnerable I was. He was motivated by the fear of damaging me further and though that the rumours of Moya would be best ignored. He had no idea that I would embark on this absurd crusade to dig up what had been long forgotten. He also agreed that now that I was stronger and coping, he should have told me.

"Does it count that I love you?" He was using my own pathetic act to win back his lover's favour. I did, with equal feebleness, give in and forgive him. Of course it counted; in essence, it was everything.

Lunch was happy. We ate pizza and salad. I refused dessert, and to Phillip's disappointment, he didn't have time to get another course in before returning to his desk. His last actions were to ask me to stay at his place again that night and to press a small piece of paper into my hand. Mick had received my list and had found one of the men I wanted to speak to. It was an easy one, really, and I could possibly have found him myself. It was just surprising that Mick sent the number to me via Phillip. The two of them seemed to be collaborating a little too freely, and I wasn't happy that they might very well have been forming a united front against me.

I agreed to stay, as it was the end of the week and we could sleep in the next day. Brendan had been out with the truck and had taken all the donations away. Stone Orchard Farm would be a little emptier and little sadder. I didn't want to return to it alone. I thought Phillip might stay on Saturday, and then we would begin the usual routine of work on Monday, January 7. In the mean time, I was in possession of my next step: a name and a phone number.

Dr. Vincent Smith had just retired and was packing up his practice. He seemed affable enough when I introduced myself to him. He had time to talk and was genuinely concerned for me.

"I remember your family quite well, Lily. It was a terrible time for your parents." That would have to have been the greatest understatement of all time, but I didn't interrupt the doctor, who seemed to want to talk.

He started by telling me how horrified he was when the bones were identified last year. He was amazed to find out that I still lived out at the farm and was sorry that my private life had been so exposed by the media. "Always looking for an angle to infiltrate someone's pain." I had to keep prompting him to go back to what had happened in this terrible time he initially referred to. I found it hard to believe that after all the patients he must have seen, he remembered so many details about Moya. She, of course, was the first and only patient of his who had disappeared under such dark circumstances. Who wouldn't remember that?

He confirmed her illness. She was unwell, and her second pregnancy was ill-advised, given the state she was in. She was, in Dr. Smith's words, out of control. He had treated her since she was a teenager for the usual things but had noticed that she was, for want of a better term, highly strung. She didn't get on with her parents, and her mischievous conduct left a huge rift in her relationship with them. She had a mental illness that these days would be diagnosed as bipolar disorder. It was treatable, controllable, and bore no stigma today, but the late '60s and early '70s were not so forgiving when it came to manic behaviour.

Doctor-patient confidentially was irrelevant at this point, and he really didn't hold back. Apparently two weeks before she disappeared, she'd given Brannen some of her medication. It was allegedly an accident, but her carelessness could have killed the little boy. Cillian was anxious that her frenzied and frantic actions were a danger to both O'Hara children.

"Of course, Lily, you were just a few weeks old. So vulnerable. Your father was at his wit's end."

This continued to sound like motive, not a disincentive, for murder. Further details emerged of a household in chaos. Moya wasn't able to breast feed because of the drugs she was taking and the drinking she was doing. She was toxic. All she talked about was killing herself. She threatened to take the whole family with her.

"I was going to commit her, but your father was afraid of taking such an action. He was hopeful that the medication would begin to work." She was psychotic and having delusions, raging about the awfulness of her life. Cillian was in constant contact with the doctor begging him to help, but five weeks after the birth, my birth, the world righted itself and calm was restored at the farm. The medication seemed to be working, and Cillian had tried to clear the house of any alcohol. The pace slowed, the rages were infrequent, and all concerned thought the storm was over, at least for a time.

When Dr. Smith heard she had disappeared with Brannen, he was deeply concerned for the boy's safety.

"Then why didn't you go to the police?" I asked. "Your evidence could have saved my father." It seemed so obvious that Mick would have seen the doctor's input as evidence, real evidence, not hearsay or the unreliable scuttlebutt of drinkers in the pub.

"I couldn't reveal your mother's condition, Lily. I couldn't violate her privacy, so her medical records were not something I could readily disclose. I was also taking up an overseas placement at the beginning of 1976. By the time the police were interested in your mother's health, I was gone." The reality, he went on to say, was that the police simply thought Cillian O'Hara was a killer, and they weren't going to look anywhere else. "By the time I got back to Australia in 1978, your father was dead. Moya and Brannen were presumed dead. What could I have done?"

"You can reveal this in a statutory declaration so I can have one reasonable shot at clearing my father's name."

He agreed but said that it really wouldn't change the coronial findings. In the earlier investigation, it might have persuaded the police to look at an alternate scenario—the possibility that my mother may have drugged Cillian and then taken her own life. And had she killed her son? It remained a question that, no matter how much circumstantial evidence and hearsay and how many facts I brought to the fore, had an answer. I hadn't meant to, but I started crying and couldn't contain my frustration. On the other end of the phone, I could sense the doctor's concern. He was encouraging me to seek help and asking about my own doctor. I was momentarily appalled that he thought I was like my mother. Inherited madness.

Constraining my feelings and burying my despair, I was able to put a slightly braver face on for the last part of the conversation. I assured him that I was all right, that I was coping, and that I had support and friends. After hanging up, I thought of Phillip but couldn't call him because I knew I'd become fretful again. I decided that ringing Mick was the better option. He would listen and not derail my resolve with his concern and declarations of love as Phillip most often did.

Mick listened to my summary of the conversation with Vincent Smith. He agreed that it was an acceptable conclusion to draw. He would not, however, concur that my alternative theory was stronger than the official findings.

"What would be Mick? What would make it stronger?"

His answer was spoken with such gentleness. I could tell he hated saying it. "It's too late, Lily. Not even an eyewitness account could turn the tide on your father's posthumous conviction, but what you believe is more important than coronial conclusions. You can believe whatever you want."

The day ended. I had so much more information about the past than I'd ever had. None of it good. None of it useful. Just more awfulness that contributed to the maelstrom. I slept fitfully with Phillip by my side. I wondered about our future. The start of our relationship had been based on the discovery of a turbulent past, a series of truths and falsehood that simply pointed out the disarray in my family's lives. Some of them lied, covered up, and ignored what was to have a catastrophic effect on them. But Phillip was right when he said that the responsibility I had was for my own life, for our lives together. I had to keep perspective lest the ruinous actions of history overwhelm me. There was little left to do, but there were others to see and other stories to hear. Someone had to be reminded that the past doesn't always stay buried and that secrets have a way of rising.

CHAPTER TWENTY-ONE

espite the extraordinary and unsettling revelations from Thomas and Dr. Smith, the days that followed saw a return to normality: working, cooking, sleeping, and reading, but now in the company of Phillip. We settled into a pleasant rhythm. Life seems to fall inevitably into to a pattern of predictabilities and routines. Time spent in contentment, even if it is only counted in days, clears the mind and steadies the heart. Chaos is returned to order, albeit briefly. I seemed to have moved into Phillip's world easily, and I returned to Stone Orchard just to check on the removal of the garbage skip and to meet with a local real estate agent to have the property valued. I wanted to know what I'd have to do to make the place more marketable. Surprisingly, the main suggestion focused on the rear gardens and orchard. Getting both of these sections of the property in order would, apparently, signal to a prospective buyer that the land was easy to manage and profitable.

A local landscaper arrived and gave a quote, and an arborist was scheduled to prune the fruit trees and restore the orchard. He gave me a stern warning about the timing for pruning. This time of the year was too early and would disrupt fruit production for the coming year. I was, however, not looking for a bountiful crop, simply a neat and seemingly fertile grove. These thoughts of expediency made me think of Darcy. They were sad thoughts. All his hard work—planting, replanting, and encouraging growth through countless seasons of drought and plenty—was reduced to this. The land, despite the fickle climate, produced many plentiful crops under his hands. My neglect these past five years would, in the tree doctor's words, do no permanent damage.

I eventually asked Eddie Towell if he would come and take a few photos of the place once the yards were restored and the place was all in order, a postscript to the generations of my family who had lived here and built this life. Helena had asked me about giving up the land and whether it was wise to sever the ties with the ancestral home. Maybe it was wiser to lease the property to someone who could work the orchard and take the profits, but it is only in happy stories about familial legacy that one has the land in one's blood. I would simply be handing on dirt and wood to the new owner. This was not a happy place for me, despite what might have been idyllic freedom in my childhood. There hadn't been happiness here for a while. Leaving behind the land meant leaving behind the past. I was happy enough to have the photographic reminders of what stood here. The photos could give future children an understanding of the place simply as it was, without its ghosts and without its pain.

Work was always an orderly distraction, and with several exhibitions visiting the museum, I was happily busy. Artefacts had to be catalogued, and research papers had to be evaluated. And it seemed that changes had to happen. Brendan's love life flourished. He was talking about moving in with his girlfriend. His personal happiness was reflected in his look of wellness and in the quality of his work. Jimmy announced his resignation and the offer of a job in Washington. One of the minor Smithsonian institutions wanted him. Helena was taking a month's leave in July to have a northern summer in London, another attempt at connecting with her son Louis. Life was shifting and fluctuating, and despite my usual loathing of change, I could see how important these alterations were and how great things can happen when we let go of the known. Phillip too was consumed by the busyness of work. He was involved in something significant that involved a number of jurisdictions, but I had few details. The explicit danger of his job occasionally made my stomach churn, but his constant affirming approach to life dispelled most of the trepidation. I recalled Mick's words to me when I met him before Christmas: "It's hard to be a copper's wife."

Behind the everyday events of our lives, Mick was making further enquiries about the band members and Roland Devine. He stayed in touch each day, and before the end of January, he had details. He had contacted three of the four original musicians who were luckily still living in Canberra. They were initially reluctant to talk and had quizzed him about the motives for the interview. After Mick had assured them that there were no legal implications, they were more receptive to a meeting with Moya O'Hara's daughter. They had seen me once when I was brand new and then again last year in the paper. I thought that at that point they would have known that someone would want to talk to them or that they would have some interest in solving the mysterious disappearance of their friend.

Mick organized a meeting for a Friday afternoon, coincidently at the café and bar where Wayfarer used to play. Mick insisted on accompanying me. I was certain it had nothing to do with keeping a watch on me, but rather it would be an opportunity for him to cast his investigative eye over the details. Phillip started checking his calendar the moment I told him about the appointment so he could join the inquisitorial team, but I simply told him no. It was bad enough to have an ex-copper with me, let alone bringing a serving detective. I knew nothing of the lives of the men I was about to meet, but I was sure a police presence might silence them on several fronts. He was not happy, but he acquiesced.

In between the start of the first week back at work and the end of the second much had happened. My friends had announced their future plans; I'd settled into a routine of living with Phillip in the city during the weekdays and going back to my place together on weekends; I'd met with Eddie, who agreed to take photos; and I'd written my list of questions for Paul, Stephen, and Sean. These were the members of Moya and Darcy's band who still lived, worked, and played in Canberra. Carl Blackberry had not been heard from for years. His strange silence commenced not long after Moya's disappearance, which may or may not have had any relevance to the story, except for the ghastly encounter Thomas West had uncovered.

Mick picked me up at the museum at five o'clock, and we arrived at the bar twenty minutes later. We had ten minutes to kill before they arrived, but before we could order a drink and some tapas to share with the group, a man approached us from one of the darkened booths near the front windows.

"Good God, you look like your mother" he said.

Given what I knew about her, I wasn't sure this was a compliment. Luckily all signs of my injuries had faded, and I had kept on my happy summer weight gain. He was good looking, and despite the balding head and compensatory facial hair, he looked years younger than he probably was. This was Stephen Doddy. He had been the band's lead guitarist and was now a music teacher at one of the local high schools. He shook hands with both me and Mick and reiterated his opening line.

"You could be Moya standing there."

He was so mesmerized by my looks that he failed to be aware of how those words might impact me. Mick broke the spell by suggesting we take seats at the booth where Stephen had left his bag.

By the time we had settled and ordered drinks and food, we had been joined by Paddy Lock and Sean Page. Paddy was, as he had been in 1975, a public servant. He was getting ready to retire, having just turned fifty-eight. He was young to quit work, but he had spent a lifetime putting his hobby on the back burner and now wanted to fulfil his life's ambition of making acoustic guitars. Sean Page owned a thriving music shop and confirmed that he'd been onto Paddy for years to give up the suit and let him sell his guitars for him. The three had remained close friends, despite the band's demise and the responsibilities of real lives. Stephen and Paddy were married and had kids, but Sean, despite a number of girlfriends, had never tied the knot. They politely asked what I did, and when I confirmed that I was fairly musical, they were collectively excited. Sean wanted me to come to one of their many sessions to play for them. The talk of music was my way into a discussion about Moya.

"I heard her voice on a tape Darcy kept," I said. I hated the fact that the little catch in my throat gave away the enormity of it. "It was the first time ever. She had a beautiful voice. Mine is a little deeper and a bit stronger." I was starting to ramble in order to gather my strength. I felt Mick's hand on my back, and I looked up to catch his expression. His was a steadying touch, and I knew it was the first time he'd heard about the tape from the concern in his eyes.

"I'm sure you know I want to ask you all about her. And about my father and Darcy." It was a weak introduction to a potentially complicated discussion, but it was better than my first emotional statement. It produced a moment of silence and discomfort that I punctuated with an understatement. "I know she was ill. Crazy." Even saying the words, I felt I was betraying her in some way. I owed her nothing, but she was still my mother, and perhaps something inside me felt I should be more respectful. "The doctor she was seeing told me she was bipolar."

This seemed to unlock the floodgates. Sean was the most forthcoming, but the other two added when he paused to drink or eat. Mick remained very quiet and let me pose questions and tease out memories when further detail seemed appropriate. When they spoke, a strange thing happened; the years between their youthful adventures as hopeful musicians and their now middle-aged existences faded. I thought the memory was meant to be fickle, clouded, and unreliable, but the remaining men of Wayfarer talked about those days as if the events they described happened only the week before. For them, it was a turbulent and exciting time that ended only with the calamity of Moya's disappearance.

"Musicians find each other." Stephen's said, explaining how the six members of Wayfarer came together.

"Why did you call the band Wayfarer?" I asked. A safe question at which they all laughed.

"Well, you know a wayfarer is a nomad or a vagabond, so it seemed to apply to our romantic notions of ourselves."

"But the real reason," interrupted Paddy, "was that Sean had bought a car to get the gear around in. It was a Chrysler Valiant

Wayfarer. We were lucky we didn't call ourselves the Vals!" It was a light-hearted moment that got them talking about the early days when the band started. They forgot that Mick was a retired detective and left in some of the details that, had they remembered, they might not have included.

It seemed that playing around the known venues in a small city puts you into the path of everyone who can sing or play. Darcy O'Hara had been known for his soulful renditions of modern pop songs. He had a six-string and a twelve-string guitar and was the only singer in town who could take a Rolling Stone's tune and make it sound like a love song. Apparently his version of "Give Me Shelter" was legendary among the live-music aficionados. I couldn't imagine Darcy singing and playing to an audience, let alone being a minor legend. The only interest in music I could remember was his silent listening to my recitals in Billie's front room and a slight disapproval of my fascination with stringed instruments. It might have been his way of preventing history repeating itself. I'll never know.

So the band grew around Darcy. Moya joined the newly forming band while she was still in high school. She finished year twelve, moved out of her parents' home, and took a bedroom in a group house with Carl, Sean, and Stephen. Paddy was just starting university and continued to live at home with his family. Darcy, of course, lived out at the lake but spent a lot of time in what became known as the "band's house." It was a pretty wild place, and I'm sure the images of partying and nocturnal arrangements were sanitized a little for both me and Mick.

Sean's story included sketchy details about Carl. He was a drug user and occasional criminal. I think Sean was about to say that it wasn't too bad, but the look on Mick's face seemed to suggest that downplaying drug use to a misdemeanour would not sit well. I did have to ask what an occasional criminal was. Apparently it was more an opportunistic one; he only pinched things that didn't take a huge amount of effort. Drinking was common, and no one in the band or anyone who was associated abstained. Moya drank a lot, dabbled with drugs, and left the rails several times. I could tell that they didn't want to say what leaving the rails looked like, but I managed to glean details such as hospital visits, weeks spent in bed, and crews sent out to locate her when she went missing. None of it painted a pretty picture. Sean silenced Paddy when he started talking about finding her covered in vomit in one of the culverts not far from where we were meeting. Too many specifics for the woman's daughter, too much disrespect for the dead, and too many details for the copper seated with them.

Looking back, they probably knew she was not well, and looking back it was easy to see she was in trouble. She was Carl's girlfriend in the early days, and they remained pretty connected over the years. She fell in love with Darcy, and he was protective of her. She was better with him—not as erratic, sober a lot of the time.

"And then she met your father," Paddy added to the story. Cillian was apparently a really quiet boy. He looked really young in comparison to Darcy, younger than the four years between them. "He wasn't interested in the life of the band, but he had a really great voice. And Darcy wanted him to sing with us."

So that's how he met Moya. Darcy had brought his brother to town to meet this wild bunch and inadvertently put Moya in his way. It wasn't love at first sight for Cillian. He was wary and introverted and only stayed around because his big brother was there to look after him. Stephen took up the story of the romance between Cillian and Moya. He said that they only sang in public four or five times. Darcy could see what was happening; they all could. Panic set in that the relationship with Cillian might wreck the band. Darcy and Carl were both jealous, and there were fights. Lots of them. They were ostensibly about music, but they all knew they were about Moya. Moya chased the younger O'Hara. What she wanted she seemed to get.

When Cillian and Moya announced that they were engaged, Darcy left the band. Moya quit too. That just left the four of them, and Carl was wavering. But everyone got it together enough to play at the wedding reception. The two were married at St. Mary's and celebrated at the church hall next door. It was a great night, except for the fact that Darcy wasn't there and Carl was so stoned he had to be hauled out of the venue before he got lynched by the locals. Not a nice person, this Carl guy.

Married life seemed to suit Moya for a while, and she lost touch with the four remaining members of Wayfarer. The three of them dutifully went out to the christening of Brannen and reconnected with Darcy, who by then was running the orchard and living by himself in a cottage on the property. Then it seemed it all started to fall apart. Paddy got a letter from Moya saying that she wanted to come back to the band and start living in Canberra. She was unhappy with Cillian, who she called boring. She also apparently hated Billie, who was always watching her and had taken over her son.

"It was all kinds of crazy talk. Your aunt Billie was one of the most serene women I'd ever met. Darcy and Cillian adored her."

It was nice that Paddy remembered Billie so fondly. Stephen and Sean agreed. Moya's feelings about Billie were not founded in fact. Billie was just trying to protect Brannen from his increasingly manic mother.

"Billie couldn't have been unkind to Moya if she tried. When I went out to the lake to see what was happening, Billie was still trying to save them all." Paddy had been more involved than the others. Billie wouldn't tell him anything except for the fact that Moya was not well and that Cillian was dealing with it. She was loyal to a fault, generous, decent, and suddenly living in a nightmare.

The five years between Brannen's birth and my own were punctuated by her visits to Canberra, erratic performances, and the band's weekly sessions. They weren't playing publicly anymore, just honing the skills and remembering what might have been. Occasionally Moya wouldn't or couldn't go home. On the nights she was too drunk or stoned to drive, one of them would ring Cillian and tell him that they'd look after her. Carl had told them that he'd been seeing Moya in Bungendore and that she was going to run away with him. A few times, they were embarrassed to tell me, she slept with Carl, whose life had gone from bad to worse in terms of his drug habit and criminal behaviour. And once or twice, Cillian and Darcy had driven into town and dragged Moya home. She would fight them, swear, and say vile things to them, and then she would retreat to her bed for weeks. Then it would all start again.

"She got better for a while. Started seeing a doctor and taking medication. She eased up on the drinking." Stephen said. His little hopeful note was not lost on me. In the calm of this brief reprieve, I was conceived. I had doubted my mother's fidelity and had misgivings about my paternity, but this lull in her madness gave me hope that Cillian was my father. "But then she lost it again soon after you were born."

And it was very soon. Apparently when I was a week old, she turned up at Stephen's house and started abusing his wife, who had a small baby of her own. Stephen was summoned home from work to find Moya ranting and raving on his front lawn. She couldn't be settled. Paddy came from work, and the two of them tried to settle her. But she was drunk and delusional.

"She was saying all kinds of crazy things." Paddy added quietly, as if the memory hurt him.

Those crazy things brought Mick forward from his chair. Moya was threatening to kill her little family. She said she had drugs the doctor had given her and she could use them to put them all to sleep. Then she would be free to make that record the band had been planning, the record that had been talked about in 1969 and was quashed soon after. It was just a drunken dream they'd fancied for a while, but somewhere in Moya's head, it was the thing that would motivate her to rid herself of a five year old, a newborn, and a bewildered husband.

Without looking at me Paddy concluded, "We rang Cillian. He rang the doctor."

Apparently Moya went home. Stephen went out to talk to my father and Darcy the day after Moya's mad visit. Stephen had finally come to realize, as had Paddy and Sean, that Moya's behaviour was dangerous. She went missing for two days after he'd gone out to see what could be done to help her.

"Your father was frantic. He had two kids, and you were just so new. He didn't know what to do."

The Valium and sleeping tablets prescribed to bring a cessation to her demons were explosive when mixed with alcohol. The whole household was imploding, but Cillian refused to contact the police. He thought that her death threats and her erratic behaviour would ensure she was committed.

"Despite the horror of what she was doing, your father loved her." Or was too ashamed to ask for help.

The confirmation of her madness was not lost on Mick. If there was a chink in the armour of that inscrutable copper's face, it appeared when he realized that Moya may very well have been less a victim of my father's anger and more a victim of her own tortured mind. It put Cillian's guilt in an entirely new light.

But my last questions had to be answered. "After this madness, she disappeared. You must have thought something had happened. Why didn't you come forward?"

As usual, the answers were not easy. The three men were not unanimous in their conclusions. It seemed that Carl had disappeared about the same time. Stephen had assumed that Moya had taken Brannen and left with him, probably up north to Queensland. His choice of destinations was Mullumbimby. Lots of musos went there, and the scene would have suited Carl's proclivities. He said it would have been just like the pair of them to be reckless and inconsiderate. Paddy thought she might have carried out her threat and killed herself and Brannen. She talked a lot about it when she was at her worst. He believed she could have drugged Cillian and then drowned herself and the boy. Sean was brief.

"She made your father's life hell, Lily. If he killed her, it would have been out of desperation." He looked squarely at Mick as if almost blaming the police for being so single minded.

"But could he have killed Brannen? And why would he if he was trying to protect us from her?"

Sean's answer seemed paltry at best. "His death would have been a mistake, a terrible accident. It had to have been."

"Did my father's suicide confirm any of this for you?" Either way, they said, he couldn't live with what had happened.

And when the bodies were discovered? What were they all thinking then? They remained divided. Stephen's theory about Carl was no longer relevant, although he continued to insist that the mad muso must have had a hand in the situation, hence his disappearance. Paddy and Sean reluctantly thought that the finds supported both theories. On two things they agreed: Moya was capable of irrational and unpredictable things, including violence, and Cillian was a loving and gentle man who would not have hurt his child. Somewhere between those two mismatched souls, a tragedy unfolded. They took one child with them and left one behind.

And there the conversation ended. Mick was as deeply engrossed in the stories as I was. He was obviously thinking about the information the men had freely offered up. He had been making notes using his iPad, having finally given up his pencil-and-paper records. As the discussion ended and it was time to part company, he asked his only question.

"Why didn't you come forward when Moya disappeared?"

Why? Initially because Darcy had asked them to stay away. He said their input would just make matters worse. And then, of course, Cillian was dead. Nothing could be achieved.

"The behaviour of the band would have been known, particularly Carl's antisocial conduct, so the police were not really our kind of people." Stephen's summary of the relationship between wild musicians and the law was another of those understatements. If the consequences of their disinclination were not so tragic, the scenario could have made me laugh.

I had one question of my own. "Did you ever see Darcy or Billie after my father's death?"

That door had been firmly shut by both my auntie and uncle. Neither of them would see their former friends. "They grew into that property like the trees in the orchard. Nothing would make either of them reconnect with the world," Sean said.

The statement rang true; I could see that. Stone Orchard was a sanctuary from the awfulness of the life that commenced when the outsiders descended upon them. They came and went from the property only when it concerned me, and as the years progressed, they became more silent and more watchful than ever. Like the boulders and rocks that littered the property, Billie and Darcy hardened and stilled. They became the flinty buttresses that supported the world in which I grew up. The only sounds were my music and the sound of time passing. In this way, they forgot about Moya. They mourned Brannen and Cillian but put hope away. If only they'd lived to see the past rise.

Dinner with Mick and Phillip was a subdued event. It wasn't unhappy, but with the three of us preoccupied with thoughts of our own, we ate fairly quietly. Mick and Phillip spoke about the meeting. I added nothing; I just busied myself with putting food on my plate that I once again couldn't eat. Then the conversation became work related. I wanted to listen to the details of the cases Phillip was working on, but other things kept distracting me, the same things that had been hammering at me for seven months. I had to believe one thing or another. The memories of those who knew my parents gave no clear indication of what actually happened but did diminish the notion that my father was a callous killer. Now, if I wanted to escape the melancholy of ignorance, I had to accept that one of them was responsible for the death of my brother. It was the sticking point in every scenario. But if I was to ever sleep again, I would have to reconcile myself to Phillip's wise words: the most probable scenario is likely to be the truth. Moya was very ill. She was threatening to kill herself and her family. She had used her prescription drugs to hurt Brannen and told others that she could use them again to silence Cillian. On the day she died, she was steady, maybe resolute. She hadn't wanted to take Brannen out on the little boat. She wanted it to be just her and Cillian, who later appeared as though drugged. The little boy would not be left at home with his aunt and wailing sister. He slept at his mother's feet, and that was the last image Cillian recalled when questioned by police—by Mick.

Cillian was a kind man who was living a tortured existence with a mad wife who had an illness that she could not recover from on her own. Babies did not make for a healing climate. They added complication to her addled mind. Moya was talented and fanciful, difficult and broken, alone inside her delusions. Even her parents had beaten a hasty retreat from Australia when they'd accepted she was marrying a carpenter. She was his problem now. They'd seen the beginnings of this in her adolescence, and instead of holding her closer, they abandoned their only child. The O'Haras were not equipped to manage the mad stranger who had roared disruptively into their lives. All they could do was stand by and protect what was left. Darcy, full of envy and anger, was finally felled by guilt. And my Billie had to do what was seemingly unthinkable, to raise Moya's child in the stead of her own lost baby.

"Lily." Phillip was trying to get my attention. He reached out and wiped the tear that had escaped. Mick politely left the table with dishes and began noisily stacking the dishwasher.

"I'm okay," I said. It was a simple declaration, but for the first time in months, I truly believed it.

CHAPTER TWENTY-TWO

The winter was coming. The sting of summer had reached its peak, and the days of March and April were marked by cool nights and the extraordinary seasonal colours of autumn. The dormancy of winter would soon send the gardens across the region into a grey period of waiting. My life with Phillip was now established, and we had made plans for a future together. When the property sold on Lake Road, we would be in a strong financial position and could make decisions about the shape the future would take for us. He was not initially keen to have my inheritance be part of our combined financial worth. Men can sometimes be strange about money, but for me it was a way of overcoming my fear of sharing and finally eradicating my preference for isolation. Relationships would always have secrets and divisions, but I wanted there to be transparency from the outset. If he decided to run off with half the money I received from selling the O'Hara land, then so be it. But I couldn't imagine Phillip doing anything dishonest, anything hurtful. Helena was a little beside herself at my naivety in matters of the heart and money. She was insisting on some legal documentation that outlined who had what, and because it was obvious to her that my assets were worth a great deal, it should be evident in some prenuptial record. I felt her own experience was influencing her advice. I thanked her but decided to take my chances. For the first time, I would trust someone unconditionally and then, if necessary, survive the crash should it come.

Phillip and I spent the last days of March at the lake. It was time for us to discuss the past that had been laid bare during my summer of discoveries. There had been a number of assumptions made in December 1975. They were, I had to agree, reasonable. But perspective is everything, and when one looks at a situation from a single vantage point, then nothing else becomes evident. The stories and secrets I uncovered were not tangible evidence, but they were proof of an alternate truth. The two of us, and sometimes Mick, weighed in on occasional debates. We could not agree on what the most probable scenario was. The two detectives in my life were immutable in their interpretation of the events, but they had moderated their understanding of the motive. For both of them, the story had been aired and reviewed, and in the absence of poof, the coronial findings would stand. The absence of proof, however, did not equate to truth. If it was reasonable to assume my father was a murderer, it was equally reasonable to assume he was not. My truth was based on memories, speculation, and storytelling— things esoteric. What I had come to know was not a forensic or legal interpretation of facts; it was something providential that comes from the heart. Love creates an axiomatic version of events. A good man could not kill his child, nor his wife in the presence of that child. And so my findings would stand. This would be what remained.

Things would change. At the cemetery I would afford Cillian the honour of fatherhood. His headstone no longer pronounced his cruel isolation from his family. The funeral mason made me a plaque that read

Devoted father of Brannen Fitzpatrick (dec) and Lily Magdelena.
Veritas liberabit vos

The truth shall set you free. And it wasn't just Cillian who had been freed; the past and all its revelations had released me too.

I wanted to honour Baby O'Hara in some way too. Her momentary place in the O'Hara history should have warranted more than a nameless epitaph. I couldn't betray Billie by etching in stone the secret she kept archived with all her other hopes and dream. I thought of another Latin inscription that was fuelled a little bit by my anger at the father's abandonment of Billie:

Infantem divina. Baby divine. Despite the spelling, the little one would have been acknowledged, at least to me, as Roland Devine's child. But I didn't have that inscribed; instead I had the bewildered engraver write *Unum prae tristitia.* One for sorrow. For all the sorrow that was to come for Billie, Darcy, and Cillian. Sorrow for us all.

Despite his misgivings, Mick eventually gave me the details of Roland Devine's whereabouts. He had, as he said in his letter to Billie, become a solicitor and continued to live in Sydney. His parents had died only in the last few years and, ironically, were buried in the same cemetery as my family. I didn't ever look at their headstones for fear of writing in permanent pen something unkind. Best not to tempt fate. But I had to ease the loathing I had for the boy who had broken Billie's heart. I had to wade through the painful and sometimes toxic waves of the past. Why should Roland Devine be excused from his contribution to the misery?

I told Phillip one more lie. I promised myself it would be the last one I would tell. I said I was going to Sydney on a course for the museum. It was two days, and I'd stay in a hotel close to the city. It was the most plausible scenario that could withstand some scrutiny. I didn't tell Mick because he would immediately have smelled a rat, and my face still hadn't learned to keep what was in my head out of my eyes. I wasn't going to attack the man, but I had to know if he felt anything when the O'Hara name came up. What went through his head when the lake's sediment finally gave up its bones? Or was he like I was a year ago—a willing participant in denial. But if the last year has taught me anything, I knew that the past is a relentless force. It will rise up, and when you least expect it, force its shape upon you.

I drove myself to Sydney in a new car that Phillip insisted I buy. He felt the old Mercedes and the rollicking four-wheel drive were not overly roadworthy nor suitable for living in the city. Economically and environmentally, he had a point, but I was reluctant to let go of Billie's Merc. She had driven it like a queen. Sedately and serenely, she would arrive, alight, and leave. It was one of the few memories that made me smile. Luckily Phillip knew a man who loved Mercedes cars and was looking for a classic model to restore for a wedding car business he was developing. I met him, and his genuine respect for the vehicle and the fact he knew my mechanic, Arlen, sold me on the idea. It was his, but it was hard to let go.

The new car was a dream in comparison, and I had to be reminded by my socially and legally responsible partner that just because the car could do 150 kilometres an hour doesn't mean that it should. The car made getting to my destination easy. Roland Devine worked and lived in Pennant Hills. He would have been the same age as Billie—mid-sixties. He was still working out of a small law firm in which he was senior partner. I'd made an appointment to see him on the pretext of needing legal advice about a prenuptial agreement. He had others to see before me, but I thought I'd arrive early and watch him come and go as he greeted his clients.

I could see why Billie might have fallen in love with him. He was tall and dark. His hair, although greying, was still chocolate brown in sections. His eyes were dark too, his skin tanned. He moved easily, despite a little middle-aged weight. When he spoke to his staff, he was warm and jovial. Nothing about him spoke of the devil I was expecting. His next client obviously knew him well. They spoke about Roland's children, the youngest having been admitted to the bar like the older two.

"A family of lawyers. That must make for a fun Christmas," the client said laughing.

A family man. Lucky him. The receptionist spoke and asked me to fill in some paper work. I thought I'd ask about her boss. See what she was willing to divulge.

"He's an amazing man. He's only working part time here at his practice; you were lucky to get an appointment. He does pro bono work for several drug rehabilitation places. It takes up most of his time."

Great, Devine is now a saint. Even as I thought this, I was struck by how ungracious I was being. I'd done the very thing with Roland Devine that I'd try to stop happening to my father. I'd allowed presumption and a single act to characterize a man I did not know. He had been not much more than a child when he was forced to abandon Billie. Who was I to berate him for a past he had obviously atoned for? And who was I, of all people, to assume he was unfeeling and able to put any thought of his tiny dead baby out of his head. For all I knew, he had been to the grave. He might have gone there when he buried the last of his parents. Perhaps the successes of his children were a constant reminder of what Baby O'Hara might have achieved. I had no tangible evidence of his true self and his motives. In my haste, I'd taken the letter he had written as confirmation of his callousness. In my anger, I'd forgotten my mantra that there was always an alternate truth.

I felt ashamed, and in the coming and going of clients, I left with the bitterness unsaid. I thought that when he called out my name he would perhaps have a stirring of memory, a moment of panic. But Lily O'Hara of Stone Orchard would not appear. He could keep his secret; it was not my business.

On the way home I checked a text. It was from Mick asking if I needed any assistance with an assault charge that came from my Sydney visit. Was there nothing the man didn't know? I happily reassured him that I'd pulled the plug on my initial plan. Roland Devine was safe and would remain ignorant of my discovery. Not everyone had to suffer, and no one needed to suffer forever. It was a lesson hard learned.

Still, there was still a shadow or two to address if sorrow was to be put away, and that could only happen on Lake Road.

CHAPTER TWENTY-THREE

n June I met the real estate agent at the property. He had a strong offer from an American who had shown interest when Stone Orchard went on the market. The money was substantial, and the settlement would take place within the month. By the end of July, I would no longer be the curator of my family home. I would have cleaned out the last of the furniture and moved to the city the treasures that Phillip and I decided could fit into our new life.

A year would have passed since the bones had been recovered and the life I was living was swept away by a landslide of secrets. It was fair to say that I'd made peace with the findings. I was happy and optimistic about the future. It wasn't a feeling I was familiar with, but it made me a better person. I didn't conceal so many of my feelings and thoughts. I had found that silence was not always a way of surviving the complexities of relationships. Sometimes you had to tell the truth, no matter the hurt it might cause. If either Billie or Darcy had had the courage to tell me about the miseries that had shaped those hard years, I wouldn't have been so fearful of the past. The O'Hara family had two histories. The first one filled the years between our arrival in 1825 and the happy life that Padraig and Patricia made for their three wild children. But the tragedy in 1975 gave rise to a second history. Times were tough for the first O'Haras, and they were poor, hard working men and women who raised the farm with sweat and faith. But the last generation failed the family. The way was lost, and the property would go.

Most of the demons had been buried, or reburied. I'd made my peace and found the truth that I could live with. But not everything had been settled. Phillip and I had experienced our first fight, and I thought I'd have a night away from him. It was not to punish him for being unreasonable but to allow myself I to have a quiet moment to think through how I was going address the discoveries about my mother. I rarely talked about her after the confirmation of her illness and unforgivable indiscretions. That was at the heart of the argument. I wasn't sleeping again, and according to Phillip, I was being fractious without provocation. He wanted to talk about whether or not I'd really addressed the issues of the past. He made the fundamental error of introducing the idea that I should see a psychologist. I felt furious that he might have been alluding to my mother's mental health issues. In my head I was hearing him say I was as mad as she was. Of course he wasn't thinking this, but at the heart of this final problem was my fear that I might inherit her illness. I looked so much like her, and I was musical like her. Even though I knew that this was where the comparison ended, I wore my trepidation like a banner. *Your mother was mad; you might go mad too.*

I had accepted in my head that my mother was the perpetrator of the accident in 1975. I could articulate that with certainty, but something in my heart threatened every hope I had of happiness. I'd not buried my anger. Moya had not been forgiven. If I was to find complete peace, I had to absolve my mother of her sins. And with the property about to be sold, I had to find the courage soon.

The late afternoon was approaching. I sent Phillip a text to say I'd be staying out at the lake. I said that I loved him and that I had to do one last thing. I omitted to say I would see him in the morning or that I'd be saying a proper goodbye to the past.

CHAPTER TWENTY-FOUR

tanding on the Lake Road side of the empty lake, I found my courage. It felt strange to know that the lake property would be sold and that the O'Hara clan would no longer be a part of Lake Road. Its history and all its tragedy had left indelible marks on the living. Perhaps those stories would continue to shape the lives of future O'Haras. Perhaps it was time to hope that I might have children of my own. Little redheads that looked like me and had their maternal grandmother's sharp green eyes or that had the dark curly hair of Cillian and his rangy frame. Or maybe they would have the blonde, blue-eyed look of the Swans. It all seemed possible now that something of my little family would emerge in a future generation.

I had always suspected that the mystery of my family would have to be uncovered, viewed in the full light of honesty and accepted for whatever it was. The last twelve months of reconstructing the events of 1975 had provided the opportunity for that cleansing breath. I have said numerous times that my grown-up life had to begin when the bodies were discovered and when everyone was gone, but I didn't realize that you can't be an adult when you refuse to look at the past and accept its impact on the person you have become. So as the last O'Hara standing, I looked out to the centre of the lake and, in the last hours of day, fixed my gaze on the eastern side where Moya and Brannen had been found. It was time for a proper goodbye. It was time to make peace with a mother I'd never known.

The chill of another approaching winter cut through my jacket and jeans as I picked my way through broken wire fences, dead blackberry brambles, and sepia-coloured reeds. Dust and seed pods rallied in the wake of my foot falls and landed softly on and around me. The light of the day was becoming golden and the horizon pink. It was my favourite time of day, regardless of the season. It was the end of the day, and no matter what had happened, it was already the past. The approach of evening signalled that the new day might just be better.

The walk across the lake bed would take forty-five minutes, so it would be dark when I returned. But the clear sky promised a moonlit path back to the house. I hadn't been out to the site before; I had just spent time looking across the expanse of lake towards the discovery. The bones had been recovered, removed, and buried appropriately. I thought I had no reason to trek out there. So now, a year on, it was time to make a first and final visit.

The lake was dry, all except a soggy middle that was merely a mud puddle. It was a simple reminder that this was once a body of water and one day would be again. The path I took was easy, and walking over cracking earth and dead plants did not impede my pace. I strode out like a woman on a mission. It felt like a race, and I had to stop myself from running. I don't know why I felt such need for this to happen, but it felt urgent. I spent the time thinking about how I was feeling. I couldn't pin a single term on the emotion. It was a combination of expectation, misery, hope, resurrection, and finality. I don't know what that might be if it had to be a single word. I hated to think it might be the illusive notion of closure. I hated that concept, as it seemed to imply that a door could be closed upon one's experiences, as if they were in some way over. I preferred the word *healing* when expressing the end of traumatic events—not over, but bearable; not invisible, but marked by scar tissue that never fully evaporates and remains as a reminder of all that has happened. It's tender to the touch and tingles as the nerves repair, but it's not painful anymore. I think about emotional scarring in the same way as a deep surgical wound. There's no denying it's there. It's a bit ugly, and it can be felt. But it doesn't hurt anymore, and it doesn't get in the way of life as it did when it was a wound. So that's what it feels like living through the impact of an injury, of a trauma. You are no longer wounded, and you return to strength; but the loss leaves its mark on you. Perhaps it is there to remind the sufferer of how strong he or she really is. It says to the world, "I am healed, and I will live the life I'm meant to."

These musings accompanied me on my walk across the lake bed. After exactly forty-five minutes, I was standing facing the indentations where the bones had been discovered. The police tape had long ago blown away or simply remained in shreds clinging to some timber pickets left by forensic investigators. The area was totally dry now. It had always been the deepest part of the lake and one of the last sections to give in to the drought. Despite the activity and the trail of official and unofficial visitors to the discovery site, the earth was strangely unmarked. No imprint of the many feet and intrusions on the location was evident. The digging and excavation of the bones from their muddy embrace was hardly noticeable. All that had happened was gone, and the physical signs were minimal. Perhaps this was the lake's closure, its healing. What had been was no longer, and when the secret was revealed, all returned to normal.

So here I stood, seeking solace or absolution, or perhaps giving it. I didn't really know. I had buried my family in the cemetery together. If solace was to be sought, surely it was there, not here where life ended so abruptly and a journey began. But I felt drawn to this spot, as if this place had to be acknowledged by the living. It seemed that here, and only here, I could forgive Moya for everything that had happened in our lives. Here I would find the final release for both of us.

The sky had darkened a little. The winter twilight was upon me as the low sun began its exit from the day sky. The last shadows were lengthening into darkness when I decided to lie down beside the place where my mother and brother had drowned, had waited, and were finally discovered. Even through my jacket I could feel the cold earth that had locked below it the promise of returning water. Deep in the land was always the promise of new life. Somewhere beneath me was the dormant growth that would shoot up and claim its share of the sun once the rain returned, once drought turned to flood, as it surely would do at some point.

I stretched my hand out over the vague impressions left by Moya and Brannan and felt the same pulse of life. I had to speak the words that, if left unspoken, would poison me. "I forgive you, Moya." I realized then that I'd always called her *my mother* or *Moya*. I'd never called her *mum*. "Mum." Said aloud, it was a profound word. She was my mother, and for all her troubles and for all my anger at this unknown woman, I would be intrinsically part of her story, as she would be of mine.

I would forever mourn the loss of the opportunity to be loved by my mother, my father, and my brother. But I also intrinsically recognized the impossibility of living trapped by the sadness of those losses. For all the other scenarios I had imagined and had so deeply wanted, I had come to rest in the knowledge that my mother was ill when she took one last look at Cillian, who had been lulled into sleep by the gentle rocking of the little sailboat after she had crushed sleeping pills into his lunch; that when she wrapped the anchor chain around herself, she had meant to take her own life in order to release us all from the demons that rattled around the inside of head; and that Brannen's death was a terrible misadventure. The little boy's chubby foot was caught in the unrelenting weight of mother and metal when it all went over the side, a silent immersion into the dark water and mud. The little boat that rocked away from this point must have been a lonely place when my father awoke to find them gone. He was consumed by guilt because he had slept through Moya's darkest moment. He had failed to protect her. He hadn't saved Brannen, and I would be alone. The darkness of this weighty truth was reflected in the darkening sky that concealed the land. Earth and sky were momentarily one, and I thought about the endless darkness that had been the last thing they had seen. And then night truly fell.

In blackness came the stars and the moon, and in that moment came the light. It was a perfect sparkling world in which the Southern Cross formed the centre piece. They had not been laying in the dark all these years; they had been watching the seasons come and go, watching the sun rising and falling. The night sky had always provided a twinkling reminder that in darkness comes the most extraordinary light.

As I lay in the strange and silent embrace of the past, another light was breaking through the dark night. A torch was sweeping back and forth on my side of the lake. Phillip was coming.

. . . .

Printed in the United States
By Bookmasters